Praise for Ripples of Truth

This debut novel held my interest from start to finish. It has everything I look for in a good book: A meaningful story with characters who come alive while making their way in a realistic setting.

Sidney W. Frost, author of *Where Love Once Lived*,
first place winner in the inspirational or spiritual category,
SouthWest Writers contest, 2007

Nell Newton is a writer who weaves together life's many threads into a tapestry of unforgettable human experience. The enthusiasm she has for her subjects is contagious and makes her work a joy to read. Nell's writing has provided me with windows to worlds I never knew existed and has never failed to leave me wondering what stories might lie behind the people and places which surround me.

Jaime Calder, Editor

Ripples of Truth is a pungent onion of a novel as the layers of the character's lives are stripped away. Mysterious secrets and deceits burst the façade of social denials like domes bursting in a mud pot. This book will capture your curiosity and the escalating intensity of psychological revelations will keep you guessing till the end.

Dr. Donald Guerrant,
Screenwriter and Script Analyst

Newton, a social worker and counselor, shows her extensive experience and knowledge to weave a mystery that grabs the reader from the very beginning, through many twists, and unexpected resolution.

Hector Timourian, author and poet,
Gifts from America; In the Beginning

A riveting tale of lonely childhoods, family secrets and tragic consequences. Newton deftly toggles between multiple locations and time periods as she weaves the fascinating tale of two half sisters, separately drawn by fate, individually driven by an overwhelming sense of loss, to understand the choices of a mother they barely knew.

Karen S. Swensson,
author of *Conversations Loosely Translated:*
A Story of Koshkonong Prairie Pioneers

Nell and I have presented several series of Life Transitions workshops together, and I am aware of her understanding of human behavior. With her training and work experience, Nell knows and understands the difficulties that many face and how complicated lives can become. I am pleased to encourage readers to delve into these characters and their suspenseful endeavors.

Carolyn Greer, ED.D.,
Licensed Professional Counselor-Supervisor
Adjunct Professor-Counseling and Psychology

RIPPLES OF
TRUTH

A NOVEL BY

NELL~EVA NEWTON

To Lisa
Best Wishes
Nell~Eva
Newton

Ripples of Truth is a work of fiction. Names, characters, places, and incidents are the products of the author's imagination or are used fictitiously. Any resemblance to actual events, locales, or persons, living or dead, is entirely coincidental.

www.abqpress.com

www.abqpress.com

Albuquerque, New Mexico

ISBN 978-0-578-40796-8

To my mother, Rita,
who ran the race set before her
with spirit, perseverance, grace, and love.

ACKNOWLEDGEMENTS

A special thank you to Randall Best, Tom Mitchell, and Karen Swensson, members of my critique group, The Talespinners, who guided, advised, corrected, encouraged, and kept me going until The End. This book would not have been the same without you.

Thanks also to author, Sidney W. Frost, for reading my manuscript, making suggestions, offering encouragement and advice, and seeing me through to the finish line. And, to author, C. Wayne Dawson, who also read my manuscript and believed in me and my book.

My deep appreciation to my husband, Gene, and my sister, Kathy, my consultants, who have been with me since inception and know why I wrote this book. Also, to my honorable children, John and Cynthia; and to my other courageous siblings Jack, Jerry, Gary, Lorita, Debbie, and Marilyn. A special tribute to Barbara, who has been in our interesting family through many difficulties and joys and remained steadfast, loving, and accepting. I love you all and hope you might see a ripple of truth.

Put not your trust in princes, in a son of man, in whom there is no help. When his breath departs he returns to his earth; on that very day his plans perish.

Psalms 146: 3-4

But the fruit of the spirit is love, joy, peace, patience, kindness, goodness, faithfulness, gentleness, self-control; against such there is no law.

Galatians 5:22

CHAPTER ONE

ALBUQUERQUE, 1920

Nine-year-old Kathleen Irene Howe stared at the open book. "Who are these children? And why are their names in my mother's cookbook?"

She heard a chair scoot in the living room, crammed the book on the shelf, then hurried back to the table and picked up her homework. The cookbook was her mother's favorite. Her dad said so when she asked him about it last night. "Don't touch it," Dad said. And like everything else about her mother, Kathleen knew not to ask him more.

The next day, she couldn't sit still at school; flunked her arithmetic test; couldn't spell flammable in the spelling bee. When the final bell rang, she tore out the door, ran all the way home, and plopped in the kitchen chair. She brushed her bobbed, brown hair off her wet forehead and looked at the clock. *Just enough time before Dad gets home from work.* She took a deep breath. *And I've got to look at that cookbook.*

She dragged her chair to the bookcase, pulled the book off the top shelf, then pressed it to her cheek and savored the faint smell of cinnamon and old paper. At the table, she turned the feathered, yellowed pages and saw stars next to some recipes and notes in margins: add more vanilla, increase sugar, reduce vinegar, add extra egg. She couldn't read some of the words, but she didn't care. Her mother had written them.

1

On the back page, she studied the scrolled words in faded black ink again. *Fancy. Like the writing in Mother's Bible:*

Walter Clayton Pruitt, Jr. July 28, 1906

Clarice Irene Pruitt, August 16, 1908

Children born to **Laura Irene Armstrong** Pruitt and Walter Clayton Pruitt,

Presbyterian Hospital, Chicago, Illinois

Kathleen's hands flew to her chest. Laura Irene Armstrong. "That was Mother's name before she married Dad. And this says she had two children in Chicago." She sucked in a quick breath. "Gosh. Gee. So that's what Dad's been hiding!" Her heart quivered. "But why?"

She rubbed her trembling finger over the writing and smiled. *Clarice Irene . . . Irene.* "The girl even has my middle name. Wow." She wrinkled her forehead. "But who is that man, Walter Pruitt?" She shrugged. *I'll ask Dad when he gets home.* Then remembering all her unanswered questions, the pain in her dad's eyes at even the mention of her mother, she knew she would never ask him. She bit her bottom lip. "I'll find out on my own."

The hum of the Santa Fe whistle floated across the valley. Soft and mellow, yet demanding, Dad's off work, it said. Hurry. She circled the four, square rooms and emptied ashtrays, folded the newspaper, pinched her nose and picked up her brother, Henry's, socks and shoes, along with his books. She grabbed a pack of pork chops out of the icebox, pulled a frying pan off the bottom shelf, and set out three potatoes. She plopped on the kitchen chair and fanned her face with her pinafore. *I've got to start supper before Dad gets home, but . . .*

She clutched the cookbook to her chest, crept to the open window, and peeked out at the towering cottonwood tree. Brittle arms reached for sky as wind whipped innocent leaves. Tumbleweed rolled across the sandy dirt to the goat pen. Her goat, Ita, looked her way. A great painful silence wafted over her while loneliness wrapped her like a shroud. She thought of her brother, Henry, and a chill slithered up her spine.

The afternoon sun pressing on her shoulders awakened something deep inside her. She looked at the pink blossoms on the cherry tree and smiled. "But I have a sister and brother in Chicago." Her heart pounded under her ribs. "And someday I'm going to find them!"

* * *

CHICAGO, 1920

Twelve-year-old, Clarice Irene Pruitt, pointed at the battered, old steamer trunk. "Where did that come from?"

Her father, Walter, glanced up from his desk. "I had it brought down from the attic yesterday."

"What's in it?" Clarice said. Not waiting for his answer, she popped the latch, but her father stopped her before she could raise the lid.

"Stay out of the trunk, Clarice."

His voice pitched high, his tone a little too precise, Clarice knew there was something in that trunk he did not want her to see.

The next day, with her father at work, and her nanny, Maureen, busy downstairs, Clarice climbed two flights of stairs to her father's study and tiptoed to the trunk. She popped the latch, rested the squeaky lid against the wall, and then waved her hands at the stench of dry wood, old paper, and stale tobacco. *It smells like Father's humidor.*

On top, lay a long, manila envelope stuffed with papers, but she could not make sense of them and put them back. She picked up an old, yellowed book with a torn cover: *The Call of the Wild.* She shrugged. *Mrs. Wright read that to us after lunch recess. Why did Father hide it here?*

She picked up another envelope and pulled out an old photograph of a wooden store. A crude sign above the door said, SKAGWAY'S BEST. Three men with brushy beards in long, dark coats stood in front. She raised her eyebrows. *Who are these men? And what do they have to do with Father?*

Underneath the photograph, lay a faded newspaper article about the grand opening of their first department store. Clarice stood in the center of some important looking men in dark suits and ties. Above their heads, the familiar bold sign: PRUITT'S. She looked at her old party dress and grimaced. *I was only seven. What a baby.*

Clipped behind the article, was an old obituary. That meant someone important to her father died, she knew, and she read:

Irene Armstrong, January 6, 1914;

survived by her daughter, Laura Irene Pruitt Howe

& son-in-law, Hartley Howe, of Albuquerque,

New Mexico; and grandchildren, Kathleen Irene Howe

and Henry Howe. No services planned.

Clarice walked to the window and held the obituary toward the light. *Survived by Laura Irene Pruitt.* "That was my mother's name!" Obituary in hand, she paced between the window and trunk. "This says my mother lives in Albuquerque. And she has another husband and another girl and boy besides me and Clay." She yanked a fistful of curls. "So, she abandoned me for them!"

She sat at her father's desk and read the obituary again. *Kathleen Irene . . .* she winced. "She even gave that girl my middle name! How could she?"

Footsteps thumped on the stairs.

Clarice stuffed the obituary into her pocket, crammed everything back into the trunk, and dropped the lid. She posed her best smile, then swirled around to face Maureen.

Maureen placed her hands on her hips. "What are ye doing, ye little sneak?"

Clarice reared her shoulders.

Red curls bounced as Maureen waved her index finger. "Stay out of that trunk, young lady, or I'll tell yer father."

Clarice cocked her head. "No, you won't. Because if my father finds out I've been in this trunk, he will fire you!"

CHAPTER TWO

ALBUQUERQUE, 1928

"Seeking information about my half sister
& brother, Clarice Irene Pruitt &
Walter Clayton Pruitt, Jr. children of Laura
Irene Pruitt & Walter Clayton Pruitt.
Please contact Kathleen Irene Howe,
P.O. Box 28, Albuquerque SW, New Mexico. Important."
Seventeen-year-old, Kathleen Howe, raced down the steps of the Albuquerque Library. A stamped envelope in one hand, her cardboard suitcase in the other, she raised her envelope in triumph. "I did it! I wrote my classified ad for the *Chicago Tribune*, and now I'm going to find my sister and brother!"

Kathleen tucked the ad into the envelope, along with two of her last three dollars for payment, then licked and sealed it. She picked up her suitcase and headed up Central Avenue; her long legs sliced the air like scissors as her shadow lengthened in the slanting sun.

Heavy footsteps approached from behind, she glanced over her shoulder and saw a man racing toward her. She tried to run, but the suitcase slowed her down. The man brushed her shoulder, knocked her suitcase to the ground, and her slips and panties spilled over the sidewalk.

The man stopped and took off his hat. "I'm sorry, ma'am," and then glanced toward the bus stop.

Kathleen dropped to her knees, shoved her underclothes into her suitcase, and snapped the latch.

The man tapped her shoulder. "Pardon me, again, miss, but I believe this belongs to you."

She looked up at the man towering over her and snatched her envelope out of his hand.

He stepped back and stared.

Kathleen stood and faced him. She had seen this look from other men. She flinched. And from her brother, Henry.

"Pardon me for saying so, ma'am, but, uh, you're very beautiful, you know."

Kathleen flinched again, and her eyes bore into him. "Well, if I'm beautiful, mister, I don't know it." She hesitated. "But, thank you."

A bus growled up to the corner, but the man still stared.

Kathleen winced at the screechy brakes and sizzling hiss as the door opened.

The man tipped his hat. "Again, please, pardon me," and he ran toward the bus stop.

Kathleen sighed. *Silly me, afraid, when the poor man was just trying to catch the bus.* She watched him board, the door clunked shut, and she wrinkled her nose at the gassy fumes. The bus roared away, and she saw a mailbox. She plopped her suitcase on the bench, cut across the street between two cars, and shoved the envelope into the box.

Back on the splintered bench, she thought about the ugly fight she'd had with Henry. *Was it only this morning?* She swallowed. *I wonder what he'll tell Dad.* Tears moistened her eyes. *You're all I have, Dad, but why didn't you protect me?* She brushed her cheeks with the back of her hand. *I don't know what's going to happen to me now. But I can't live at home anymore with Henry there.*

Busses growled up to the bench. Passengers got off and on while Kathleen wondered about her sister and brother in Chicago. *What do they look like? Do they know about me?* She grimaced. *And why didn't Dad ever tell me about them?* She rested her head on the bench and gazed at the giant circle of Albuquerque sky. In the west, remnants of gold dimmed into soft yellow fingers over stunted volcanoes. To the east, the craggy peaks of the Sandia Mountains turned watermelon pink in the setting sun. She hugged her chest. *My mountains. They wrap their giant arms around me and . . .* wind whipped hair danced across her face; she tucked it under her collar.

Alone on the bench, "What am I going to do now? I left home. I quit school. And I only have one dollar left to my name." Kathleen stood, picked up her suitcase, and gazed at the mountains. "But I have a sister and brother in Chicago. And now, dear God, I'm going to find them!"

* * *

CHICAGO, 1928

Twenty-year-old, Clarice Pruitt, sat at her desk and skimmed the *Chicago Tribune*, then pulled out her competitors' ads: Sears Roebuck, Montgomery Ward, and Marshall Field's. She scrutinized each one. *Montgomery Ward and Sears beat us on prices this week, but we beat them on style. Marshall Field's?* She frowned. *I'm working on them.* She slammed the newspaper on her desk. "But their women's fashions have nothing over us this week."

Her intercom buzzed. "Your friend, Felicia Bradford, is on the telephone, Miss Pruitt."

Clarice tapped her fingernails on her desk. Felicia almost never called her at work. "Put her through, please, Miss Watson."

"Sorry to disturb you," Felicia said.

"Is something wrong?"

"Did you read this morning's classified ad?"

"You know I don't read the classifieds."

"Column three in the personals," Felicia said. "Then call me back."

Clarice hung up, then picked up the paper and searched through the personals: men wanting companionship, women seeking the perfect mate, both looking for lost loves. "Ridiculous." She snickered. Then halfway down the third column she saw her name. "Seeking information . . . children of Laura Irene Armstrong & Walter Clayton Pruitt . . . Important."

She read the ad again, and then buzzed Miss Watson. "Hold my calls, please."

"Your father has some questions about the inventory."

Clarice's face grew hot. "I've been doing inventory since I was sixteen. And he questions me?"

"Uh, well, yes, ma'am. What should I do?"

"I said to hold my calls."

"For how long?"

Clarice gritted her teeth. "Until I tell you, Miss Watson." She hung up, then walked to the window and looked out at morning's gloom hanging over Lake Michigan. Below, long ribbons of automobiles lined State Street, while miniature people scurried back and forth juggling packages. "Shoppers." She smiled. "And thank God a lot of them are coming our way."

Back at her desk, she recalled the day she discovered her mother had abandoned her for another man, and she had a new family. She grabbed the telephone and dialed Felicia. "It's that damn girl in Albuquerque! My sister, ha."

"What do you think?"

"That my mother might be afraid to search for me herself, so she made that girl do it."

"Well, perhaps . . ."

Clarice banged her fist on her desk. "Well, Miss Kathleen Howe can tell my mother that I still live in the same house I did when she abandoned me. And she would know that if she had bothered to come back."

"What are you going to do?"

Clarice balanced the telephone on her shoulder and stabbed her pen into the inkwell. Black blobs splattered as she scribbled "Go to Hell" across the ad. "Mail it back to Albuquerque," she said, and then decided, "No. Why give her the satisfaction?" She ripped the ad into pieces and dropped it into the trashcan, "That Kathleen Irene Howe can search all she wants. But she will not find me!"

Ripples of Truth

CHAPTER THREE

Walter and his head Buyer, Gilbert, studied pictures of the new spring line of women's apparel. "Hemlines are dropping, and waistlines are rising," Walter said. "Good thing we cleaned out last year's inventory."

"Right, sir, our managers don't like mark-downs."

Walter pointed to a stack of papers on his desk. "Business is booming now, yet they still hung back on their orders."

"Like I said, sir, they don't want to get stuck with end-of-season merchandise."

"Stuck, huh? Well, I increased most of their orders by ten percent."

Gilbert frowned. "I'm not sure about that, sir."

Walter flipped his hand in the air. "We'll sell it all. Mark my word. I'll have Clarice look at the hats, though."

"Good idea, sir."

Walter grinned. "Funny how Clarice never seems to care what she wears, yet she has good instincts for what will sell. She even sits at a window table in restaurants, so she can look out and see what the women are wearing."

"Miss Clarice knows her stuff." He nodded toward Walter. "Seems to come natural."

"She studies Harper's Bazaar, Vogue and the rest, and she swears by that French woman, Coco Chanel." Walter made the sign of the cross. "Bless Madame Chanel for bringing the practical to America." He nodded toward the stack of orders on his desk. "And we're selling the hell out of it!"

Gilbert stood. "I need to get back to the floor, sir."

Gilbert left, and Walter pulled his envelope of college pamphlets from his top drawer and sorted them across his desk. *Clarice knows her stuff all right, but I haven't worked this hard for her to pound her heels on these floors the rest of her life. And she agreed. Two years at the State Street store, then she's off to college.* He brushed the pamphlets aside. *And her part of the deal is almost up.*

Walter leaned back. *Clarice doesn't see it now, but college will move her to a higher element where she can meet someone with class instead of some bloke off the street. She might climb to the top of the social ladder.* "Hell, money, class, that's what I'm aiming for her."

He walked to the window and gazed at the greenish, gray lake. The sailboats were gone, and he'd hardly been outdoors all summer. *Maybe Clarice and I—*

His intercom buzzed.

"It's your daughter, sir."

Clarice strode through the door.

Walter turned to greet her, then saw the look on her face and frowned. "What's wrong?"

"Where is your *Tribune*?" she said.

He pointed toward the shelf beside her.

Clarice shuffled through the newspaper, tore out the classified ad, and thrust it toward him.

Walter read the ad, and his throat tightened. He loosened his tie and took a deep breath. "Well, it seems that someone is trying to find you."

"*Someone*, Father?" Clarice's face reddened. "You know who she is."

Walter swallowed. "Calm down."

Through gritted teeth, Clarice said, "I won't calm down until you tell me what happened to my mother."

Walter stood and faced her. "We've been over this before. Your mother left us when you were a baby, and I have nothing more to tell you."

"But you know she went to Albuquerque, and we both know that this girl is her daughter."

Walter's head throbbed. "You don't *know* anything."

Clarice's voice softened. "I found my grandmother's obituary in your old steamer trunk when I was twelve. It showed Laura Pruitt of Albuquerque as her daughter. My mother! And it said she had another husband, a boy named, Henry, and a girl, Kathleen."

Pain like a shard of glass shot through Walter's chest. He threw up his hands. "Good Lord! Why didn't you say something?"

Clarice reared her shoulders. "You forbade me to ask about her, remember?"

"Forbade?" Walter snorted. "When did that ever stop you?"

"It did where *she* was concerned."

"But you've been perfectly happy without her."

"Happy, Father?" Clarice's voice quavered. "I've only been longing for her every day of my life."

Walter groaned. "This is the first time you've said that, Clarice."

"I want to know what happened."

Walter's face grew hot. "Your mother walked out on us when you were a baby. And you are the better for it."

"And is Clay better off?"

Walter shook his fist in the air. "If not for your mother, Clay might have played outdoors like other boys instead of shutting himself in his room like a monk. He could have gone to public school, he—"

"You took Clay out of school."

"And I took care of you both after your mother left and never looked back."

Clarice looked at him steadily. "Maybe she's trying to find us now through this girl."

Walter glared. "That girl wants something: money, our stores, our house, something. You can bet on it."

Clarice dropped onto the sofa, kicked off her high-heeled shoes, and let out a long sigh. "I can't deal with this now. I'm exhausted."

Walter sat down at his desk and picked up the ad. "What made you read the classifieds?"

"Felicia called me."

"Felicia?"

"Well, she saw the ad first and—"

"Damn woman."

"Felicia was my mother's best friend."

"She was a poor influence on your mother and on you, too."

Clarice leaned forward. "What is it with you and Felicia?"

Walter waved his hand in dismissal. "I didn't approve of her back then, and I don't approve of her now."

Clarice's eyes narrowed. "There's something going on between you two . . . or there was something."

"Find a friend your own age."

"Why are you so stubborn about her?"

Walter dug his fingers into the back of his neck. His energy expired as seconds ticked away on the gilded clock.

Clarice shrugged. "It's the German in you, I guess."

Walter tightened. "What are you going to do?"

"I could answer the ad. . . ."

She's willful, obstinate. Do not challenge this headstrong girl. Walter gave her his trusting smile. "Let's go over the inventory."

Clarice stood, flattened her hands on his desk, and looked him in the eye. "Damn the inventory. What happened to my mother?"

CHAPTER FOUR

Walter stood as the dark clad waiter ushered Felicia to his table in the far corner of the dining room. He noted the admiring glances of other diners as she walked by. *That walk, that luscious red hair, that woman.*

Diamonds sparkled on her slender neck as Walter pulled out her chair. "You look ravishing, my dear."

Felicia glanced up at him. "Why, thank you, Patrick."

Walter sat down across from her. "So, that's the way you want to play it. I'm Patrick Roark again, eh Annie?" He smiled. "But then your wit and charm are what attracted me in that saloon in Fairbanks all those years ago."

"It was the six beers that attracted you, as I recall."

Walter made a sweeping gesture with his hands. "Ah, well, Patrick Roark and Annie Parsons together in the finest restaurant in Chicago."

Felicia's emerald eyes shined. "Right. The dancehall girl and the thief."

Walter's jaws tightened. "Only part of that is true you know."

"That's because you didn't have the guts to take the money yourself, did you? And you didn't have the guts to take me with you when you left Fairbanks."

Walter frowned as the waiter appeared with menus.

After a moment's study, "A cup of tea, please," Felicia said, "and the maple cottage pudding with maple syrup."

"A slice of the green apple pie and a cup of coffee," Walter said.

The waiter hovered over Felicia. "Will there be anything else, ma'am?"

Felicia smiled. "No, thank you."

Hands trembling, the waiter picked up the menus and left.

Walter snickered. "Darn nuisance, that one."

"He's anxious to please. Just learning I'd say."

"He's anxious for a handsome tip." He shifted in his chair. "I thought we agreed the Alaska chapter in our lives was closed."

"We never really agreed on anything. We just both kept our mouths shut, and that's not the same thing."

"So, let's continue to keep our mouths shut," Walter said.

The waiter returned with their orders.

Felicia took a bite of maple pudding and nodded her approval.

Walter sipped his coffee and remembered the first time they'd met again in "Chicago's polite society" at a charity dinner. When Robert Bradford, one of the richest men in Chicago, introduced her as his wife, his heart nearly stopped. She'd offered her hand as if for the first time, while all he could think was: How in hell did she get here? He winced, wishing he could have handled their meeting again as smoothly as she had. Instead he'd faked a cough and departed.

Felicia touched her chin. "What were you thinking just now?"

Walter grinned. "About the first time we met at that charity dinner, and how I wondered how you got there."

She tilted her head. "The same way as you, perhaps."

Lilac lingered in the air. He took a deep breath. "I remember that fragrance."

Felicia smiled. "I stay with the things I like."

Walter lifted his spoon. "Touché, my dear."

"So, Patrick, or excuse me, Walter. Why did you invite me here?"

Walter leaned forward. "Because you've seemed bent on being part of Clarice's life. And I want to know why."

"It's not *my bent*. Clarice is the one who calls me."

"And you always make yourself available to her."

"She needs a woman's influence."

"And what makes you think she needs *your* influence, for heaven's sake?"

Felicia's eyes glistened. "What she needs is a mother's influence. She's aching from the absence."

Walter's stomach tightened. "The matter of Laura is over."

"Why do you speak of Laura as if she will never come back into Clarice's life?"

"She won't. Take my word for it."

"Your word?" Felicia's voice quavered.

"I've always kept my word with Clarice."

"And your son?"

Walter's jaw ached. *Damn woman.*

Felicia looked at him for a long moment. "I've never understood the discrepancy in the way you treat your children."

"Clayton is not open for discussion. Especially with you."

"You'll have to tell the truth about Laura someday. If not to me, then to them."

He glared at her. "Why did you call Clarice's attention to that classified ad?"

"It's a public record. Someone else would have. I should think you'd be happy for her."

He looked across the dining room at a dark-haired, young woman in a bright blue, bias-cut skirt draped over her legs. A red cloche hat sat in a sassy tilt as she laughed. He grimaced. *Those hats sell like hotcakes. But they're unappetizing all the same.* He moved a bite of pie around his plate, stabbed his fork into the crust and said, "So, Annie, you've come a long way from that saloon in Alaska."

"No thanks to you."

"Again, touché, my dear, yet I wonder how you hold your tongue around that husband of yours."

Felicia smiled. "A lady has no need to hold her tongue." She took a sip of tea and looked at Walter. "Robert loves me. He believes in me."

"And what does he believe?"

She raised her eyebrows. "Well, what did you think the first time you saw me here in Chicago? Did you fall in love with me again?"

Walter's eyes darted toward the nearby waiter. "He can hear you for heaven's sake."

Felicia let out a soft laugh. "My, might there be a little of Patrick Roark left in ye?"

Walter cheeks grew hot. "We were Patrick Roark and Annie Parsons in Fairbanks a long time ago. And we both have a stake in keeping them there."

"Perhaps."

"You manipulated your way back into my life through Laura, and now you're doing it with Clarice."

"Clarice is the one who seeks me out. I've found that quite ironic since she knew nothing about you and me, once upon a time."

Walter pointed his fork at her. "Stay away from Clarice."

"She's a grown woman. You can't control her anymore."

"And neither should you."

Felicia took the last bite of pudding and dabbed her napkin on her lips. "It will be as it was with Laura. I will not initiate contact with her, but neither will I turn her away."

"You told her about that classified ad."

"Clarice had a right to know." She shrugged. "However; she doesn't want anything to do with the girl or her mother either, so you can relax."

"Relax? Hell, you can't predict what Clarice will do." He gulped his coffee. *Damn this prohibition. I could use a real drink right now.* He looked at Felicia. "I wonder who has the most to lose here."

"And why should Clarice be the loser?"

The lunch crowd had dwindled. The delicate clink of fine china filled the room as waiters cleared tables. Walter beckoned, and their waiter brought the check on a silver tray.

"Leaving so soon?"

Walter signed the check, stood, and looked down at her. "You make sure Clarice doesn't answer that ad, or you'll see who the loser is."

CHAPTER FIVE

Walter rode in the backseat of his black Packard Eight Sedan while his driver, Tom, drove south on Lake Shore Drive. Now that he'd settled on a location for his new store, he scribbled cost projections for his meeting with his accountant on Monday.

Since seeing Felicia, he had negotiated a deal with a supplier about a defect in his last order of sweaters, soothed his furrier's hurt feelings, and settled a dispute between his Jewelry and Women's Wear managers. He winced. *Working with people is the hardest part. The rest is easy.*

As they crossed over State Street, ornate stores towered side-by-side while people poured out of cable cars and packed the street and sidewalks. A few brave drivers inched their automobiles through elbowing crowds as bicycles darted between them. "State Street," Walter said, "the world's most famous bazaar."

"And your store stands with the best of them, sir."

Walter reared his shoulders. *Along with my Madison Street store, and another one planned on the outskirts along with Marshall Fields, Wieboldts, Montgomery Ward and the rest.* He leaned back on his seat and stretched his neck. *I Wonder what my old man would think of me now?*

And his thoughts drifted to the rat infested flat in Chicago's Bridgeport community where he grew up as Patrick Ryan Roark, only child of Egan and Paulette Roark, second-generation Irish immigrants.

Egan, or "Big Red" they called him for his russet curls, worked at the stockyards slaughtering cattle during the day then settled in at the pub at night with fish and chips and his pint. Under the spell of Irish whisky, he spun tales of leprechauns, banshees, fairies, and witches. And like his Irish ancestors, the stronger the whisky, the more he embellished his tales until they were barely recognizable from one tellin' to the next.

Patrick never liked the colorful characters in his father's stories nor appreciated their wealth of rustic Irish imagery. He didn't understand the man's devotion to Ireland where his parents nearly starved to death in the potato famine. To Patrick, Egan was a drunkard who wasted what little money he earned on whisky, while his family barely survived in a stinking flat.

Paulette was Black Irish, descended from the wreck of the Spanish Armada, or so everyone said. She married Egan at fifteen and did his bidding, except in the raising of Patrick. Every day, she scrubbed Patrick's clothes on a wash board, hung them on the line across the alley, and pressed them with her flat iron. She refused to send him to the barbershop and cut his hair herself.

Paulette hated Egan's love of the pint and cried when he left her alone at night. After years of watching her neighbors die from the fever, flu, childbirth, and consumption, she clung to her only child who was at least six inches shorter and fifteen pounds lighter than other boys his age, and she kept him home from school at the first sign of a sniffle. "You're all I have, Patrick," she'd said, "you're the only one that I love."

Bathed in Paulette's affection, Patrick wanted to stay home every day, because after school gangs of boys taunted him: "Mama's boy; mama's little funny boy." As he grew older, their taunts turned to beatings.

One afternoon, a gang of boys circled, pushed him back and forth as each one took a lick, and then pinned him on the sidewalk and kicked him.

"Hey! Not a fair fight," someone shouted from across the street. A red-haired boy pushed through the circle of boys, offered Patrick his hand, and the gang fled.

Patrick looked up at Ferris McKenzie, a boy from his fifth-grade class, who had helped him once with his homework. But with his red hair and freckles, Ferris reminded him of his father, and he waved him away.

After the beatings, Patrick always avoided Egan, which was easy because the only thing the family did together was attend Sunday Mass. Patrick dreaded the dark sanctuary with the twisted statues, musty candles, and Latin chants. He cringed when the nuns stood over him at catechism, and the priest pressed him at confession. He hated the church, but every time he looked at Egan, he hated being Irish even more.

One hot sticky night, a rare night when Egan was home, Patrick heard his parents' voices and tiptoed to the kitchen door.

"What are those bruises on the boy?" Egan said.

"Och, those Faraday boys from down the street and the Sheridan's. Did you not see the bruises before?"

Patrick drew his fist to his lips, because when Egan was home, he might ask him about school, remind him of chores and homework, but mostly ignored him. He had often watched in fascination while Egan talked in animated gestures with neighbors and friends, yet at home he was silent.

"Did he defend himself?" Egan asked.

"There were too many," Paulette's voice squeaked. "All he could do was run."

"Run?" Egan's heavy footsteps thumped across the kitchen. "My boy ran like a yellow-bellied coward?"

Paulette shushed him. "Don't be hard on him, Egan."

"Hard on him?" Egan sputtered. "I should give him a licking myself. Tis a blessing my father didn't know him."

Patrick had often studied the faded photograph of Egan's father. The man's narrow face, framed with dark curly hair, a bushy beard and mustache, looked like one of those Puritan preachers he had studied in American history. Yet Egan told him his grandfather had worked at the lime plant and died of consumption when he was fifty-three.

"Ye won't lay a hand on him," Paulette said. "He's been hurt bad enough."

Hurt? Pain cut across Patrick's bruised shoulder as he crept back to his bed and pulled the sheet under his chin. He lay as if strapped to his bed and smelled rancid grease, cooked cabbage, and urine from down the hallway. From his open window, he smelled horse droppings, a whiff of garbage from across the street. The streetlamp flickered as a peddler called out his wares. Mothers shrilled for their children. A siren blared in the distance.

The bedroom door creaked open. Patrick closed his eyes and heard the soft rhythm of footsteps across the room; felt the dark presence of his father looming over him. His tongue tasted like rusted nails. Waves of shame washed over him. *I will be a better man than you are someday. And I will take care of my mother.*

* * *

When Patrick was fourteen, Egan quit his job at the stockyards to work for the local ward. He quickly moved up the political ladder from ward heeler, to boss, to alderman where he controlled government money. With payoffs, kickbacks, and his own operations on the side, he finally had some money, power, and local fame.

Now, when the boys who had bullied Patrick passed him on the street, they left him alone. He had even started to feel safe, until one day a boy he didn't recognize shoved him onto the sidewalk.

"Leave him be," a deep voice shouted as Ferris McKenzie came up behind them.

The boy snarled. "Why should I let the puny bastard be?"

"Because his father is Big Red Roark, and Red won't like you pushing his boy around."

"What the devil?" The boy laughed. "A man like Roark with a sap like this for a son?"

Mucus, like a wad of sour grease, clumped in the back of Patrick's throat. Anger burned quick as a flame as he pushed himself up, thrust his head forward, and splattered the glob of spit on the boy's face.

The boy reared back his leg.

Patrick grabbed his other leg and twisted him to the ground. The boy pushed up, but Patrick kicked his chin and he fell flat. Patrick laughed, waved to Ferris McKenzie, and walked up the street toward home.

As Patrick grew older, Paulette suffered bouts of pneumonia, influenza, and whooping cough. She had forgetful spells and rarely left her rocker. She cried to Egan every day: "Surely now you have money to move us out of here."

"Bridgeport is my power base," Egan always shouted and banged out the door.

Eyes bleary, she begged Patrick. "Help me, son, or I will die."

At the thought of his mother dying, Patrick grew more obsessed with moving her out of the flats. He had watched the money come in, stuffed in large briefcases, hurriedly collected and uncounted. Late afternoons, two men with guns strapped inside their jackets, tipped their hats to his mother, then followed his father into the bedroom and shut the door.

One day they came through the door muttering. Egan's face was red as his hair as he ushered them into the bedroom.

Patrick tiptoed to the door and pressed his ear over the keyhole. "Raid . . . move headquarters, tomorrow . . ." and he knew he had to get at that money now, or it would be out of his reach.

He locked his hands behind his back, paced, and thought about his hero, Buffalo Bill, scouting Indians for the army; cowboys waving their hats riding broncos. *What can a "yellow-bellied coward" a "mama's boy" do against three armed men?* He recalled Ferris McKenzie who had rescued him from the gang of boys and stopped. *Ferris would know what to do.*

Patrick went into the kitchen, splashed water on his face, and grabbed a dish towel. As he dragged it over the stove, the end of the towel caught fire, and he stomped it out with his boot. He tightened. *She left the stove on again. She could have started a fire.* He started. *Fire! Damn. That'll get 'em out.*

He grabbed a handful of dishtowels and flung them on a rack behind the stove with the edges dangling close to the open flame. *I'll grab that money and run, or I'll burn this stinking building to the ground. Doesn't matter which. But I'll save my mother.*

He closed the kitchen door and crept to the sofa.

Paulette dozed in her rocking chair.

After a short while, Patrick smelled burning cotton, heard flames crackle as smoke pushed under the kitchen door. He opened it, and ribbons of flames climbed up the wall behind the stove. He shouted, "Fire! Fire!" And the men burst through the bedroom door.

"What the devil," Egan shouted, as they tore off their jackets and started pounding the flames.

Patrick slipped into the bedroom, grabbed fistfuls of money, and crammed them into his coat pockets until they were stuffed. He went back to the living room, shoved his coat under the sofa, then grabbed another coat off the coat rack and joined the men beating the flames.

Paulette screamed.

"Take care of her," Egan shouted.

Patrick threw his coat in a corner and ran to Paulette. "Don't be afraid, Mother."

Egan shoved him aside. "Get a wet towel, damn it!" He scooped up Paulette in his arms and carried her out to the stairwell.

Patrick came back with the towel and watched as Egan cradled Paulette in his arms like a child and kissed her cheeks and forehead. His raspy voice somehow gentle, he murmured, "Don't cry, sweetheart. Everything's going to be all right." He jerked the towel out of Patrick's hand and shouted, "Move her chair by the window."

Egan lowered Paulette into the rocking chair, pulled threads of black hair off her forehead, and wiped her face and neck. "The fire's out, darling. You rest here till I get back."

"Don't leave me," Paulette whimpered, "please, don't . . ." her voice trailed away.

Egan glared at Patrick through swollen eyes, "Take care of her," he ordered, then dashed to the bedroom with the other men and stuffed the money into briefcases.

Patrick crept back to the kitchen. The wall hissed through the black murky mess while steamy smoke rose.

Egan grabbed his shoulder and spun him around. "What the devil happened here?"

"The stove; she forgot to cut it off."

"You were supposed to watch her."

"I did, but . . ."

Egan bent down and picked up the coat Patrick had used to beat the flames.

Patrick froze.

"Let's go, Red!" One of the men shouted.

Egan's eyes fixed on the coat. "Something's not right here, Son. You had another one on when—"

"We gotta' get out before the cops come, Red."

Egan glanced at the men, then back to Patrick and shot him a fierce look. "Tend to your mother," he said. "We'll settle this when I get back." He tossed the coat in a corner, gave Paulette a quick kiss, then tore out the door behind his men.

Patrick laid Paulette on the bed, covered her with a quilt, then ran next door and told Mrs. Gilbert to look after her. Sick from smoke, his shirt blackened from flames, he grabbed his coat from under the sofa, slipped out of the building, ran until his sides ached, then caught the first cable car north.

He got off near an abandoned warehouse. Seeing no one around, he pried the door open, searched the building until sure he was alone, and blocked the door with tires found piled in a corner. He dropped to his knees, separated the bills, and his eyes bulged at the stacks of hundreds. Hands shaking, he counted. He turned the last bill and sweat popped on his forehead. He swiped it with the back of his hand and counted again.

Patrick stood and stared at the piles of bills. Heart thumping, he pulled his knotted fists to his chest. "What am I going to do with eighty-nine thousand dollars?"

He remembered the look in Egan's eyes when he'd held up the jacket, and fear stabbed him like an ice pick. He wanted to grab the money and run but thought of his mother and knew he had to go back.

Money crammed into his pockets and boots, Patrick turned the corner to his flat. Neighbors stood in groups around the front steps. Two police cars were parked at the curb.

Mrs. Gilbert shrilled from the second-floor window. "Patrick! Lord in heaven. Where have you been?"

Patrick perched to run, but Mr. Gilbert grabbed him. "Ye won't be runnin' this time, ye little snot," and he pushed him up the front steps.

Mrs. Gilbert met them in the hallway. Tears streamed down her cheeks. "Oh, Patrick, it's ye father."

Patrick broke away from Mr. Gilbert and tore up the stairs. A police officer stood by his open door. A second officer, pen in hand, sat on the sofa next to his mother.

Paulette looked at him and screamed, "Patrick, oh Patrick, they killed yer father!"

Three weeks later, talk had died down, the police quit badgering Paulette with questions, and the neighbors stopped bringing food. Lifeless, Paulette sat as if glued to her rocking chair and stared out the window. Patrick watched her grow weaker every day and knew he could not wait any longer. He knelt beside her and held her limp hand in his.

Tears slid down her cheeks. "Patrick, oh, Patrick."

"Don't cry, Mother. I'm going to move us to a new place on one of the avenues, just like you always wanted."

Paulette's mouth quivered. "I don't want to leave."

Patrick stroked her hand. "But you begged me to move you out."

"Yer father might come home, and I won't be here."

Patrick felt like he was the parent and her the child. "He won't be back, Mother."

Paulette blinked. Her dark eyes now pearly gray, she gazed at Patrick. "I love him."

Patrick started. "You said I was the only one you love."

"I loved you because he wasn't here. You took his place."

Patrick's eyes stung. All those years of, "You're all I've got, Patrick; you're the only one I love." He recalled the heroic thoughts her words had generated, and comprehension came. *She loved him. Oh, my God, she loved him; not me.* He dropped her hand, then stood and looked down on his mother as if she were a stranger, and his childhood disappeared.

Two weeks later, on Patrick's sixteenth birthday, Paulette did not wake up. "Heart failure," the doctor said. Without tears, Patrick buried her next to Egan in Niles Cemetery and knelt by his father's grave. *Was it my fault, Father? Did they kill you because the money was short?*

The next day he found the spot where Egan was murdered and pressed his hands over the bloodstained sidewalk. *You were ashamed of me, Father, yet you got gunned-down on the street by thieves.* A chill wind brushed his face. *Everyone said it was thieves, but did they know I helped myself first?* He stood and looked at his father's blood. "I don't know where I'll die, but it won't be on a cold sidewalk where people walk on my blood as if I were never here."

The next week, Patrick sold what belongings he could and gave away the rest. He stuffed the money into the innersoles of his sturdiest boots and sewed the rest into the lining of his warmest coat. He packed a satchel with dried salami, crackers, cheese, and an apple, then headed to Union Station and hopped the first freight train headed west.

CHAPTER SIX

In Chicago, Clarice had paced the floor for two nights. Should she tell Clay about the classified ad Kathleen published? One part of her said, yes. *He has a right to know that their mother is in Albuquerque with another man, and they have another brother and sister.* The other part said, no. *Clay might retreat even further into his shell and never come out.* She scratched her neck. *But if I don't tell him now, he might find out on his own, and he'll hate me.* She clenched her fists. *Damn! How long will this secret haunt us?*

She climbed the stairs to Clay's room and pressed her cheek on the thick oak door. It felt warm; or did she only imagine it so because Clay was on the other side? She knocked twice then three more quick knocks, and Clay opened the door.

"Hi, little brother." Clarice zipped past him to the bed and pulled off her shoes and socks.

Clay pinched his nose at the imaginary odor.

Clarice stuck her finger through a ragged hole in his blue, flannel shirt. "You shouldn't talk. Bet you've been wearing this rag for a week."

Clay threw up his hands. "Hey, it's my best shirt."

"It's awful, Clay."

"It's comfortable."

"Well, I'm going to bring you some new shirts. We do own two department stores, you know."

"You and Father do."

"Come on, Clay. You know the three of us are partners."

"For business purposes; to save on taxes."

"Well, we're partners all the same."

He waved his finger at her. "You and Father are, and you and I are, but the three of us? No."

"True. But that leaves me to take care of your share of the business." She stood. Clay was a head taller, and she brushed his shoulder with the back of her hand.

Clay smiled. Only it wasn't a smile really, just a lopsided curling of the corners of his mouth, yet it comforted her. She glanced around the room that her father had made for Clay and drew comfort from it, too.

She had always likened Clay to a fawn as he moved lithely from his chair to his desk to his bed. With his hazel eyes and hair the color of wheat, his golden skin blended with the soft greens and browns adorning the room. *As if he lives in a forest.*

Clarice admired her brother with his slender neck, high cheekbones, and chiseled face. *His mind is like a sieve, sifting and sorting everything.* She looked at his bookcase piled high with notebooks, newspapers, and books. *To think that old bat of a teacher in public school called Clay feeble-minded. Just because he wasn't like the other boys.*

Their father had removed Clay from school in the middle of fourth grade and hired "Old Mister Leonard" to teach him. She pictured Mr. Leonard now, with his pinched face and round glasses that dangled from a string around his bony neck. She'd always thought he looked like a crab. Yet Clay studied so hard for the man. And she realized now how much Clay had loved his old teacher.

After Mr. Leonard came, builders knocked out the wall to the next room and made Clay a study. Mr. Leonard made a list, and Father filled shelves with dark leather-bound books. They cut a hole in the bookshelves and made Clay a desk with an inkwell and a special box for his pens. Now, cluttered with books, maps, pencils, and paper, Clarice had not seen the top of Clay's desk in years.

A mahogany four-poster bed stood on the far wall. When Clarice was little, Clay used to boost her up on the bed and read to her. Then, feet dangling, they talked.

Clay's eyes narrowed. "What's going on in that bright head of yours?"

"I was thinking how when you were little this room seemed to dwarf you, and now you've just sort of grown into it."

"Do you think Father knew I would be over six feet tall?"

"Well, he's six feet."

"I'm not like him," Clay said. He pulled out his chair, sat down at his desk, and pushed his notebooks aside.

Clarice pulled out a chair and sat next to him. "What are you studying now?"

"Canada."

"Canada?" She stifled a laugh. "Who cares about Canada?"

Clay gave her a stern look. "That's precisely why I'm studying it. Do you know that Canada is the second largest country in the world?" He spun his globe past China, Europe, Africa, the United States and pointed. "Canada sits right on our northern border, yet most Americans know nothing about it."

Clarice wrinkled her nose. "You're so serious about these things."

Clay raised his eyebrows. "Can you name the ten provinces of Canada?"

She tapped her forehead. "Well, I know Ontario and Manitoba are on the border, oh, and Quebec. That's about it, I guess."

"I bet most Canadians can name our forty-eight states."

Clarice shrugged. "Why do you care so much about that kind of stuff?"

"I want to know about other parts of the world. What the people are like and their cultures."

Clarice bristled. "Well, you might learn about the world if you came out of this room."

Clay spun his globe again. "I will when I'm ready."

"And when will that be?"

"I still have things to learn," he said.

Clarice squinted at him. "Father is so set on *me* going to college, but you're the one who should go."

"You know better than that, Sis."

Clarice wanted to scream: How are you ever going to get out of here then? But the words lay thick on her tongue.

"Father is right," Clay said. "At college, you can learn about history, art, economics, things like that."

Clarice sniffed a laugh. "I find it strange that my going to college is the only thing you and Father agree on."

Clay turned away from her. "For different reasons, I think."

Clarice paced across the room then back to Clay. "All I want to do is run our stores on my own someday, but Father says a woman has no place in business. That people will think—"

"Father cares too much about what other people think."

"And you?"

"The more you try to please others, the less you might think of yourself."

Clarice sighed. "Why are you always so serious?"

Clay yanked her curl.

Clarice shook her head. "You know how I hate these curls. And when it's damp like this they do what they want." She grabbed a fistful and pulled it straight. "I'm going to cut them off someday. That would fix Father, wouldn't it?"

"Now that's my ornery little sister. Remember how you used to drive poor Maureen to fits?"

"Poor Maureen? Ha. I got sick and tired of her telling me what to do all the time."

Clay's eyes twinkled. "You gave her plenty to talk about."

"She should have minded her own business."

"She was responsible for you."

"And she made my life miserable."

Clay rolled his eyes. "Like you gave her such joy. Remember when you used to run up here and hide under my bed?"

Clarice laughed. "And Maureen was too chicken to come in and get me. But seriously, Clay, it must have been hard on Father to raise us by himself. I guess he needed someone to help him."

Clay tapped his fingers on his desk. "We've been over this before, but I still think it strange he didn't have relatives to help."

Nor our mother, Clarice wanted to say, then said, "You'd think at least an old aunt might have shown up occasionally."

"Father told me he was an only child, and that both of his parents died when he was sixteen. I asked what they died of, and he said his father got shot in a street robbery, and his mother's heart gave out. I asked if he had photos, and he said he threw them away." His eyes shot to the ceiling then to Clarice. "Why would Father throw their pictures away?"

Clarice shrugged.

Clay fingered his chin. "There was more to it, I think . . . just the way he said it."

"Well, I don't care about old pictures."

"Don't you ever wonder what our grandparents looked like?"

"Why should I care about dead people?"

"Well, sometimes I wonder where I got my light hair. And you have dark hair like Father's, but you don't really look like him. And where did your curls come from?"

Clarice yanked a handful and pulled it straight. "Well, if I knew, I'd give them back."

Clay laughed. "But we were saying how Father needed someone to help him, and no one did except Maureen."

"I wonder why he kept her around for so long."

"Because she ran this house like a business. You should appreciate that."

"She was only a nanny, but she ordered me around like she was my mother."

Clay looked at his empty hands. "Mothers don't act like that."

"I'm sorry, Clay. But how would I know how a mother would act?"

"You can't," he said. "But I remember her. Or her presence at least." The corners of Clay's lips curved up. "I remember her holding you in the rocker and singing. I remember her sitting by my bed at night running her fingertips over my eyelids to put me to sleep. But I opened my eyes as soon as she stopped." He looked at the ceiling, and then at Clarice. "But, I can't remember her face. I've tried, but I can't remember what she looked like."

Clarice pressed her hands on her stomach. Clay's old memories were all she had of her mother, and she turned on him. "Well, at least she left you something!"

"I'm sorry, Sis." He stood.

Meaning discussion over, Clarice knew. Her voice cracked. "I didn't mean to start this again. But she left you too."

Clay nodded. "Yes."

Clarice's eyes flashed. "Then why aren't you angry at her?"

"I can't explain it, Sis." He walked to the window, pulled the green, velvet curtain back, and looked out into the darkness.

Clarice's chest tightened. *Tell him; tell him now.* Her mouth quivered. "I need to tell you something."

"Not now, Sis. I have to study."

"I saw an ad in the *Tribune* and . . ."

Clay held up his hand. "I said I have to study."

Clarice felt a familiar knot in her stomach. *Clay and I can talk about anything. Yet we can't talk about, her.* She touched Clay's shoulder, picked up her shoes and socks, and tiptoed out.

In the dim hallway, she rested her head on the door. She'd wanted to tell him. She'd tried. But how could she tell Clay about the ad, when just those few words hurt him so?

And if I ever see that girl, Kathleen, I'll tell her how our mother wounded Clay and of the pain she caused me and my father.

CHAPTER SEVEN

The kitchen was only a corner in a little square adobe house just like most all the little square adobe houses in Albuquerque. But in this one, a room jutted out back where the four children slept. And as Kathleen stood over the black iron stove stirring a bubbling pot of muddy brown pinto beans, she thought how the dark murky mixture reflected her mood.

She glanced at the calendar. *Why haven't they answered my ad? Maybe they didn't see it. Maybe I should send another one.* It was almost four months since she'd left home and placed her classified in the *Chicago Tribune*, and then spent the night in Morningside Park. *There wasn't even a moon.* The next morning, she'd pulled the *Albuquerque Journal* out of a trashcan, searched through the help-wanted ads, and took a bus to Blount's Hardware Store where Mrs. Blount hired her on the spot.

She earned five-dollars a week to care for four children ages five through eleven with Sundays off. But she had a bed in a corner that must have been meant as a closet, and she had been happy to have it. And she'd tucked every cent she made into and an envelope marked, "Trip to Chicago".

The children's happy voices from the backyard told her all was well, yet she felt the need to check on them. She gave the pot a final stir and went out the back door. The yard was a field of sandy dirt with one cottonwood tree and a few juniper bushes. Eleven-year-old Lonnie ran up to her with the three girls close behind him. "Ah, Kathleen. Do we have to come in?"

"Fifteen more minutes," Kathleen said.

"Yay," they chorused. Lonnie pitched a can in the air with one hand, caught it with the other, and they sprinted across the yard.

Kathleen smiled. *Children are so constant. Hugs, a drink of water, a cracker, a bandage for a hurt knee, always something.*

Back in the kitchen, she looked at the boxy brown sofa, Mr. Blount's over-stuffed, olive green chair, the wooden dome of the radio where freshly scrubbed children circled at night. Her world now. Evenings with Mr. Blount reading the *Albuquerque Journal*, Mrs. Blount ironing her clothes for work the next day, while Kathleen cooked supper, washed dishes, set out school clothes, checked homework, and planned the next day's meals. She sighed. *I wish I were home.* She felt the familiar chill up her spine. *But Henry is there.*

The wall clock showed three-thirty. She mixed flour, cornmeal, salt, and baking powder in a glass bowl then took an egg out of the icebox and placed it on a saucer. Her stepmother, Beatrice, always said, "Eggs should be room temperature before you prepare to bake." With the cornbread preparation started, she gave the beans a final stir, turned off the burner, and went outside.

Five-year-old Janie waved. The other three paid her no attention. "Watch me!" Janie cried, as she kicked the can into the neighbor, Mrs. Warfield's, yard, and they all raced after it.

Kathleen ran to the edge of the yard and called them back.

Mrs. Warfield stood on her back porch with her hands on her hips while Kathleen treaded carefully among cacti and juniper bushes and retrieved the can.

Mrs. Warfield waved her approval.

Kathleen waved back. And standing among her four young charges, with their dirt-smeared faces and happy voices, she tried to remember how it felt to have nothing more important than getting her next shot at the can.

She gathered her flying hair and twisted it under her collar, then walked back to the concrete step. She rested her head on the door and soaked in the afternoon sun. Lonnie counted, feet scuffled, the can popped while her thoughts drifted back to another game of kick the can when she was thirteen, Henry, twelve. Her friends Jill and Edward wore the happy faces. They were not her stepsister and stepbrother then.

Kathleen, "It," she'd placed the can on the ground, covered her eyes and counted. Jill and Edward scattered. Henry's boots scuffled around the corner. At count of ten, she'd headed toward the cotton-wood tree hoping to find Edward, but he dashed out from behind his father's blue Ford, raced her back, then skidded to a stop and hollered, "Hey! Where's the can?"

Jill came from behind the cottonwood tree.

Henry came around the corner and pointed to Kathleen. "She threw it in the bushes."

Jill put her hands on her hips. "Kathleen wouldn't do that."

Henry smirked. "She's trying to show off for Edward 'cause she's sweet on him."

Hands still on her hips, "You're lying," Jill said.

Kathleen walked up to Henry. "You did it. I heard you."

Henry drew back his fist. "Prove it."

Edward stepped in front of Kathleen, and Jill pulled her back.

Edward beckoned. "Let's see how brave are you now, chicken."

Jill hollered, "Get 'em, Ed!"

Henry was taller, but Edward was faster; they scuffled, circled, while fists flew. Henry lunged. Edward dodged him, and Henry fell flat on his face.

"Ha ha, Henry," Jill taunted.

Henry pushed himself up, brushed off his pants, and waved his hands at the angry trio. "It was a joke. Okay?" He stepped into the bushes, pulled out the can, then dropped it on the ground. "Are you happy now?" He turned as if to leave, then swung back around and crushed the can with his boot.

Jill hollered, "You're weird, Henry."

Henry took off, Edward and Jill chased him, while Kathleen basked in the warmth of Edward's intervention.

Tears stung now as she pulled hair out from behind her collar. *Poor Edward. Poor dead Edward. All your beauty was destroyed in that awful car crash.* She winced. *That old jalopy, the twisted metal, the smashed roof.* She brushed her cheeks with the back of her hand. *Edward, my Prince. You were supposed to save me from Henry.*

Janie screeched.

Kathleen jumped up, but Lonnie was already at Janie's side. He held her in his thin arms until she stopped crying, then boosted her on a rock and examined her knee. Kathleen watched as Lonnie wiped Janie's knee with the corner of his shirt, pronounced it well with much aplomb, and she skipped away. Kathleen squeezed her eyes shut. *Why couldn't Henry treat me like that?*

Back in the kitchen, tears streamed down her cheeks as her thoughts returned to Clarice and Clay. *If they don't answer my ad, I'll keep saving my money and go to Chicago and find them.*

She cracked the egg into a small bowl, beat it lightly with a fork, then pulled the milk out of the icebox and poured it into a measuring cup. She poured the milk and egg into the cornmeal, mixed, then spooned it into the cast iron pan and placed it in the oven.

There was a knock at the front door. Kathleen opened it and found her dad on the step, hat in hand, smiling. "Hi, Kats."

Her heart raced as she smiled back.

Hartley held up his index finger. "Let me get Beatrice."

Kathleen's smile faded as he walked to his touring car, held the door open, and guided Bea to the front step.

"How did you find me?"

"We wormed it out of Jill," Bea said. "She's worried about you." She looked around the sandy front yard and pointed to a rusted metal chair. "That thing needs a coat of paint." Then, in the curt tone, normal for her, she said, "Well, Kathleen, aren't you going to invite us in?"

Kathleen held the door open, Hartley and Bea came into the house, and the three stood in the tight little room studying each other. Hartley always reminded Kathleen of a lost boy trying to find his way home. A simple man, his face like an upside-down pear with deep-set, almond shaped eyes the color of sky. Thoughtful eyes, an honest face, and how Kathleen had yearned for the sight of her dad's face during her long nights staring at the ceiling.

She started to reach out to him, but would not, could not, with Bea standing there. Yet when he smiled, Kathleen went into his open arms and hugged him.

Hartley held her at arm's length in front of him. "You haven't put on any weight I see, still skinny as a stick." He hung his hat on the rack then sat on the sofa. Lithe, he hardly made a dent.

Bea sat next to him with her back rigid and chin held high.

Kathleen pulled up a chair and told them about Mr. and Mrs. Blount and the children.

Hartley nodded. "So, you're settled then?"

"I have a job," she said.

Hartley fingered his chin. "Your grandmother is coming to visit next month. And she, uh, she will expect to see you."

Kathleen's face tingled. *He wants me to come home.*

Hartley patted his leg in an irregular rhythm, while Bea rearranged the doily over the sofa arm. "Maybe you could, well, come for a visit," he said.

Kathleen blinked. Her grandmother . . . tiny pint of a woman who invaded their home every summer to "tend to this household" and then proceeded to tear it apart. Her bun was pinned so tight her eyes slanted as she swished her broom, swung the mop, and bucket in hand, issued orders. And she adored Henry.

"I need to check on the children," Kathleen said, then walked to the back window where, knees crossed, they sat in a semicircle under the cottonwood tree with their little arms in animation. She pulled a handkerchief out of her pocket and wiped her eyes. "Tell Grandmother I have a fancy new job that keeps me so busy I can't take time off."

Hartley chuckled. "I doubt that will convince her." He came to the window beside her and looked out at the children. "They're quiet enough."

"They're good children."

Back on the sofa, Hartley's eyes danced. "We went to that new Kimo Theater last night, and boy was it something with fancy lights and hand rails, even murals on the walls."

"I haven't been to the Kimo yet," Kathleen said, hearing the longing in her voice, but too late to hide it. "What movie did you see?"

"My Best Girl. I thought it was great, but Bea didn't like it."

"I don't care for Mary Pickford," Bea said. "And I like the old theater better."

"We went there last week for Bank Night," Hartley said. "Why there was over fifty dollars in the pot." He slapped his hand on his thigh. "I almost got it that time, Kats. My ticket was only two numbers off."

Kathleen smiled hearing about their Wednesday ritual. "They'll draw your number someday, Dad."

Bea sniffed. "That's what we think every week." Then she told Kathleen about Jill's new job at the telephone company. "She dresses up in high-heeled shoes. She has her own desk and typewriting machine."

"And she has a fella," Hartley said. "Seems she was standing at the bus stop, and he pulled up in his car. He must have talked fast, because he brought her home, and they've been courtin' ever since."

Kathleen loved her dad's impish grin, but Bea's eyes shot daggers at him. "He's not her *fella* yet," she said. "And he won't be if I have anything to do with it."

Hartley saluted in his courteous mocking gesture. "Yes, my love."

Kathleen enjoyed this ritual. *How else to deal with Bea?*

"He has been married before," Hartley said. "His wife died and left him with a little girl. She's about ten, I think."

"Eleven," Bea said.

Kathleen glanced to the ceiling. *Poor Jill, she'll have her hands full with her mother now.* "Jill's smart," she said. "She knows what she's doing."

Hartley laughed. "Oh, she's smart all right. She's practically moved me out of my own house."

Even Bea laughed now. "Oh, Hartley, you never give the girl a rest."

Hartley's eyes sparkled as he opened his hands in helplessness. "She's spread out all over the place: shoes, stockings, combs, and those curlers and bobby pins." He touched his imaginary hair. "She brushes her hair so much, the other day I told her, 'No use to brush, Jill, because it doesn't help.'" He ducked in an exaggerated gesture. "I thought she was going to throw the brush at me."

Pain rippled through Kathleen's chest. Jill, her beautiful stepsister with shining black hair, creamy skin, and dreamy blue eyes . . . *and now she has my father too.* Then she felt sudden remorse. *Jill and I played dolls together.* She looked at Bea. "Tell Jill hi for me, please."

She looked at her dad. "How is Henry?"

"He's gone."

"Gone where?"

Hartley shrugged. "I wish I knew. Oh, he came home last week. We fed him, gave him money, and then he disappeared again."

"Henry's so smart. He got hundreds on his report cards, while I struggled."

"Henry may be smart," Bea said, "but he looked like something the dog drug in."

Kathleen pictured her brother sleeping in a field, hungry, dirty, worse.

"His eyes looked like a wild man," Bea said.

Kathleen shivered. She knew that look well. "Please don't tell him where I am."

Hartley shook his head. "Of course not."

"I told your father that Henry should go into the army," Bea said. "They will teach him discipline. He'll have to behave."

Kathleen heard the slight pleading in Bea's voice. "I don't think discipline will help," she said. Yet she didn't know what might help Henry, either.

Bea stood. "I have supper to fix, Hartley."

"Supper?" Hartley walked to the stove and lifted the pot lid. "These beans sure look good."

Kathleen looked at Bea. "I made them the way you taught me, with chili powder and onion and a pinch of garlic powder and cumin."

Hartley smacked his lips. "They'll be good then." He put the lid back on the pot and rubbed his stomach. "And the cornbread sure smells good."

Kathleen grabbed a potholder and yanked the pan out of the oven. "I almost forgot."

Hartley took his hat off the rack, held it over his chest, and bowed to Bea. "I'm ready, my love."

The trio stood outside in the driveway in awkward silence.

Mrs. Warfield cut across the yard and walked up to them. "Thank you for keeping those children out of my yard, Kathleen. I don't want them tramping on my flower beds."

"I know," Kathleen mumbled. After a moment, she said, "This is my father, Hartley Howe, and my stepmother, Beatrice."

Mrs. Warfield extended her hand. "Oh, well, glad to meet you. One can never be too careful, with these young girls now, I mean."

Hartley stammered. "I, uh . . ."

Mrs. Warfield stared at the touring car. "Are you from around here, Mr. Howe?"

"We live over on La Vega Road."

"I see, well, pleased to meet you, Mr. Howe, Mrs. Howe," and she walked across the yard to her house.

"Well, goodbye, Kathleen," Bea said and held her arm out to Hartley.

Hartley helped Bea into the car, then opened the back door and pulled out a cardboard box. "We brought your things," he said and set the box on the porch.

Kathleen winced. *This is all? My things, some questions so they can feel better, no mention of my coming home.*

Hartley pulled folding money out of his wallet and pressed it into her hand.

Kathleen handed it back to him. "I don't want it."

"Please, take it, Kats."

"Thanks, Dad, but I earn my own money now."

Hartley's face crumpled. "Maybe you'll come see us when your grandmother comes."

"Maybe," Kathleen said. "On one of my Sundays off."

Hair flying in the breeze, Kathleen stood in the middle of the road as her father drove away and felt herself shrinking, like a paper sack just emptied. The sun pressed on her shoulders as she gathered her hair, tucked it her under her collar, and wiped her tears with the back of her hand. *They don't want me . . . what if Clarice doesn't want me either?*

* * *

Hartley looked at Kathleen in his rearview mirror and remembered a raggedy little girl of eleven chasing after his car crying, "Daddy, Daddy, don't leave me."

He had just wanted to get away for a couple of hours for a picnic and enjoy the company of a young woman. Yet Kathleen's wary eyes had watched him all morning while he baked a chocolate cake, made potato salad and turkey sandwiches. He'd dished up plates for her and Henry then patted her shoulder. "Be a good girl, and I'll be back before you know it."

But she'd followed him to the car pleading, "Don't go, Daddy, please don't go."

Yet he'd steeled himself, closed the door, and headed out the long driveway. He'd glanced to the side and saw Henry with his hands in his pocket, leaning on the cottonwood tree, laughing.

His chest ached. He could barely breathe. *Oh, my child, I shut you out of my mind and left you on the road, begging. What kind of a father would do that?*

Bea touched his leg. She shared his pain, she understood, and he was thankful. *Yet, would she understand if she knew?* His shoulders drew up. *Dear God.*

He turned right and glanced across the seat at Bea. Her pointed chin held high, sun sprayed over her soft brown hair and slender neck. *She's patrician.* He liked the sound of the word though not sure of its exact meaning. He had read it in a book once describing a woman with regal bearing and great beauty. Like the barren beauty of this high desert. *Patrician; yes, it suits her.*

He sighed. But not like Laura, his Laura, with her shining blue eyes, curving lips, and glossy black curls. And the old pain hit, not sharp anymore, yet always there, ready to grab him.

I knew I would lose her. I should have prepared myself. And then she was gone. Tears welled. *Dear God, after all these years.* He looked at Bea again. No, never anyone like Laura. Not Bea. Not Miriam. No one.

And for the first time in a very long while, he pictured his second wife, Miriam's, pale face, her anxious gray eyes and sloping chin. *Ah, Miriam, if I had only known your eyes were masking pain. Timid little bird you were. I married you to mother my children, and you knew it. But you got back at me by dropping dead in the last verse of Blessed Assurance at Broadway Christian Church.*

He remembered her hymnbook falling to the floor, her body crumpled over the pew, the horrified faces of his children. That was what he remembered when he thought of her at all.

He felt Bea's sharp eyes boring into him. Not ready to acknowledge her yet, he stared straight ahead. *She's complicated. When angry, her face is firm like a rock, and she's unmovable. Yet she has been hurt, too, when her husband, Van, took off with that other woman and disgraced her. And then her son, Edward, killed in that car crash.* His chest tightened. *A fine young man . . . bright and full of promise. Where was the fairness of it?* He stiffened his back. *Where was fairness when Laura left me with two little children?*

Bea had known trouble all right. Yet beneath her chiseled exterior, he'd found softness, kinship, and strength. Though he didn't need her softness, he did need her strength.

They were almost home when Bea spoke. "You must feel better now that you know where she is."

It was a statement and a question. Hartley did not answer.

She spoke again. "Why do you torture yourself? You tried everything you knew how to do with those children."

"I tried, yes, but it wasn't enough." His words hung in the air between them.

He glanced across the road at the turgid waters of the Rio Grande. *Oh, I disciplined them, though it didn't take much for Kathleen, just a stern look, a pointed finger, or a good spanking now and then. But with Henry—warnings, scolding, spankings, to bed with no supper—nothing worked.*

And then the day that haunted him still. He had struck Henry across the face, and then felt so dreadfully sorry he grasped him to his chest and cried, "Son, my Son, why do you do these things?" Henry broke away from him. His face crippled with rage, he'd screamed: "I don't know why. Can't you see that?"

The crushing weight of weariness washed over him. "That boy drained me; consumed every drop of my energy and left nothing for her."

Bea touched his leg again. "You did the best that you could."

"By whom?"

"Well, by him, her, both of them." Her voice sounded raw with impatience.

Hartley squeezed the steering wheel and stared straight ahead. "By him, maybe, but not by her!"

CHAPTER EIGHT

Clipboards in hand, Clarice and Walter walked the lonely aisles of Pruitt's. The last customers gone, doors locked, and lights dimmed, they made their last swing: Walter through Bedding and Bath and Clarice through Women's Wear and Jewelry.

They had put in fine jewelry just last year and were pleased with the sales and large markup. Diamonds and gemstones long since in the safe, Clarice ran her finger over the glass countertop, and it left an imprint in the dust. She grabbed a pad and left a note for Mrs. Grey.

In Women's Wear, she stopped in front of a manikin and straightened "Molly's" skirt. When Clarice was a little girl, the store was her playhouse, and the manikins were her friends who posed in stiff gestures during the day, then went home to their families at night. She had named each one, but as their stores expanded she'd lost track, so the brunettes became Mollies and the blondes, Veronicas. Her father even let her dress little Mollies and Veronicas in Children's Play Wear. She pretended to be their mother and dressed them in the latest style of school clothes.

For Clarice, this store had always been her real home. She was happier here than anywhere else. She'd followed her father around the store and saw how people listened when he spoke and then did what he said. She'd worked beside him and polished counters, straightened shelves, broke down boxes and stacked them in the back room. Anything. Just to be with him.

She stepped back now to assess Molly's plaid skirt and blue sweater, then dashed across three aisles and came back with a lilac silk scarf, cameo pin, and a black leather purse. She draped the scarf around the manikin's neck, fastened it with the cameo, and placed the purse in her open hand. She stepped back and nodded. "You're ready to go now, Molly."

In a fitting room, an ivory, silk blouse lay crumpled on the floor. Clarice hung it up and wrote a note for Miss Fisher. Back in the center aisle, she stopped to admire a display of woolen sweaters in vivid blues, greens, and dark rose. She counted the ones remaining and smiled. Time to reorder. She knew the sweaters would sell when she saw them at Market last month, and she felt proud that something she chose turned out the way she'd hoped.

She met Walter at the back of the store. "The perfume counter needs straightening," she said, "and the jewelry counter needs dusting. I left a note for Mrs. Grey."

"Everything looked good on my end except Bedding."

"Bedding?" Clarice said, surprised.

"I spent most of my time straightening sheets and pillowcases." Walter hummed. "When Dubois works, we never seem to have a problem. He wasn't here today."

"Funny how we can walk through this store most any time and notice these things. Why can't they?"

Walter tapped his clipboard. "Well, we may have to make some changes if they don't." He gazed across the store. "This is my favorite part. Seeing great displays, full shelves, and polished floors."

"And money locked in the safe," Clarice added.

Walter grinned. "I can't argue with that."

"It's like this store is alive" Clarice said. "Like it has a life of its own, and we're only caretakers. Sometimes I feel like it just wants us to get out of here, so it can rest." She raised her eyebrows. "Some might think that's pretty strange."

"Sounds like a merchant to me."

"Right," Clarice said. "And I'm going to run this store someday."

"Not until you finish college," Walter snapped.

Back in Walter's office, Clarice flopped on the couch and sorted through her notes.

Walter sat at his desk and sorted his.

Finished with her notes, Clarice studied him. *He's a perfectionist; stays on top of things and never stops.* She thought back to her lonely childhood. *When it's my turn to run this store, I'm going to have fun.*

As if feeling her quiet assessment, Walter looked up. "End of a long day," he said.

"Everything's going well, isn't it?"

"Pretty well, I guess. I just hope it stays that way."

"You're such a curious mix of optimism and pessimism."

"What do you mean?"

"Well, Chicago is booming, sales are great and we're expanding, yet you don't seem to embrace it."

Walter smiled. "It took optimism to get this far. But it's my more prudent nature that keeps things running smooth."

"True," Clarice said. "But I remember when this was our only store."

"Sometimes it seems like a dream, doesn't it?"

Clarice stretched out her legs. "How did you get money to start? You never told me."

"Borrowed from the bank, of course."

"What did you use for collateral?"

Walter shuffled through his notes. "I didn't have much of anything. They just took a chance on me."

Clarice pictured the pillared bank with cold marble floors, men in dark suits bent over mahogany desks. "I can't imagine any of those men taking a chance with *their* money."

He looked up. "Well, they did. And look at us now."

"Right," Clarice said. "So you can pour over ledgers, and then spend your nights on this couch."

"Only when I must," he said.

Clarice sighed. "When I was little, I wished you were at home more."

Walter frowned. "It's been a long time since you've said that, Clarice. I thought you, well, you might understand now."

"I do, sort of. Yet sometimes I wonder what drives you."

"Money," Walter said. "And power and pride, of course. They go together."

"And control?"

"I don't deny it."

Clarice yawned. "I'm tired for some reason."

"You asked what drives me," Walter said. "And I'm wondering what drives you?"

"I've been following you around this store since I was a little girl. I've never known anything else."

"Well, if I'd realized I was making a merchant out of you, I would have made you stay home."

Clarice let out a soft laugh. "Oh, you knew all right, and you brought me anyway."

Walter nodded. "I wanted you with me."

"And you don't, now?" Clarice's voice quavered.

"I want more for you than just this store."

Clarice sat up straight. "It's all I've ever wanted to do, and you know it. And besides, I want to prove I can run this store as well as you can."

"Prove it to me?" Walter said. "Or to yourself?"

Clarice stroked her chin. "To me, I think. But to you, too, and all the rest of the men in this business."

"Nonsense. You're going to Harvard."

"Women go to Radcliff, Father. Don't you know that?"

Walter's eyes brightened. "Well, to Radcliffe then. The money is already in the safe."

Clarice stood. "What if I change my mind?"

"You agreed. Two years in this store, and then you're off to college." He pointed at his calendar. "And you have six more months."

"Why is my going to college so important to you?"

Walter walked to his bookcase and ran his fingernails across a row of leather-bound books. "Successful men send their children to college."

"So, it's a status thing for you."

"And for you, too." He shrugged. "Who knows? You might meet someone with means and marry well."

Clarice's face grew hot. "If I do marry, Father, it will be on my terms. Not for money or status."

Walter walked back to his desk. "I need a couple hours to finish up, so you might as well go home." He sat down. "In fact, I'll just sleep here tonight, so I can check out the warehouse in the morning."

* * *

Walter stood at the window and watched Clarice get into the taxi. *She's independent as hell.*

He smiled. *And more like me than I even imagined.*

Yet he had sensed something different in his daughter tonight. Old words, but new thoughts, perhaps. Lights shimmered off the shoreline. A full moon illuminated the clouds as the taxi headed up State Street. There were times when he wished he could tell her who he was, and how he got here. Lift the guilt hanging over him like dense fog. Yet even as he thought it, he knew it would be impossible, dangerous even, for her to know.

Back at his desk, he opened the ledger book. His eyes flitted from column to column, seeing, yet not absorbing, and he slammed it shut. "It's that damn classified ad! It's changed things. Changed her." He loosened his tie, hung it in the closet along with his jacket, and pulled out his pillow and blanket. *But at least she hasn't said anymore about that ad. Felicia did her job, I see.*

He patted the cracked, brown leather sofa. *So many nights together old friend with icy roads, holiday sales, inventory, or just pure exhaustion.* He lay on his pillow as moonlight's white silk streamed through the window. His desk became a somber block, his file cabinets tall rectangles, his bookcases dark grids. This, with no ringing telephones, accountants, salesmen, and customers, was his only time free from being Walter Pruitt.

CHAPTER NINE

In 1892, sixteen-year-old Patrick Roark hopped freight trains across Illinois plains, was rolled and pitched off by a bum outside St. Louis, got staggering drunk on Irish whiskey, and was cheated out of most of his "boot money" by Big Jake, a seasoned Faro dealer. His initial spirit splintered like an abandoned scarecrow, he tramped his way to Wichita and bought his first gun and horse.

In the Texas Panhandle, he learned how to rope calves, brand steer, eat sowbelly beans, and make sourdough biscuits. After his first night in the bunkhouse with bedbugs and lice, he wrapped his boots inside his coat for a pillow and slept under the stars with the other hired hands. He went to town with the men on payday but remembered, Big Jake, at the Faro table and showed only small bills. He stayed in one place long enough to make a few dollars, then moved on.

Skirting towns, Patrick roamed the west Texas desert, camped by mountain streams in New Mexico, tended horses in Colorado and lived in mountain caves. After five years, he had grown seven inches and gained thirty pounds. His face lean and chiseled, with his coal black hair and mustache, more than one woman looked his way.

California beckoned as he sewed the last of his money into a new topcoat and boarded the Santa Fe, a paying customer. The train headed down the pass into the San Bernardino Valley enclosed by snow-capped mountains, some jutting up over ten thousand feet high. The sweet fragrance of orange blossoms filled the air, and by the time the train reached Redlands, Patrick got off and found the closest orange stand. Tart, yet sweet, pulpy yellow juice dripped down his chin as he ate his first orange.

The late April sun warmed Patrick's shoulders as he walked up palm tree lined streets with gingerbread houses and wrapping front porches. He bought an old horse and rode out to the long rows of Eucalyptus trees planted for windbreaks and found pockets of old California ranchos, along with packing sheds and fruit stands.

He spent time with Amos Seymour, an orange grower in Riverside. "Oranges need warm days and cool nights," Seymour said. "Our winters are near perfect, though I had a scare last year when the temperature dipped into the twenties." He looked toward the mountains. "But like a farmer, an orange grower takes his chances."

"How'd you get your start?" Patrick said.

"Paid five dollars for my first naval bud stock from Mrs. Tibbets in Riverside. Everybody said I was touched in the head to pay that much for a bud, but navels are sweeter than other oranges and they're seedless." He chuckled. "Shipped my first load to St. Louis and sold out soon as they unloaded. But we're still experimenting. Oranges take time and tending to."

Patrick camped by the edge of the Santa Ana river bed and was tempted to stay. Seymour had offered him a job come picking time. For five years, he had scrounged for food, trudged through fiery deserts and freezing snow, and survived by his own grit. Yet he still felt the massive figure of his father looming over him. "My boy, run? Like a yellow-bellied coward?" And he was still running. He dug a stick into the last embers of his campfire. *But I'm going to show Big Red—and all those other bastards who treated me like I was nothing.*

He just didn't know how yet.

The next morning, Patrick packed his gear, traded his old horse for a fresh nag, and headed north. The gold rush was almost over, yet he found San Francisco wild, with more gambling, women, and drink than he'd seen anywhere. He got a job cleaning horse stalls and washed dishes in a hotel dining hall for his keep. After six months of getting nowhere, he threw his apron on the floor.

"Can't blame you none," the owner said. "Ain't nothin' here for a smart young fella like you." He tugged his beard. "Me, I spent months on my hands and knees in that icy American River. Got just enough gold to go back and forth to Hangtown for supplies, so's I could do it all over again. Was about to quit and go home when a nugget slid into my pan like manna from heaven. I cashed it in and bought this place, and I ain't been back since."

The old man's voice rattled with excitement. "Things was booming then. Place was full every night." He rubbed his palms together. "Wish I had some of that dough now."

Patrick heard the regret in the old man's voice. "You by yourself?" he asked.

"Had a family back in Omaha, two boys and a girl. Little girl was only three when I left, but she must be courting by now." His eyes glazed over. "Meant to send for 'em but when I finally got money, the wife had done took up with some other fella." His shoulders slumped. "Don't blame her none."

Having stifled the loss of his parents, Patrick felt the hollow ache in his chest and the old stabbing pain. *When I have my own family, I won't abandon them like this creature did his.*

"If I was yer age, son, I'd be on the next freighter to Alaska. Fella I know from Seattle said six or seven men came in with three million worth of gold in their satchels. They're supposed to be on their way here, that's if bandits don't get 'em first."

* * *

Fresh off the steamer in Skagway, Alaska, a crowd of eager men absorbed Patrick as he headed up Moore's wharf toward town. A man in a three-piece suit and derby hat tapped him on the shoulder. "I'll send the family a telegram for five dollars, mister."

"Don't have a family," Patrick muttered.

"Must be somebody needs to know you arrived safe."

"Nobody," Patrick said, and then stopped and stared at the man so earnestly vying for his five dollars. He looked businesslike, yet something told Patrick the man was not what he appeared to be. Another man grabbed his arm. "Carry yer bag for a dollar, mister." This one looked less prosperous, and Patrick shook him off.

In Skagway, crude, wooden buildings and pole-tents lined narrow streets, which were more like muddy creeks scented with horse manure and fresh-sawed lumber. Some of the men walked the plank sidewalk to Greensby's Dry Goods, while others went straight to Clancy's Saloon. Patrick found a bank to deposit his money, then found a bath and a dollar-a-day bed.

The next day, with his stomach full and pockets light, he went to Clancy's. The piano bounced as raggedy women danced with boisterous men. A hand-blocked sign over the bar said: One Dollar a Dance. "Over here, Gert," a white sleeved bartender called out, and a ruddy-faced woman with greasy strings of brown hair pulled away from a table of mud-caked men and weaved her way to the bar. The gambling tables were six men deep. Remembering Big Jake in St. Louis, Patrick sat at a far table and ordered a beer.

A few beers later, Patrick headed out the door to the sidewalk and bumped into a grizzly man with shaggy, gray hair hanging over his face and down his neck and shoulders. His brown eyes were barely visible through two slits above his nose. His teeth looked like rusted nails as he spat a sticky glob on the boardwalk.

"How long you been here?" Patrick said.

"Long enough to be a sourdough, son; meaning I made my mistakes and stuck." He stared at Patrick. "Yer just off the steamer, a cheechako. In a year or two, you'll look like me. That's if you stick around."

Patrick reared his shoulders. "I'm going to strike it rich."

"Me, I never did. But this place keeps me here. Not sure why. Just know I like it here better than any place else." He stopped. "Hell, I'm the freest man on earth."

They walked together in silence past Greensby's, a two-story hotel, a drug store, and a watch maker shop amongst half-finished buildings.

"Clancy's is quite a place," Patrick said.

"Yep, Soapy and his men are already at work."

"Soapy?"

"Soapy Smith. He runs the place. That woman, Gert, and the rest will get those fellas drunk, take 'em up to a room and clean out their pockets, then go on to the next one. Them they don't get, Soapy's men will rob 'em on the street. Those lucky enough to get on the trail with money and supplies, will likely be met by his bandits."

"Where's the law?" Patrick said.

"Ain't no law here but Soapy's. He runs it all from Clancy's, and now he owns Jeff's Place down the street. Passes himself off like a gentleman, but his men meet cheechakos at the boat offerin' to buy 'em a drink at Clancy's, and then they'll fleece 'em. Hell, he even opened up a travel bureau and sells maps for a dollar, so he can see inside their wallets."

"Some fellow offered to carry my bag," Patrick said, "but I didn't like his looks and turned him down."

"You'd a never seen yer bag again, if you had."

"Guess I was lucky."

The sourdough looked Patrick up and down. "If you made it this far with yer money, you ain't lucky, yer smart." He turned into Jeff's Place and looked over his shoulder. "By the way, son, there ain't no telegraph lines in Skagway."

The next morning, Patrick bought a horse and saddle, headed to Greensby's, and loaded up with enough supplies and food for three months. He stood on the plank sidewalk and looked up the mud slogged road toward Clancy's and smiled. *I'm going to strike it rich. I feel it. And I'll hang onto my money, then go home and show those bastards.*

* * *

The cheechakos trudged through icy streams. Wind whipped their faces as they clawed up jagged mountain glaciers, while glaring sun reflected off ice and burned their skin and eyes. Horses, half-frozen and delirious, slid to their deaths on icy banks, and snow slides claimed their masters. Those left, drove on, most to return empty-handed. The rest might never be heard from again.

Halfway up the first glacier, Patrick's eyes burned as if stabbed with a branding iron, his face was on fire, his feet and hands stung as if stuck with a thousand, pointed knives. Barely able to grasp the next rock, fear choked him like a hangman's noose, as horses and screaming men slid past him down the rocks to the ice below. Half-frozen, numb, and delirious, Patrick shot his horse, abandoned most of his supplies and turned back while he could, then took the first bed he could find.

Three days later, his face puffed like a blister, eyes pools of blood, feet and hands still numb, Patrick dragged his aching body to the dining hall and ravished his first hot meal in three weeks. In the gloomy dusk of eighteen-hour days, he walked the plank sidewalks, talked to sourdoughs, and amused himself by watching fools parted from their money at Clancy's and Jeff's. Killings averaged one-a-day. One night he watched the "telegraph man" shoot a sourdough in the middle of the street.

Patrick was frugal, but living in Alaska proved costly. After six months in Skagway, he paced back and forth by his rented bed. *What am I doing here? It's dark all the time; there's thieves everywhere; people gun-down each other on the streets.* He slammed his boot on the side of the bedpost. "Damn! I didn't even get halfway up that mountain!"

With just enough money to get to Seattle and purchase a train ticket east, he headed to Moore's Warf where he'd landed six months before. "Two months 'till the next steamer can get through," the ticket master said. "Maybe more."

Patrick gathered what supplies he had left and took them to Greensby Dry Goods. "Don't need 'em," Mr. Greensby said. "Try selling 'em yourself when the next load of suckers come headed out, he spied a "Help Wanted" sign in the wind off, and handed it to Mr. Greensby. "When do I start?"

* * *

It didn't take Patrick long to find where the real fortune lay. Endless streams of gold seekers seemed oblivious to prices they paid for mackinaws, picks, flannel shirts and coffee, and Patrick worked hard to accommodate them. By the end of his first month, he called all his regular customers by name and knew which men had their families with them. By the end of his third month, Mr. Greensby patted him on the back. "You have a good feel for what people want. You do the ordering from now on."

Whether working with customers, unloading freight, stocking shelves, Patrick never wasted a move or touched a piece of paper twice. By the end of the year, he was running the place while Greensby went back and forth to his family in Seattle. Like the other businessmen, Patrick maintained an "understanding" with Soapy's men who demanded money for their "Missionary Fund" or the town's "Defense Fund." Yet it rankled him. He grew alarmed when gold seekers started landing in Dyea, a rival port, six miles north.

It all came to a head when Soapy's men extorted a sizable "contribution" for the town's favorite preacher, and then had his men rob him that night while he slept. The town formed a Committee of 101 and published an order to "all con men and other objectionables to get out of town while the gettin' was good".

Soapy countered with his own Law and Order Committee of 303 and posted, "No blackmailers or vigilantes will be tolerated," then he promptly returned to his old ways. After one of Soapy's men fleeced a cheechako at Jeff's Place, the Committee of 101 demanded return of his take. Soapy stormed to the wharf ranting where someone shot him in the chest and killed him. The committee of 101 promptly rounded up the rest of Soapy's men and drove them out of town.

With Soapy disposed of, honest citizens established civic activities suitable to a law-abiding town. Ladies from the Literary Society came to Patrick for donations, and he showed them his new bolts of fabric and ribbons and gave their children peppermint candy. Mr. Greensby spent most of his time in Seattle now. "I had confidence in you from the start," he told Patrick, "I'm giving you a big fat raise."

But Patrick didn't want a raise, for a banker from Fairbanks, Mr. T.L. Guthrie, had approached him and offered a loan. Just in time for spring thaw, Patrick opened Skagway's Best, six doors down from Greensby's. Opening day, Greensby shook his fist. "Damn Irishman! Should've known better than to trust one of 'em."

Patrick met the cheechakos at the boats, guaranteed the best prices, and delivered. He joined the YMCA Debating Club, gave money to the Women's Christian Temperance Union, and discarded his Catholic upbringing and joined the Methodist-Episcopal Church. He'd lured most of Greensby's regular customers away, and Mr. Greensby closed his shop and went back to Seattle for good.

He saved every penny and abhorred waste of any kind. One day, while watching his new clerk wrap a package, Patrick stopped him mid-sale and demonstrated the frugal use of paper and string. He worked eighteen-hour days, seven days a week, slept on a cot in the back of the store, and dreamed of ways to make money. One night, he woke up with his mouth watering. The next morning, he wrote to his friend, Amos Seymour, and Patrick was the first merchant in Skagway to receive a load of oranges. They sold out immediately at three dollars each. "Oranges; imagine that," the townspeople said, and they flocked to Skagway's Best.

A prized customer at First Bank of Fairbanks, Patrick paid off his loan to Mr. Guthrie in less than three years. He walked the plank sidewalks, his shoulders square in a gentleman's suit. A local politician even approached him to run for mayor. Amazed, Patrick considered the offer, but his goal was to make money and go home. Being mayor might be a distraction.

In his search for profits, he'd read how the United States government set up an agricultural station near the new gold field in the Tanana Valley near Fairbanks. He recalled the bedraggled face of the hotel owner in San Francisco who stayed long after he should have left and wondered if Skagway's boom might soon be over.

The following month, order books tucked in his satchel, Patrick followed the Chena River into Fairbanks and rented a room. A riverfront town, he found larger mining operations in Fairbanks than in Skagway and the citizens more savvy. Mr. T.L. Guthrie was still president of First Bank of Fairbanks, the most prominent bank in town, and he owned the main trading post. He rode out to the agricultural station where long summer daylight produced enormous turnips and rutabagas which were tender and tasty. He liked the lettuce and radishes, and the potatoes looked promising. He rode back to Fairbanks, his head swelling with possibilities.

He went into every retail store and checked prices, merchandise, and store conditions. He called on mining operators about their need for tools and supplies, and then went through his order books and presented them with a list of the goods and services he offered. He even found a suitable building. He walked the wharf in the summer twilight, hung around saloons, and listened to men talk. People were here from Nome and Dyea. He even recognized a few faces from Skagway.

All Patrick's instincts told him to sell out in Skagway and open a new store, or maybe keep his operation in Skagway and open a second one here. Yet he had learned from Greensby. A man should run his own operation. He thought of Fred, the young man he'd left in charge of Skagway's Best and decided to sell out in Skagway and open a new store in Fairbanks. Elated, he ran a comb through his hair, smoothed his mustache, and headed to the nearest saloon. He didn't want to overlook a potential customer.

* * *

The first thing Patrick noticed was her auburn hair. The second thing, as he sat at the table across from her, was her warm, soft, yet throaty voice. "I'm Annie," she said.

"And I'm Patrick Roark."

"Irish, huh? My grandfather was from County Roscommon. He told me stories about Banshees and Leprechauns."

Patrick grimaced, and then ordered two beers. He drank. They talked. He drank. They danced until his head whirled, and Annie guided him back to the table. "Where are you from, Patrick Roark?"

Loosened from six beers, "Chicago," he said, then added, "but I've been traveling the west the past few years."

"I'm from Kansas City, that's Missouri," Annie said, "and I'm going back as soon as I can." She pulled a lock of auburn hair off her shoulder, twisted it around her finger and said, "Do you want to go up to a room?"

With little money in his pocket and nothing to lose, Patrick ordered another beer, put it in Annie's steady hand, and followed her up the stairs.

He leaned back on the headboard, held out his open hand, and Annie handed him his beer.

She pulled pins from her hair and red curls bounced over creamy white shoulders.

Patrick's years of wandering, his emasculation by his father and final betrayal by his mother, had marked him like the cattle he'd branded in the Texas panhandle. He had bedded whores, but women meant weakness and deception and he avoided them, relieving his throbbing groin over sagebrush.

In his quiet triumph tonight, he had approached Annie without thinking. In his alcohol haze, he watched her back up to the bed, brace his boot between her legs, and yank.

Patrick's head exploded as he drew his other boot to her buttocks, shoved, and Annie tumbled across the room. He'd spent too many years guarding his boots!

Heart racing, he jumped from the bed and found Annie

sprawled on her back with her hair circled like a crimson fan. Her cheeks were as red as her hair and her eyes shot daggers at him. He offered his hand, but she drew her foot to his chest, pushed, and and he stumbled across the room.

Drunken pinwheels swirled through Patrick's head as he thudded against the wall and slid to the floor. Tears rolled down his cheeks while he drew his knees to his chest and rolled back and forth in bawdy, raucous laughter. His face tingled. He pushed up and walked around the room, a new man.

Annie stood with her arms folded, shaking her head. "This one has lost his mind," she said and guided him out the door.

The next afternoon Patrick slipped back into the saloon and found Annie at the window table with a customer. He took a seat at the bar and studied her with new appreciation. Her auburn hair flowed down her back like a foaming waterfall. With her pearly white skin, her high cheekbones, and soft green eyes, he imagined her a treat for any man. *What could she be doing here?*

The man left, and hat in hand, Patrick approached her.

Annie smiled. "How about a drink, Mr. Roark?"

Patrick groaned. "I'll pass."

Annie nodded toward the chair, and he sat across from her.

"Didn't mean to drop out on you last night," he said. He took her hand in his and slipped a ten-dollar gold piece into her palm.

Her eyes slanted toward the bartender, then she handed it back to him.

"Take it, please."

Annie's eyes twinkled. "All you got was a good chuckle, Mr. Roark, and me a sore bottom." She winked. "Besides, I had a good laugh over it myself."

Patrick liked the saucy tilt of her chin, her impish eyes, the two rosy dots on her cheeks. The sun illuminated her face, and he saw a faint scar above her left eye and wondered how she got it. Without thinking, he said, "I'd like to buy you supper, Annie Parsons." He glanced toward the bartender. "If that's all right."

"It's all right, Mr. Roark."

Later that afternoon, her plate piled with roast rabbit, mashed potatoes and cornbread, Annie ate heartily.

"Will this get you in trouble?" Patrick asked. "I mean me seeing you out of the saloon."

Annie shrugged. "I'm on my own time now."

Patrick gazed at her ivory hands, her long arms and wondered how it might feel with them wrapped around him.

Annie placed her fork on the table and looked up. "Are you thinking of moving your operation here, Mr. Roark?"

Patrick started. *What the hell!* "My, uh operation?"

"My best friend, Lucille, says you own the largest dry goods in Skagway."

"Lucille?"

"Lucille Cartwright. She works at First Bank of Fairbanks and says that you're one of their largest depositors."

Patrick relaxed. "Used to be, maybe. I got my first loan from Guthrie."

"According to Lucille, you still are." She leaned across the table and whispered, "But Lucille says Guthrie's a crook." Her square chin and high cheekbones lent a youthful authority to her face. "I moved my money last year," she said. "You might want to move yours."

Patrick paid the bill, guided her out to a side street, and stopped in front of an abandoned drug store. "What else does this Lucille say?"

"Well, she shouldn't be telling me things, of course, but she knows I'm saving my money to go back to Kansas City and open a dress shop."

"Why does this Lucille think Guthrie's a crook?"

"Well, Mr. Guthrie handles all the out-of-town accounts. Lucille says he comes back from his business trips with loads of money and gives her a list of deposits to post, but she thinks there's something funny about it."

"Funny?" Patrick said.

"Because she doesn't know any of them. She knows the names of the other depositors, but she doesn't know the ones on his lists. Every so often, she sees a withdrawal slip, but she knows the person has never been in the bank, and it didn't come through the mail. Lucille doesn't think they really exist. She calls them her phantom depositors." She shrugged. "But now you're here, so maybe they do exist."

Patrick searched her face but saw no guile. "Why are you telling me this?"

As if asking herself the same question, she paused. "I, well, I kind of like you, and I thought you should know."

"When can I see you again, Annie Parsons?"

"I'm off for the next three days."

Early the next morning, Patrick went to Guthrie's Trading Post. "Mr. Guthrie is out of town," the clerk said. "He'll be back the end of next week." He bought clean clothes and walked across the street to the bathhouse. Soaking in the steaming tub, his thoughts swirled. *Maybe this Lucille got my name wrong . . . maybe she's just a blabbermouth clerk trying to sound important.* And mostly: *What is Miss Annie Parsons up to?*

That afternoon, a young guard stood near the front door of First Bank of Fairbanks. The bulge under his suit told Patrick there was a gun strapped to his side. A woman with faded brown hair pulled tight from her round face looked up from her paper-strewn desk then walked to the teller cage.

Patrick noticed her dark clothes did not disguise her lumpy figure. "You must be Lucille," he said and gave her his best smile.

"How may I help you?"

"I'm Patrick Roark," he said. "I want to check the balance in my account."

Lucille pulled her spectacles from a string around her neck then slipped them on the end of her nose.

"I met with Mr. Guthrie in Skagway," Patrick said. "We're going to start a new business here in Fairbanks."

Lucille raised her eyebrows. "What kind of business, Mr. Roark?"

"A drug store," Patrick said, surprising himself with his quickness. "Mr. Guthrie wants everything drawn up before he gets back next week."

"Well, the last one shut down." She huffed. A string of limp, brown hair fell over her pasty face, and she hooked it behind her ear. Her thin lips, narrow eyes, and straight hair reminded Patrick of his mother. He forced a smiled and said, "Mr. Guthrie spoke highly of you."

Lucille harrumphed. "I need proof, Mr. Roark. Something to show you are who you say you are."

Patrick opened his wallet, pulled out the receipt for his rented room, a bill of sale for his horse, and a faded deposit slip from First Bank of Skagway.

Lucille examined each piece of paper, and then handed them back to Patrick. "I need something to prove your connection with *this bank*, Mr. Roark. Like your account number, your birth date, or a deposit slip."

"1043-0-PRS," Patrick said, surprising himself again by reciting the loan number of the account he had paid off to Guthrie a year ago. "My birth date is April 16, 1876."

Lucille glanced over her shoulders at the guard now asleep at his desk. "I can give you your account information, Mr. Roark, but you will have to wait until Mr. Guthrie gets back to make a withdrawal." She fingered through her ledger, jotted on a piece of paper, and handed it to Patrick.

He glanced at the paper and tipped his hat. "Thank you, Lucille. And I'll be sure to tell Mr. Guthrie how efficient you are."

"It's Mrs. Cartwright to you, Mr. Roark. And please, do not tell Mr. Guthrie *anything* about me."

Back in his room, Patrick stared at the piece of paper. Ninety-thousand dollars was still in his account he had settled after he'd paid off his loan to Guthrie. He did not understand banking, but he knew about debits and credits and knew this credit could be withdrawn.

The next morning, he found a lawyer. "I have a business in Skagway," he said, "and I need you to check something."

He went back to Guthrie's Trading Post. A different clerk was on duty, and he asked again for Mr. Guthrie. "Back the end of next week," the young clerk confirmed. Patrick filled a basket with crackers and cheese, a bottle of wine, a tin of candy, and he showed up at Annie's door.

They ate lunch on the back steps of the Methodist Church overlooking a graveyard. Annie saved the candy for last. "A luxury," she said and brushed a trace of peppermint off her lips.

"Here we are in gold country, yet you deprive yourself."

"I'm saving every cent to go home to Kansas City," she said.

They walked among gravestones, most weathered to the same mottled gray. Annie knelt next to one of the stones and brushed off caked dirt. "He was only twenty," she said and pointed at the row across from them. "Some of those were even younger."

"Chasing gold," Patrick said. "I learned early that wasn't for me."

"I wish my daddy had," Annie said, fiercely. "He came home one day and told Mama he'd missed out in California, but he wasn't going to miss the Klondike strike. Mama begged to let us stay with my grandmother, but he wanted us to be together. Mama cried all the way here."

They walked back to the church and sat on the steps. "Daddy found us a room at the boarding house and then headed for the slopes." Annie's lips quivered. "Only he never came back. Some man told us later that Daddy slipped on ice and fell down a bank, and his mule landed on top and crushed him." She wiped a tear from the corner of her eye. "Mama died six months later. Of a broken heart, I guess. I stayed with a woman for a while, but then her husband died, too, and she only had money to get herself home. That was three years ago. I was fifteen."

"And you had to survive."

She gazed at the gravestones. "I survived their deaths, yes." She looked at Patrick. "And I will survive this."

They spent two days together.

Annie took him to the trailhead where she last saw her daddy. Her chin trembled. "Why would a man tear his family apart to chase after gold?"

"My old man died chasing another kind of gold, and my mother wasted away like yours did. I was sixteen, alone, so I hopped a freight train and headed west."

Annie grinned. "We're a lot alike, Patrick Roark."

And they had three nights.

Slithery bliss of tongue and warm kisses, writhing rhythm of coming together, parting, and coming together again. Her silken hair, the cup of her breast, her soft thighs, her long arms enclosing him, Patrick was sated; reverent. And waking up with their legs entwined, her auburn hair tangled over her pillow, was somehow more intimate than the night's passion. The burning loneliness in his chest eased. He wanted to take Annie in his arms and never let her go.

But she's a whore, my friend.

Patrick picked up the coffee pot and filled their cups. "I met your friend, Lucille, at the bank," he said.

Annie's eyes flashed. "You didn't say anything about me, I hope."

"Nope. But she seemed afraid to give me information about my own account."

"Like I told you, Mr. Guthrie handles the out-of-town businesses."

"She acted like she owned the place."

Annie sipped her steaming coffee and set her cup down. "Lucille's lonely, I think, and needs to look important. Her husband brought her here from St. Louis and dropped her at the boardinghouse just like Daddy did us, and she never heard from him again. So, she's stuck here like me. That's how we became friends."

Patrick lifted her hand and kissed her fingers. He loved her soft skin, her mellow voice, her courage. And it scared the hell out of him. "I have some business to take care of," he said. "I'll be back as soon as I finish."

At the lawyer's office, Patrick learned that Mr. T.L. Guthrie was still the legal owner of Skagway's Best. That the document he had received through the mail from Guthrie was fake. He could take Guthrie to court, but it might take six months for a territorial judge to get to Fairbanks, and Guthrie would no doubt buy him off. "That son of a bitch stole my money," Patrick said and slammed the door on his way out.

He walked the wooden sidewalks and thought back to the kitchen fire he'd set and grabbed his father's money and took off. Dirty money, illegally got, and he saw the irony of it.

Back at the bank, the young guard nowhere in sight, he told Lucille, "I've got a good deal on a building. And I need my money now."

Lucille reared her shoulders. "Like I told you, Mr. Roark, there is nothing I can do for you until Mr. Guthrie returns."

Back at Annie's, he grasped her hands. "How would you like to go to Kansas City?"

She laughed. "How many beers have you had Patrick Roark?"

"I'm serious," Patrick said, and then handed Annie the piece of paper Lucille had given him. "Lucille is right. Guthrie's a crook. I paid off my note to him over a year ago, but he kept my store in his name and kept my money. I bet he's done the same to plenty of others, too."

Annie's eyes seemed to examine him. "How does this get me home?"

"It's my money," Patrick said. "But your friend Lucille won't let me make a withdrawal until Guthrie comes back. If that happens, he'll hide it again, and my money and my store in Skagway will still be his."

Annie pressed her finger to her cheek. "Lucille's my friend, but she can be stubborn."

"How bad does she want to get out of here?"

"Nearly as much as me."

"Do you think five thousand dollars will appeal to her?"

Annie's eyes widened. "That would get her back to St. Louis for sure." She hesitated. "But Lucille won't take something that doesn't belong to her."

"Neither would I," Patrick said. "But it's *my* money, and it will be a gift from me to her."

Annie face sobered. "Guthrie will send that guard after you and some hired guns, too."

Patrick grinned. "I spent five years hiding out west. I can lose that guard and anyone he might send."

"But where will you go?"

"Well . . . how about Kansas City?"

Annie's eyes brightened. "Do you mean what I think you mean?"

"We'll go together."

She searched his face. "But you hardly know me."

"I like what I know," Patrick said, simply.

Annie collapsed on her kitchen chair. "But you only know part of me; I want a different life when I go home."

Patrick sat across from her and held her hands. "We both know we want to get out of here. Lucille too, I hope."

"Oh, I hope so," Annie said. "I really do hope so."

"Then you'll do it?"

Her face brightened. "I'll ask her," she said, then hesitated. "But Lucille's awfully smart. What if she wants more money?"

"Get me a pencil and paper," Patrick said. "I've got a plan."

* * *

Three days later, Annie waited in her room with her bags packed while Patrick filled out a withdrawal slip for ninety thousand dollars at the First Bank of Fairbanks.

Lucille counted the money into two piles. Eighty thousand in one and ten thousand in the other. Lucille had been a tough negotiator, doubling her share. But Annie had done it, by damn.

Lucille handed the thick envelope to Patrick, then slid the thin one under the counter and into her handbag.

He tipped his hat. "It's been a pleasure doing business with you, Mrs. Cartwright."

Lucille smiled. "And with you, Mr. Roark."

Patrick rode out of town quietly, just as he came in nine days before. He stopped on a snowy ridge and looked back at the Chena River. He could just make out the saloon where he'd met Annie, the steeple of the Methodist Church where they ate their picnic lunch, and Annie's rented room. *She's walking the floor now, looking out the window and wondering. Or maybe she's already at the bank checking with Lucille.*

He wanted her. Her luscious red hair, the green silk of her eyes, her curving arms, the way she made him feel.

But take a whore home with me?

He sat in his saddle seeping in the somber gray twilight. *There'll be a woman someday; one worthy to introduce to my friends, perfect enough to bear my son, and to enthrone my home.* He pulled his reins to the right and angled up the narrow ridge. The hollow ache in his chest came back, along with the loneliness and pain.

In Skagway, he withdrew his savings from First Bank of Skagway, cleaned out his till at Skagway's Best, then handed his keys to a startled Fred and wished him luck.

Back in Chicago, Patrick made up a dignified name with German heritage, found a lawyer, and legally changed his name to Walter Pruitt. Some months later, he read in the *Chicago Tribune* about a banker in Fairbanks, Alaska, Mr. T.L. Guthrie, who was found guilty of embezzlement. During Guthrie's lengthy trial, irate townsfolk learned he had moved their money between accounts for years and siphoned it off for his own use.

There was no mention of the disappearance of Mr. Guthrie's head cashier, Lucille Cartwright, a whore named Annie Parsons, or a man named Patrick Roark.

CHAPTER TEN

In Albuquerque, Kathleen picked up a crumpled doily, smoothed it over the arm of the sofa, and wondered: *Why haven't Clarice and Clay answered my classified ad?*

It had been six months today. Six months of children's messes, settling squabbles, washing dirty faces. The black iron stove, her taskmaster now, she stirred the demanding pot of bubbling stew. The corners of her mouth curved up. *But, I've saved enough for my train ticket to Chicago. In a few more months, I'll have enough to stay at the YWCA. And I'll find them.*

She glanced at the clock. Time for homework, and she went out to the back step and called Lonnie.

"Aw, come on," he whined. "Just a little bit longer."

"You've had your little bit longer," Kathleen said.

There was a knock on the front door, so she held up her open hand. "Five more minutes," she said, and little voices cheered.

She opened the front door to Henry, and fear jerked her by the throat.

His brown eyes were slits, his light hair lay in greasy clumps, and Kathleen didn't know whether to scream or cry. She held tight to the side of the door. "How did you find me?" she said.

"Dad's address book. He hid it under the lining of his sock drawer. He got real mad when I found it and told me not to bother you." He grinned. "But I wanted to see where my big sister lives."

"I don't live here, Henry. I work here."

"I just want to talk to you."

73

"I can't have visitors at work, Henry. You need to go."

"Please, Sis—" Henry grabbed her wrist.

Kathleen twisted free, slammed the door and locked it, then ran to the back step and shouted. "Lonnie, get your sisters and come in."

Lonnie begged, "Just a few more minutes."

She ran to Lonnie and grabbed his hand. "Get the girls in the house. Now!"

Henry came around the corner and stopped.

Lonnie broke loose from Kathleen, and the three stood staring at each other.

"Who are you?" Lonnie said.

Kathleen whispered. "Take your sisters into the house, please."

Lonnie looked at Henry, hesitated, and then gathered his sisters together. "Time to wash up," he said and urged them toward the back step.

"But that man," Janie cried as Lonnie ushered her through the doorway.

Kathleen glared at Henry. "You need to go."

"Can't we talk? Just for a minute."

"Not while I'm working," she said.

"Then I'll wait out front."

Kathleen shouted. "Just go, Henry, *please*."

She went into the house, bolted both doors, locked every window, and pulled the curtains tight. The children settled at the kitchen table, and Kathleen dipped a fresh cloth into the wash bucket and wiped Janie's face.

"Who's that man?" Janie said.

"Maybe a salesman."

"You know him, Kathleen. You called him, Henry."

Kathleen sighed. *I should tell them he's my brother, but I'm ashamed.* She kissed Janie's wet forehead. "Don't worry. I won't let him hurt you." She dipped the cloth back into the bucket and handed it to Lonnie. "Finish washing the girls, please."

Kathleen peeked out the back window just as Henry came around the corner.

"Let me in; let me in," he shouted.

"Like the big bad wolf," Janie squealed, ran to the window, and parted the curtain. "Not by the hair of my chinny chin chin."

Lonnie pulled her back. "Be quiet, stupid."

Kathleen sat at the head of the table and held out her hand. "Now let me see those spelling lists."

The children busy with their spelling, Kathleen crept to the front window and parted the curtain. Henry sat in the rusted chair with his legs parted, his hands fumbling with his blue jean buttons.

Kathleen groaned.

Janie jumped up. "What's the man doing?"

Kathleen closed the curtain and looked at the four frightened faces. "Just keep at that spelling," she said, and then parted the curtain again.

Henry's head bobbed. His hands clasped over his groin, he thrust up and down, jerking, groaning, moaning.

Kathleen clamped her hand over her mouth. *Dear God. Not here. Not now.*

The chair rocked. Henry grunted.

Mrs. Warfield screamed from the next yard. "Get out of here, you maniac!"

Lonnie jumped up. "What's he doing?"

Kathleen closed the curtain. "Everything's all right," she said. "He won't . . ."

There was a bang on the back door, Kathleen unlocked it, and Mrs. Warfield burst into the kitchen waving her hands in the air. "There's a lunatic out there. He's jerking himself, he, he's mastur-ba—"

The girls screamed.

Kathleen put her hands on her hips. "Stop it, Mrs. Warfield. Right now!"

"What does masterba' mean?" Janie cried.

Kathleen pointed at Lonnie. "Take the girls into the bedroom, please, and keep the door closed."

After the children left, Mrs. Warfield announced, "I called the police."

Kathleen groaned. "We don't have a telephone, so go call my father, Hartley Howe, on La Vega Road. The operator will know how to reach him."

Mrs. Warfield twisted her hands. "Those poor little children. What a thing for them to see."

"They didn't *see* anything," Kathleen said. "Now, please go call my father."

Five minutes later, a patrol car pulled into the front yard with siren blaring. The children burst through the bedroom door. "It's the police," Lonnie said. "Wow."

"Get the girls back in the bedroom!" Kathleen ordered.

Janie ran to the window. "But that man . . ."

Lonnie pulled her arm, then ushered her and the other two girls back to the bedroom and shut the door.

Kathleen parted the curtain again. An officer stood on each side of Henry, yanked him up, jerked his hands behind his back, and slapped handcuffs over his wrists. A tall officer pushed Henry's cheek into the cottonwood tree and jabbed a nightstick on his back.

Mrs. Warfield ran across the yard with her arms flailing. "There are children inside!"

The shorter officer motioned. "You the one who called?" he said. Mrs. Warfield nodded, and he pulled a notepad out of his pocket.

Hartley pulled into the driveway. Still dressed in his work overalls, he hurried toward Henry and the officers.

Mrs. Blount's car spun around the corner and parked next to Hartley's. She rushed up the front steps, and Kathleen met her at the door. "Where are my children?" she said.

Kathleen pointed toward the bedroom.

At the sound of their mother's voice, the children burst through the door. Lonnie's eyes shined. "The police are here, Mom. They had their siren on."

Janie grabbed her mother's skirt. "Where's that man?"

"Go back in the bedroom and stay there," Mrs. Blount ordered. The children complied, and she brushed past Kathleen and out to the officers.

Kathleen glanced at the children's closed door, then walked out to the front porch. Seeing her dad, she felt a flicker of hope. *He seems calm.* She bit her bottom lip. *But this is nothing new.*

Henry jerked away from the officer and ran to Kathleen. "Don't let them take me, Sis."

The tall officer spun Henry around, marched him to the patrol car, and splayed his face over the dusty, blue hood.

Kathleen clenched her fists. *Dear God. Will this ever end?*

Mrs. Blount walked up to the short officer. He jotted more notes, put the pad in his pocket, and motioned to Mrs. Warfield and Hartley. The officer did most of the talking while Hartley nodded, Mrs. Blount shook her head, and Mrs. Warfield looked over her shoulder and glared at Kathleen.

Back at the patrol car, the tall officer pulled Henry up from the hood, and they stood face to face.

Reading him the riot act. Kathleen sighed. *But what good will it do?*

Hartley placed his hand on Henry's shoulder, whispered in his ear, and then bent down and buttoned Henry's blue jeans. The officer cupped his hand over Henry's head, shoved him into the back seat, and they drove off.

Hartley spoke to Mrs. Blount for a moment, and then walked to Kathleen. His blue eyes dark as chocolate, he said, "They're going to hold him overnight."

Kathleen grabbed her stomach. "He'll come back!"

"They going to release him to me in the morning. I'll clean him up and take him downtown to the army recruiter. That was the deal they offered. The officers I mean." He placed his calloused hand on her shoulder. "What do you want to do?"

Kathleen looked at him for a long moment. "This is my job, Dad. I can't leave the children, now."

Hartley rubbed his upper arms. Tears glistened as he kissed her on her forehead. "I'll let you know when Henry leaves for the army." He walked back to Mrs. Blount, said a few words, then got into his car and drove away.

Mrs. Blount walked into the house to the children's room and shut the door behind her.

Kathleen went to the kitchen, tied a fresh apron around her waist, and then measured the ingredients for biscuits. She was almost finished mixing when Mrs. Blount came out of the bedroom. Gooey dough clumped on her spoon as Kathleen turned around. "I'm sorry Mrs. Blount, but the children didn't see anything."

Mrs. Blount's face bunched up like a knotted fist. "And I'm sorry you didn't tell me you have a lunatic brother."

Kathleen's eyes stung. Family pride, fealty, gravity welled. "Please don't speak about my brother that way."

Mrs. Blount snorted. "Well, *your brother* has tainted my children."

Kathleen's mouth quivered. "My brother has some problems, yes. But I didn't know he would—"

"Well, your father knew. From what the police said, this has happened before." She placed her hands on her hips. "And to think that I trusted you with my children."

"The children wouldn't have known about it if Mrs. Warfield hadn't gone hysterical."

"Well, it's a good thing she did. Who knows what might have happened."

"I would never let anyone harm these children."

"You couldn't control your lunatic brother."

Kathleen's eyes burned. "Henry is not a lunatic."

Mrs. Blount waved an accusing finger toward the window. "If he's not one now—he will be. What he did out there, it makes a man go insane. For all I know, you could be insane too."

Kathleen steadied herself on the edge of the table. "But I take good care of your children."

"Well, I won't take chances with their safety." She glanced at the clock. "Mr. Blount will be home in an hour. He'll give you one extra week's pay, and you can leave in the morning."

Kathleen stared at Mrs. Blount and could not believe this was the same woman who had befriended her six months before, who trusted her to take care of her home and her children. She sighed. *I should be used to this by now, and yet, still, it hurts.* She glanced toward the bedroom door. "I want to say goodbye to the children."

Mrs. Blount's eyes blazed. "You stay away from my children."

Kathleen walked to the front window and parted the curtain once more. The late afternoon sun sprayed a purple-pink haze over the yard. The innocent chair where Henry had done the unthinkable lay on its side as if wounded. Henry—the Presence; dark, looming, permeating her life. She never felt comfort. She never felt ease. She always jumped at the sound of a banging door. She always had an escape plan.

She turned around and faced Mrs. Blount. "Tell the children goodbye for me, please." She untied her apron and folded it over the kitchen chair. "I'll pack my things and leave now. And I don't want your extra week's pay."

CHAPTER ELEVEN

After leaving her father to spend the night at the store, the taxi driver dropped Clarice in front of her house, then sped away with screeching tires that jarred an owl. She entered the foyer where the coat rack cast a shadow on the wall like an ancient, gnarled tree. *It's like crossing over a moat into a medieval castle.* She winced. *And I'm no princess.* She scratched her neck. *Maybe Father sleeps at the store so he won't have to come home to this monstrous house.*

In the parlor, the Oriental rug swirled with reds, blues, and deep purple flowers with gilded leaves and lazy green ferns. She smiled recalling how she and Clay used to twirl around the gyrating patterns until dizzy, then dropped to the floor, laughing. She sat in the rocker and looked at the cherry wood end tables anchored to the oak floor with permanence. Their lamps looked like melted licorice; their shades forgotten hats on a top shelf to be worn another day.

This room, like all the rooms in this three-story house, had looked the same for as long as Clarice could remember. Once, as young teenagers, she and Clay took everything off the tables, shoved furniture to unfamiliar places, and rearranged their father's pipes, books, vases, even his miniature busts of unknown presidents. Delighted, they sat cross-legged in the middle of the floor and admired their "new room". But when Maureen saw it she'd screamed, ran for the gardener, and by the time their father came home, everything was back in its place, and Clarice and Clay's furniture moving days were over.

Clarice pictured her father with his back stiff in his leather chair reading the *Tribune*. *It's as if he's not real in this house. He's only real at the store.* She squeezed her eyes shut. *Why doesn't he sell this place and move closer to town?* Yet, even as she thought it, she knew: Her father had built this house, in all its grandeur, for the man he'd wanted to be.

She opened her eyes. *And why am I still here when I can lease my own apartment downtown?* She looked toward the darkened staircase leading to Clay's room, and she knew why. Her hands gripped the arms of the rocker. *Clay said our mother used to rock me here . . . her arms rested where mine are now.* She eased back and felt the weight of unsaid words pressing down on her.

As a child, she used to picture her faceless mother gliding down the balcony in a flowing white dress or sitting in this chair or that chair knitting a sweater. *Mother's knit sweaters, don't they?* And she recalled the day when she sneaked through her father's trunk and found the obituary revealing her mother was in Albuquerque with her new family. She'd hidden the obituary in her drawer and often pulled it out just to see their names in print, to remind her they existed.

Everything changed on her fourteenth birthday. Esther had baked a white cake with pink frosting, and presents were piled high on the dining room table. Father, and even Maureen, remarked how smart Clarice was, and how fast she was growing up.

And that's when she decided.

The next day, she'd pulled the obituary out of her drawer and studied it again. *Hartley Howe . . . he must be from Chicago, and he might still have family here.* She thumbed through the telephone book and called all the Howes she deemed were close enough, so she could ride the Elevated. "Do you know Hartley Howe?" was her one sentence request, not knowing what she might say had the party answered yes. The last woman she called suggested she try Howe's Grocery and Delicatessen on Western Avenue.

Now, at twenty-one, Clarice brimmed at her audacity. "Let sleeping dogs lie," her father always said when she asked him about her mother. She hadn't known what he'd meant then, yet the look in his eyes told her not to ask him more. But she had been fourteen, for crying out loud, and she'd wanted answers.

* * *

She remembered the day vividly.

Bells jingled as Clarice walked boldly through the front door of Howe's Grocery and Delicatessen and wrinkled her nose. *It smells like old salami.* And like all the stores in this neighborhood, it was dark, deep, and narrow. She suspected the owner lived upstairs.

Groceries were stacked neatly on side shelves. Barrels of flour, sugar, beans, and rice clustered in the center. At the end of the counter, bulbous jars of peppermint and twisted black licorice tempted her. An old woman in a limp gray dress, her hair pulled back in a matching gray knot, stood behind the counter adding up an order. To her right, a thick-shouldered man sliced meat from a round tube and wrapped it in white paper. He opened an icebox door and set it on a shelf next to some milk bottles, pint jars of cream, and butter tubs.

The back wall was stacked high with ribbons and bolts of fabric. Clarice walked to the back and sorted through the ribbons.

"What are you doing, young lady?"

Clarice whirled around and faced the old woman who was only slightly taller than she was, yet she felt the woman's authority. And to her horror, she stammered, "I, I'm trying to match some threads," she said, then reached into her pocketbook. "But, well, I forgot my piece of fabric."

"Then why are you fingering my ribbons?"

The old woman's face looked like a dried apple, and despite the age difference, she reminded Clarice of Maureen. "Oh well," Clarice shrugged. "I'll just look for the closest match."

"And you have no money with you, I suppose."

Clarice lifted her chin. "My father owns a whole department store, madam. I can buy all of your threads if I want to."

"Why are you here then?"

Clarice cringed. "I . . ."

Bells jingled again as a tall man in a blue topcoat walked through the front door. "Good afternoon, Sybil," he said and waved a sheet of paper in the air.

Sybil motioned to Clarice. "Come up front with me, young lady."

Clarice made a face and followed. *I do not like this woman, and she does not like me.* When she reached the front counter, she pulled a nickel out of her pocketbook and headed toward the licorice jar.

"Afternoon, Max," Sybil said.

Max handed her a list. "Mildred needs a few things."

Sybil walked through the store and placed cans and jars in a cardboard box. She came back to the counter, jotted prices on a sheet of paper, and then added them up. "That will be three dollars and thirty-two cents, Max."

"Put it on my account, if you will. I'll be back payday and settle up." Max started toward the door, then turned around. "Is Hartley still in Albuquerque?"

Clarice's heart thumped.

"Still there, unfortunately. But thank goodness he works for the railroad and gets free train passes. In fact, he's trying to get time off next month when the children will be out of school."

"Those kids must be pretty big now."

Sybil's voice rang like a melody. "Henry's almost twelve. A fine-looking boy and smart. He gets one-hundreds on his report cards."

"And the girl, Katherine, is it?"

"Kathleen," Sybil said. "She's getting tall and lanky."

"Think you'll ever get Hartley back home to stay?"

"Believe me, I've tried. But he loves that godforsaken place." She shrugged. "I don't understand it. Only thing there is sand and sagebrush and those gosh awful mountains." She shrugged. "But at least he's happily married to a fine woman."

Clarice gritted her teeth. *A fine woman who abandoned her husband and children.* She ached to announce herself, tell Sybil who she was, but the boulder in her chest held her down.

"Well, if I don't get back while Hartley's here, tell him hello for me."

"I'll do that, Max."

Max left, and Clarice placed her nickel on the counter and pointed to the licorice jar, "Two, please." She felt Sybil's sharp eyes examining her as she handed her the licorice sticks.

"What is your name, young lady?"

"Clarice."

"And do you have a last name?"

"Thank you for the licorice," Clarice said, and then walked out the jingling door.

* * *

Most every day the next month, Clarice stood in the shadow of the bakery across the street from the Howe's Grocery. Smells of baking bread wafted as people passed by. She wondered if anyone thought it strange, her standing there so long, but no one seemed to notice her. The owner questioned her once, so she bought a chocolate muffin. She'd told Maureen she was doing research at the library. She'd looked suspicious, but would she tell her father? And Clarice wondered what he would do if he found out where she was.

After nearly two weeks of waiting, she was about to give up when a taxicab pulled up to the grocery. A man sat in the front seat next to the driver, and there were three more heads in the backseat.

Sybil came out of the store. "Hartley, oh Hartley."

Clarice's stomach lurched.

The man got out of the taxi and hugged Sybil.

A boy stepped out.

"And my Henry," Sybil cried.

The boy gave Sybil a quick hug, and then followed the taxi driver to the trunk and took charge of the bags.

Clarice frowned. *His sleeves are too short, and that coat gaps open. Bet he can't even button it.*

A girl stepped out from the back seat. Her pale, green dress hung like a limp rag around her ankles. Clarice winced at her bobbed, brownish blond hair and bangs.

A man came out of the store, placed his hand on Hartley's shoulder, and they embraced.

Clarice recognized him as the butcher who sliced the salami.

Hartley opened the back door of the taxi, held out his hand, and a woman stepped out. Her wide-brimmed hat cast a shadow over her face, and sun shined on her white neck.

Clarice stood as if glued to the side of the bakery. *It's her . . . my mother.*

Sybil hugged the woman. They locked arms, and then walked up the steps and into the store. The men and the boy followed with the suitcases while the girl shuffled behind them and closed the door.

Clarice gulped a breath. Her heart pounded. *I saw my mother, but I couldn't see her face!* She stared at the closed door and ached to go in and announce who she was, but she pictured her father's face and ran toward the safety of her home.

The next day, Clarice stood again in the shadow of the bakery. After a while, the girl came out carrying a notebook. She wore the same green dress, her bobbed hair lay plastered over her ears, and her stubby bangs looked like they were trying desperately to grow out. Clarice decided she must cut them herself. She had tried to picture this girl, and in her envy, she'd created someone haughty, beautiful even, someone at least worthy of Clarice's abandonment. Never had she pictured this waif, this nothing of a girl, who sat on the bench and gazed aimlessly up the street.

Clarice stiffened. *Enough of standing in the shadows.* She stepped out on the sidewalk.

The front door jingled, and Sybil's head popped out.

Clarice ducked behind a parked car.

"Your mother's been looking for you, young lady. Come and set the table." Sybil held the door open, and the girl disappeared into the store.

Clarice marched across the street and up to the door. She reached for the doorknob, noticed the abandoned notebook on the bench, and picked it up. On the cover was a crayon drawing of tall mountains with white caps of snow. At the foot of the mountains stood a yellow house with a picket fence. Blue curtains draped the windows with boxes of colorful flowers. Behind the house, a rainbow arched over a river. *Their house?* Clarice wondered.

"Thief!" a male voice shouted.

Clarice jumped, clutched the notebook in her hand and took off, while the boy chased after her. In her panicked state, Clarice easily outran him and ducked into an alley until he ran past. Panting, she slid down the side of a trashcan and opened the notebook: "Poems, by Kathleen Irene Howe."

With only a touch of guilt, she read poems about clouds and flowers, her favorite teacher, Mrs. Cowie, and laughed at a poem about, Ita, the goat. On the last page, Song I sang in the sixth-grade play: "I love you a little on Monday, on Tuesday a little bit more, on Wednesday I simply adore you . . ." Clarice slammed the notebook shut. *She's just a dreamer. Like those stupid girls at school who gaze out the window and write ridiculous poems about glamorous lives they will never have.* She stood and brushed off her skirt, picked up the notebook, and headed back.

As she approached the store, a deep voice called from behind her. "So, the thief is returning her stolen goods."

Clarice whirled around to face the boy, the brother. *Her brother?*

He stood a head taller than her. His eyes shown light brown, his hair the color of dry ashes, and his skin looked like ponds cold cream. Clarice searched, but she did not see a pimple. "Who are you?" she said.

"I'm Henry Howe. Who in heck are you?"

Clarice lifted her chin. "None of your business."

"You have my sister's notebook. That makes it my business."

Clarice shoved the notebook behind her back. "I found it."

"You're a poor liar," Henry said. "But no matter, my sister's scribbles are stupid, aren't they?"

Surprised by a touch of defensiveness, Clarice said, "Why do you talk that way about your sister?"

Henry smirked. "Because she's a devil."

Clarice thought of Clay's loyalty, his calm assurance in her no matter what she did.

"Why are you staring at me?" Henry said. "And why are you interested in my sister?"

"I'm not interested in her, or in you either."

Henry crossed his arms over his chest. "You're interested all right. I've seen you watching us from across the street." He dropped his arms to his sides. "What are you doing in this part of town?"

"Maybe I live here," Clarice said.

Henry pointed to his wrist. "Your watch. No kid around here wears one. Your clothes are store bought, and your black leather boots are special-made."

Suddenly uncomfortable in her favorite plaid skirt and green sweater, Clarice wanted to pull off her boots and throw them at this boy. Yet, wanting to take charge, she said, "Well, you're not from around here either."

"I was born here," Henry said. "But we live in Albuquerque."

"What's it like in Albuquerque?" The strange word stuck on Clarice's tongue.

Henry's sharp eyes seemed to appraise her. "Dry. Sometimes hot and sometimes cold, with lots of mountains and desert. Not crammed together like Chicago."

"So, why are you here?" Clarice said.

"We're visiting my grandmother."

"We?"

"Me and my sister and my mother and father."

Clarice's throat tightened. *My sister . . . my mother.* How eerie these words sounded and to hear this brother say them. Damp curls clung to her neck. This boy had control, and she did not like it. "You don't seem to think much of your sister," she said.

"I told you, she's a devil."

"And your mother?" Clarice's voice quavered.

Henry's eyes lit up. "My mother's an angel, she—" He grabbed Clarice's arm, and twisted. "You're a strange girl," he said, "and you ask too many questions."

Clarice felt his hot breath on her face as she stared at this brother, who did not know he was her brother and saw herself. She felt kinship, and as they looked each other up and down, she sensed that he felt it too.

"Henry!" Sybil's voice shrilled from across the street.

Henry let go of Clarice's arm. "Over here, Grandmother."

Sybil walked up to them. "Where have you been, Son? Your supper's ice cold." Her eyes locked on Clarice. "You again."

"We were just talking," Henry said.

Sybil's face softened. "Come in and I'll heat up your supper." She glared at Clarice. "And you, miss, whoever you are, go home and don't come back."

Clarice handed Kathleen's notebook to Henry.

Henry mumbled, "thank you," and then followed his grandmother into the store and closed the door.

* * *

Still in the rocking chair, Clarice opened her eyes and shook her head to clear it. She had pushed the memory with Henry to the back of her mind and rarely allowed herself to think about it. On the few occasions she did, she remembered every detail: Henry's pale brown eyes, his haughty intelligence, their strange camaraderie. She wasn't sure why, but she knew it had something to do with her complicated feelings for Clay, and this disturbed her. She ached to purge herself of this poison permeating her mind.

She gripped the sides of the rocker and wondered how.

CHAPTER TWELVE

The following afternoon, Clarice sat across from Felicia at Manny's Diner.

"Let me get this straight," Felicia said. "You saw your sister and mother and you actually talked to your brother?"

Clarice nodded. "That's about it, I guess."

"You guess?" Felicia frowned. "We've been friends a long time. Why did you just now tell me?"

Clarice looked away, but Felicia's piercing green eyes pursued her. "I was afraid, I think."

"You? Afraid? I don't believe you."

"It was complicated," Clarice said. "I just pushed it out of my mind. But then when I went to that store and saw them all together, well, I felt like a sneak."

"You're brash, impetuous, a little too smart, maybe." Felicia rolled her eyes. "Hell, you do what you want and let the world be damned. But you have never been sneaky."

Clarice looked at her empty hands and sighed.

"You're like an iceberg," Felicia said. "Only a tiny part is visible while the rest lies chilling beneath the surface. That part causes damage, you know."

"I know," Clarice said. She looked at Felicia "Everything was fine until I read that damned classified ad Kathleen published."

"And what do you call, fine?"

"Well, I had a father I practically worshipped, a brother I adored, and—"

"Why has that changed?"

"Because I had to think about my mother again. And I had to confront Father, which made him more determined to ship me off to college."

"And Clay?"

Clarice barred her teeth. "I, well, I feel guilty, like I should tell him or something."

"You can't protect Clay forever."

Clarice's eyes stung. "You don't know Clay. He has this idealized image of his, of our, mother, and I won't ruin it for him."

"Then I'm sorry I told you about the ad."

"I'm sorry, too."

Felicia tapped her fingernails on the table. "I see . . . poor little rich girl."

Clarice's cheeks grew hot. "You say that? When you're married to one of the richest men in Chicago?"

"And one of the most decent and honest."

Clarice pulled her sweater from the back of her chair and draped it over her shoulders. Telling her story to Felicia had left her naked, vulnerable. "I used to wish she were dead," she said. "That way she didn't really abandon us." She lowered her eyes. "See how awful I am, to wish my mother dead."

"Just human, I'd say."

"Even when I found out my mother had another family in Albuquerque, it didn't seem real. But when I saw them together in front of that store, I figured, Clay and me, we weren't good enough for her." She pounded the table. Coffee sloshed over the top of their cups. "I hate that girl."

The waiter rushed up to them. "Is anything wrong?" He dabbed the spilled coffee with a cloth napkin. "May I get you another cup?"

"Please," Felicia said.

The waiter finished cleaning the table, then returned with two fresh cups of coffee.

"Thank you," Felicia said, and then looked at Clarice. "I see why you might be angry at your mother. But the girl, well, she's an innocent."

Clarice rested her chin on her hand. "I hate her because she has *my mother!*"

"Hate," Felicia said, softly. "It takes a lot of energy."

Clarice let out a long sigh. "And I'm exhausted."

Felicia eased back in her chair. "You know, Clarice, there is a whole big world outside of Chicago. And guess what? It isn't even about you."

"The only world I care about is here."

Felicia's eyes danced. "Do you know that in Los Angeles, the sun shines all year long, and you don't even need a sweater?"

Clarice shrugged.

"Robert believes the future lies out west. He wants to investigate land out there, but he can't seem to get away to do it." She raised her eyebrows. "Perhaps you could make a preliminary trip for him. Get a feel for the place. Look at some suitable land for him to develop."

Clarice stiffened. "What makes you think I could do that?"

"Robert's seen how capable you are. Your store conditions are always top notch, and you've increased your sales by almost thirty percent."

Clarice cocked her head to the side. "How could he know that?"

"Don't give me that look. Robert's a businessman. And he's aware of what it takes to run one." She paused. "He has his ways of knowing these things."

"Robert's smart, but . . ."

"He would pay your expenses, of course, and send one of his secretaries with you for a companion and to take notes." Felicia's voice gathered momentum. "Who knows? You might want to expand Pruitt's out west someday. You could take the Santa Fe, make a little vacation of it. It stops in Kansas City, my hometown, the 'Wild West' and all, and you might see some cowboys."

Clarice stiffened. "Father would never allow it."

Felicia smiled. "There are some fine colleges out west like Stanford, Claremont, The University of California. You might want to visit them."

Clarice looked at her warily. "Who's being sneaky now?" She shook her head. "And besides, Why give her the satisfaction?"

"The girl, you mean, or your mother?"

"Both," Clarice snapped.

Felicia reached into her purse, pulled out a copy of Kathleen's classified ad, and handed it to Clarice. "And the train stops in Albuquerque."

CHAPTER THIRTEEN

Clarice had three great weeks in Los Angeles riding streetcars and buses, haunting downtown department stores, and driving around the suburbs in her rented car. Using Robert's letter of introduction, she met with chamber of commerce presidents, city planners, zoning commissioners, and real estate brokers. Out of respect for her father, she'd visited the University of Southern California and Claremont College and even squeezed in a visit to the San Gabriel Mission.

Walter had objected to the trip, of course. Yet Clarice persisted, saying it was about Pruitt's expansion out west someday and to visit western colleges. And he had finally, reluctantly, at her insistence, agreed.

On the trip home, Clarice braced herself as the train hissed and groaned up to the Albuquerque station. She moved across the aisle to the window and looked out at the towering mountains and recalled that old woman, Sybil, talking about "those gosh awful mountains". Her stomach felt like grape jelly, her chest as if were clamped with a vise. *Should I get off? Should I try to find her?*

The train hissed and groaned again with cars being added and taken off. Clarice looked at the station with its domed tower and red tile roof gleaming over an arched arcade. *Beautiful; like the California missions.* She twisted her watch and thought of Henry. "Your watch. No kid around here wears one." Felicia's face floated before her. "There's a whole big world outside of Chicago . . . and it isn't even about you." She clenched her fists. *It is about me.* Charged with an unexpected surge of energy, she grabbed her sweater and purse and hurried down the steps. I'll look around at least.

Crisp, cool air caressed her face as she walked toward the pebbled arches. Indians sat by blankets displaying silver and turquoise rings, pins, and necklaces, along with intricately carved pottery, woven baskets, and shawls. Clarice scanned the people lined up. *They can't wait to buy something.* She tapped her foot. *Pretty slick marketing.* She looked at the attached Alvarado hotel with its shaded portals, bell towers, and fountains and wondered what kind of stores are in Albuquerque.

On the platform, brown-skinned people hugged one another in greeting jabbering a strange language while children scurried around them playing tag. Seeing their joy in each other, Clarice blinked back tears. She closed her eyes, but the happy voices assaulted her senses. *Will my mother be glad to see me?*

Clarice opened her eyes and raced back to the train car. "Go ahead without me," she said to the startled secretary. "Tell Mrs. Bradford I'll catch the next train home."

* * *

Clarice only had a name and post office box number, but a search through tax records got her an address. The taxi headed west on Central Avenue, crossed the Rio Grande, turned south at Five Points, and left on La Vega Road.

"What do they call those mountains," Clarice asked.

"The Sandías," the driver said. "Means watermelon in Spanish. They turn pink at sunset. You'll see tonight."

"I won't be here tonight."

The driver stopped in front of a dusty field and pointed. "It's the house at the end."

"Wait here, please," Clarice said, then got out of the taxi and walked toward the house. She kicked a rock and thought of that old woman Sybil again, "Only thing there is sand and sagebrush."

Sybil was right. But she forgot the cactus and weeds. She reached back and felt her curls hanging loosely down her neck. *But I like my hair here.* The wind nipped her face, and she wrapped her sweater about her. *And it's windy like Chicago.* At the end of the field, a cottonwood tree hovered over a little square adobe house. At the side was a cellar with a wooden door held firm by an iron lock. In back, stood a wire pen with three clucking hens and a goat. She remembered Kathleen's diary and wondered if the goat was, Ita. She wrinkled her nose. *Goats? Chickens? Cactus?* She kicked. *And this blasted sand?*

She stared at the house. *I shouldn't have come here.* Her stomach churned as she took a deep breath, walked up to the front door, and knocked. *What if she doesn't answer?* Clarice knocked again. *And what if she does?* After several long minutes with no answer, she wasn't sure if she was disappointed or relieved.

She walked to the goat pen and tried to pet Ita, but the goat screamed and backed away. Behind the pen, lay remains of a vegetable garden fed by a large drainage ditch. She followed the ditch back to a row of thick green bushes and juniper trees and heard the whispering whoosh of the Rio Grande. *I wonder if Kathleen and Henry played in the river?*

Back toward the house, she passed a pile of weathered boards. A small shack stood a few yards from the back door, and she grimaced. "Ugh! An outdoor toilet." A tumbleweed rolled up from behind and grabbed her sweater. She tried to pull it free and pricked her fingers. A mottled-brown, lizard slithered across her foot. She kicked, missed, and slammed her toe on a jagged rock. She grabbed her foot and hopped on her other foot until she collapsed on the rock. Her toe throbbed, her fingers stung, as she glared toward the craggy mountains and shook her fist. "Lord, they're grasping toward heaven for relief!"

A woman walked across the field and up to Clarice. Her long black hair was tied back with an orange and yellow scarf. Her brown and yellow striped skirt bounced from her ample hips. "I am Maria

Lopez," she said, then pointed to a man hoeing weeds. "That is my husband, Juan. We keep watch here during the day."

Clarice pushed herself up from the rock and pointed toward the pile of boards. "What was that?"

"The old summer kitchen."

"A summer kitchen?"

"She cans food from the garden so she don't heat the house. He is going to build her a new one." She shaded her eyes with her hand. "Who are you?" she said. "And why are you snooping around here?"

Clarice's stomach churned. "I'm not snooping. I'm looking for Mrs. Howe."

"She in Chicago."

Clarice grabbed her throat. "In Chicago?"

"She has people there. She goes all the time."

People? How about two children and a husband?

Mrs. Lopez stepped toward her. "What do you want here?"

Clarice stammered, "I, well, I came to see Henry."

"Henry?"

Clarice noted the surprise in her voice.

"Henry go in the army. And a good thing he did."

Surprised at the hollow feeling in her chest, Clarice realized how much she had wanted to see Henry again. She shuffled her feet. *How stupid to think he would even remember me.* "When will Kathleen be home?" she asked.

"Miss Kathleen no live here."

Clarice opened her hands. "Where is she?"

"At the mansion." Mrs. Lopez frowned. "Poor Kathleen, after all Henry did to her, no wonder she leave."

Clarice stared at her feet. Her mother is in Chicago, Henry's in the army, and Kathleen is living in a mansion. She raked her shoe across the sand. *How could I think they would all be at home waiting for me to knock on their door?* She looked at Mrs. Lopez. "What about Mr. Howe?"

Mrs. Lopez eyes lit up. "Mr. Howe a good man. He work all the time." She pointed to the irrigation ditch. "He dug it all the way to the river, and he shares the water with us." She shook her head. "But Mrs. Howe never happy. He bow and say, 'yes, my love, yes my love.'" She shrugged. "Easier to do what she say, I guess."

Clarice turned away from Mrs. Lopez and gazed across the dusty field to the outdoor toilet, the dried remains of the vegetable garden, rubble of the summer kitchen. She tucked her hair behind her ears. *This is it? My mother is a griping bitch?* She bit her lip and turned back to Mrs. Lopez. "Where is the mansion?" she said.

"Up by the Country Club. Real fancy with wide streets and trees in the middle." She hesitated. "Are you Kathleen's friend?"

"We, uh, we're like sisters."

"No one ever came when Henry was here."

Why? Clarice wondered, and then smiled for the first time. "Do you have her address?"

Maria Lopez looked Clarice up and down. After a long moment, she said, "Kathleen give me her address in case something happens."

"I need to see her," Clarice said. "It's important."

She looked her up and down again. "Miss Kathleen is lonely over there, I think. You wait. I get you her address."

* * *

The mansion stood at the end of a wide, tree-lined street surrounded by cottonwood trees. The red tile roof gleamed in the sun, and a thick adobe wall enclosed it. The taxi driver called it a courtyard. Clarice clenched her fists. *I'm not going to watch from the shadows this time.* "Wait here," she said, then stepped out of the taxi, unlatched the iron gate, and knocked on the front door.

A young woman wearing a green uniform with a white lace apron opened the door. "May I help you?" she said.

Clarice admired the contrast of her ebony eyes and hair with her creamy white skin. "May I speak to the lady of the house, please?"

The young woman squinted her eyes. "Lady of house?"

"The lady who lives her," Clarice said, impatiently. Receiving no response, she said, "Kathleen Howe, please."

The young woman smiled. "Ah, Miss Kathleen." She beckoned for Clarice, walked to the end of the porch, and pointed toward a brick pathway. "Miss Kathleen in back."

Clarice passed rock gardens, lush with palm and cacti in green and yellow pots. A bubbling fountain spilled into a small pond ringed by rocks. A white wooden cross stood at the side of the pond and she wondered about it. Another brick walkway curved around more cactus gardens, each enclosed by low ornamental brick walls. The house, the yard, the prickly plants were foreign to Clarice, yet she admired their spare beauty.

Behind the house, a young woman lay on a slatted, wood lounge chair holding a book in her hand. At her side, stood a baby carriage with a pink bow draped over the top.

Clarice sucked in a quick breath. *It's her. And she has a baby.*

A muffled cry came from the carriage.

Clarice slipped behind a tree.

The woman arched her back and lifted her face to the sun.

Clarice clamped her hand over her mouth. *She looks just like Clay!* Transfixed by her long and wavy bronze hair, her high cheekbones and golden skin, she thought of a shiny new penny and yanked her own springy black curls.

The woman lifted the baby to her shoulder and murmured, "Go to sleep little baby . . ."

Struck by the rich resonance of her voice, Clarice clenched her teeth. *She has all this, and a baby, while I . . .* she opened her mouth and closed it. *I shouldn't be standing here spying . . . but, she placed the ad to find me.* Weak with anger, curiosity, yearning, she leaned on the tree, and her sweater caught on a piece of bark and snapped.

The woman clutched the baby to her chest. "Who's there?"

Clarice's head roared. Hands shaking, she jerked her sweater loose, and tore up the path with bark dangling from her sweater.

The woman clutched the baby to her chest and followed while Clarice shot across the front yard, pushed through the gate, and jumped into the back seat of the taxi.

The driver wiped his eyes. "You okay, lady?"

"Take me to the train station," Clarice ordered. "Now!"

* * *

Kathleen cradled the baby in her arms as the taxi drove away and bit her lower lip. *Who was she? And what did she want?*

Back in the house, Mrs. Wendell asked, "Who was that?"

"I don't know," Kathleen said.

"Maria said she asked for you. Were you expecting someone?"

"No, ma'am. She was hiding behind the tree, I think. I heard something snap, and then she took off. All I saw was a head full of black curls and a blue, checked skirt."

"That's strange, don't you think?"

"Very strange."

"I'll talk to Maria about letting strangers in the backyard. We have to be careful with Mr. Wendell gone all week."

"But nothing happened," Kathleen said.

Mrs. Wendell motioned, and Kathleen placed the baby in her open arms. "Wait here while I put Sarah down for her nap."

Kathleen felt a twinge in her stomach. *Am I in trouble?*

Mrs. Wendell returned and sat in a chair across from her. "You seem happy here," she said.

Not sure if it was a statement or a question, "This is the best place I've ever worked," Kathleen said.

"Good. Because next week you will have been here six months, and like I said when we hired you, we're going to raise your pay to twelve dollars a week."

Kathleen clasped her hands in a childish gesture. "Oh, thank you," she said, then looked at the ceiling and calculated figures in her head. "With the raise, I might have enough by this spring to take my trip. That's if I can still take some time off. Without pay, I mean."

Mrs. Wendell looked puzzled for a moment then said, "Oh, yes, your trip to Chicago. We can work something out, I'm sure." She hesitated. "I like to see people set goals, Kathleen. They give us reasons to live."

"I surely have my reasons," Kathleen said and crossed her fingers. *But they're mine alone. Until I find them, that is, and then I'll shout to the world that I've found my sister and brother.*

Mrs. Wendell smiled. "You're the best nanny we've ever had. You take care of my Sarah like she was your own."

"I love her," Kathleen said.

Kathleen loved Mrs. Wendell's smile. Tall, graceful, her austere face lent a regal air about her. When she smiled, her mouth curved up to two bright dimples, one on each side of her cheek. Life is good, her smile said. The world is steady and safe.

Kathleen used to lock herself in the bathroom and practice smiling like Mrs. Wendell. She curved her mouth at the right angle, but her teeth did not align, and her lips were crooked. So, she developed her own smile, which did not affect such a radical change as Mrs. Wendell's, but it pleased Kathleen all the same.

And yet, Mrs. Wendell had her dark times when she closed her bedroom door in the middle of the morning and did not come out until late afternoon. Maria tiptoed. Kathleen shushed Sarah. Those first months had been puzzling, with Mrs. Wendell watching Sarah's every move one moment, then handing her to Kathleen and disappearing into her room the next. But no matter, a kind, kind lady.

"Maria agreed to switch days off with you next Saturday." Mrs. Wendell said.

"What about the baby?"

"Maria will help. We'll manage."

Kathleen clasped her hands together. "Thank you. It's my dad's birthday, and I want to surprise him."

After supper, Kathleen went into the kitchen where Maria was washing dishes. "I hope you didn't get in trouble," she said.

"No trouble. Mrs. Wendell, she is too nice."

"What did the woman look like?"

Maria held soapy hands out from the side of her face. "Blue eyes and black curly hair sticking out."

"What did she say?"

"First, she says, 'lady of the house' and I don't understand. Then she say your name, so I showed her out back."

"Did she say anything else?"

Maria's forehead wrinkled. "No, nothing else."

Kathleen started toward the door, and then turned back around. "Thank you for working for me on Saturday. If you want to leave early Friday, I will fill in for you."

"What about the baby?"

"Her nap, remember? We put her down late on Fridays, so she'll be wide-awake when Mr. Wendell comes home."

Maria smiled. "Then I think so, yes."

"I envy you," Kathleen said. "Going home so often, I mean."

"Mama, she misses me." She hesitated. "You should go home more too."

"That's what my dad says."

Maria rinsed her hands under the faucet and wiped them on the towel tucked at her waist. "The girl at the door," she said. "She was like you."

Kathleen's heart quivered. "How?"

"Long arms and legs like you and little tummy. Not short and fat like me."

A thought flickered. Kathleen squelched it. Yet it flickered again and flamed. *Could she have been Clarice?* Her heart raced. *But how did she find me? And why would she run away?*

CHAPTER FOURTEEN

On Saturday, Kathleen sat at the familiar kitchen table with her hands clasped around the warmth of her favorite cup. "Happy Birthday, Dad."

"Thanks for the tie," Hartley said and held it up to his neck.

"The red and blue stripes look good on you. Wear it to church on Sunday."

Hartley set a plate of muffins in front of her and handed her a heavy Mason jar. "Try some of Bea's last batch of cherry marmalade. The trees came in heavy this year. If you like it, you can take some with you."

"No need to taste," Kathleen said. "If Bea made it, I'll take it." Her stomach tightened. *I should tell him about that girl. But how, after all this time?*

Hartley pulled another jar of marmalade out of the cupboard and set it on the table next to her.

Kathleen made a sweeping gesture with her hands. "I like what you've done to the living room, and you've added a fireplace, no less."

Hartley grinned. "Well, Bea did the designing, and I did the work. She tried to help paint, but her hands drew up so bad she couldn't."

"What did the doctor say?"

"Arthritis. The crippling kind." His shoulders drooped. "And there's nothing he can do for her."

"I was hoping she'd get better."

"Me too," Hartley said, and then glanced around the kitchen. "Next, I'm going to give these walls a fresh coat of paint, and when Bea comes home from Chicago, she'll make new curtains on her old Singer. Her fingers still work when she sews, thank goodness."

Kathleen rubbed the seasoned, yellow oilcloth. "I hope you don't get rid of this though, it's been around for years, or one like it anyway."

With a sheepish look on his face, Hartley rubbed the oilcloth, too. "I expect she'll get rid of it." He stirred his coffee. "But the next big job is the bathroom."

"A bathroom? Wow. You're coming up in the world."

Hartley grinned. "But don't expect I'll get to use it much between Jill and her mother."

"Are you still giving Jill a tough time?"

"Only when she's not working at that telephone company or out with Dan."

Kathleen touched her cheek. "Do you think she'll marry Dan? He's so much older, and he has the little girl."

"I expect she will," Hartley said. "But she'll have to do battle with her mother first." He dipped his knife into the butter and spread it over his muffin as if frosting a cake. He spooned a glob of cherry marmalade on top, caught the drippings with his fingers, and licked. "For my part, Dan seems a decent fellow and should make Jill a good husband. But the little girl, well, Bea's already made her mind up, and she hasn't even met her."

No surprise there, Kathleen thought, but she did not say it. "I miss Jill," she said. "But it's hard for us to get together with her shifts at the telephone company and my job."

Hartley pressed his sticky hands over his ears. "I can hear the chatter now."

"Remember when we practiced being acrobats, and Jill did a somersault and broke her toe?"

"Lord, yes. She squealed like a pig."

Kathleen laughed. "And that ended our circus careers."

Hartley hopped up. "I'll make more coffee and heat up these muffins. I love marmalade over melted butter."

Sipping the last of her lukewarm coffee Kathleen gazed out the back door and recalled the first time she saw Jill, a wiry girl of eleven with her nose pressed to their screen door.

"Hi, I'm Jill. My dad's out back with your dad." She held her index finger to her lips and whispered. "Dad's out of cherry wine. He made me wait in the car last time, but this time your dad saw me and told me to come in."

Kathleen opened the door, and in a heartbeat, Jill's sharp eyes took in everything. "This place looks like fun. Do you get to climb the cherry trees? Do you get to pick the cherries?"

"I practically live in those trees, Kathleen said. "And I get to eat all the cherries I want. One time I ate too many and threw up red globs on my stepmother, Miriam's, lap. She wasn't happy."

"Do you get to milk the goat? Do you get to feed the chickens?"

"She's my goat. Her name is Ita. I milk her in the mornings before school while my dad feeds the chickens."

"Do you help him make wine?"

Kathleen's chest had puffed. "I get to crush the cherries in the barrel. He won't tell what he puts in it, but it has to set for a while, and sometimes I help cap the bottles."

"Boy! My mother would never let me do that." Jill looked around. "Where is your stepmother now?"

"She died three years ago."

"Oh, I'm sorry," Jill said and went on excitedly: "My dad's name is Van and my mother is Beatrice, but everyone calls her Bea. Dad owns a gas station with a trailer park behind it. Me and Edward, that's my brother, we clean up after the trailers leave. Edward's a dreamboat, by the way. Maybe you'll meet him sometime."

The men came in then. Van looked like he had just stepped out of the movies, flashing, tall, handsome, and Jill obviously adored him. Kathleen felt guilty comparing him to her own slight father.

Hartley discovered Bea was from Chicago and invited Van to supper. It wasn't long before Van invited them back, and a fast friendship began. They played Pinochle every Friday night with Hartley's friends, the Patchells', and Hartley found another audience for his corny jokes. Yet he always seemed to have more in common with Bea than he did with Van. They even shared recipes.

Then came the terrible day when Kathleen went home with Jill, and they found Bea crying. "Jill dear, your father has left us for another woman!" And then the day Kathleen came home from school to find boxes all over her kitchen and Jill and her mother moving in. She and Jill were so embarrassed, for if there had been a wedding, they had not been invited. She shared her cramped little room with Jill. Henry moved into the kitchen. Bea took over their lives, and Hartley let her.

Kathleen winced. *That man's leaving changed everything. Now Jill and Bea live here, and I don't; Henry's in the army; and poor Edward died in that car crash.* She rubbed her eyes. *I was going to marry Edward.* She looked up and Hartley was leaning over her with the pan of warmed muffins.

"Daydreaming again?" he said.

Kathleen smiled. "I was thinking of the first time I met Jill."

Hartley poured more coffee and sat down across from her.

"Have you heard from Henry?" she said.

"He's almost finished with basic training. They gave him a bunch of tests, and he's supposed to go to Infantry Training." He fingered his chin. "A shame, smart as Henry is in math and all, but maybe the discipline will do him good." He sighed. "Hope so. It's his last chance."

"I hope so too, Dad. You can't know how much."

"Speaking of Henry, some girl came looking for him the other day. Mrs. Lopez said she was out back snooping around, so she came over to check."

"What day was it?"

Hartley tapped his fingers on the oilcloth. "Let's see . . . she caught me on my way in from work. It was Tuesday, I think, yes, because Bea called that night, and I remember telling her about it."

Kathleen's stomach fluttered. "What did the girl want?"

"She asked for Bea first. Mrs. Lopez said she seemed real surprised to hear she was in Chicago. But then she asked for Henry." Hartley tapped his fist against his lips. "You know Henry didn't keep friends for very long."

Kathleen made a steeple with her hands. "That's interesting. Someone came looking for me last Tuesday, too. I was out back with the baby, and she must have been hiding behind a tree. I heard something, but then she ran and took off in a taxi."

"Wonder who she was?" Hartley said.

Kathleen searched his face. *I should tell him about the ad.* She looked at her hands wrapped around her coffee cup. *I'll find them myself first.*

Hartley brightened. "Bea's coming home next Wednesday." He glanced around the kitchen. "Guess I'll have to spiffy up around here."

"It looks fine to me, Dad."

"Well, you know Bea. Everything has to be just so."

"I know," Kathleen said. She looked at the tea pot clock above Hartley's head. "I need to go if I'm going to catch my bus. I've just enough time to say hello to Mrs. Lopez."

"I'll drive you," Hartley said.

"I like to ride the bus. A new way to get around."

Hartley reached across the table and grasped her hand. "Come home, Kats. You can finish high school, and—"

"There's no room for me here, Dad."

"Jill can clear out some of her things, and with Henry gone—"

"That's not the kind of room I'm talking about."

Hartley sighed. "Well then, thanks for the tie, but best of all for you."

Kathleen walked across the road and found Mrs. Lopez in her front yard.

"I saw the girl snooping around, so I went to check," she said.

"Did she say her name?"

She shrugged. "I forgot. She said you were like sisters. That is why I gave her your address."

"What did she look like?"

"Kind of pretty with black, curly hair and white skin. She did not sound like anyone around here, and she wore one of those scratchy sweaters".

"What color?"

"Blue, I think, and her skirt was blue too. She asked for Mrs. Howe first, and then she asked for Henry." She placed her hands on her hips. "No one like her ever came when Henry was here. I told her he went in the army, and then she asked for you. She knew all your names, so I gave her your address. I hope that is okay?"

Kathleen frowned. "I don't want Henry to know where I am."

"Don't worry, I won't tell him."

Kathleen's thoughts whirled as she walked up the road toward the bus stop. *It must be the same girl. But how did she find Dad's house?* Her pace quickened. *And why would she ask for Bea and Henry?*

Mrs. Wendell was in her bedroom when Kathleen got home, and Maria was rocking Sarah. Seeing Kathleen, Sarah reached for her, "Ka Ka." Kathleen set the Mason jar on the table and took Sarah. "I've got her now. You can start supper."

It was one of Mrs. Wendell's dark days. Not as often now, yet somehow, they seemed worse. Sarah yawned, and Kathleen stroked her forehead. *They've been so kind, treat me like family; Mr. Wendell even thanked me the other day, though I'm not sure what for.* She carried Sarah toward her room. As they passed Mrs. Wendell's closed door, Sarah reached out her hands and touched it. *Tiny little one . . . yet you understand.*

And Kathleen kissed Sarah on the forehead.

* * *

Back in Chicago, Clarice slammed the ledger book on her desk. "These figures don't make sense!" She buzzed for Miss Watson.

No answer, and she buzzed again. *Where can the woman be?* She walked to the outer office just as Miss Watson came through the door.

"Where have you been?" Clarice said.

"I was out of carbon paper and went down to Supply."

"They're supposed to deliver those things."

"They usually do, but they were busy and—"

"I expect you to be at your desk when I need you."

Miss Watson hung her head. "Yes, ma'am."

"Call accounting for me, please, and tell Mr. Schwartz I want to see him right away." She went back to her office. *What's going on in Supply, anyway? And why can't that accountant do his job?*

Her intercom buzzed. "Mr. Schwartz is at the Madison Street store, Miss Pruitt."

"He's supposed to be here today."

"Yes, ma'am, but there was a problem, and he left around two-thirty. Do you want me to try and reach him?"

"Do that, please. Tell him to be in my office first thing in the morning and bring August sales reports."

"What year?"

"This year, August 1929. What year do you think?"

"Well, he's been looking at last year's reports, so I thought—"

"August, this year."

"Yes, ma'am."

Clarice gritted her teeth. *May I never have a job where I have to say, "yes, ma'am".* She let out a long sigh. *Nothing's gone right since I got off that train in Albuquerque. How stupid to go off half-cocked without a plan, and then run away like a coward.* Anger flowed like lava. "Damn. Why did I go there anyway?"

She scratched her neck. *But if Henry had been there, I might have revealed myself and been done with it.* And she realized how strong the old feeling of kinship she'd felt, and how much she had wanted to see Henry again. She tapped her foot. *I just might see him again, but next time I'll have a plan.*

She thought of her meeting with Robert and Felicia when she'd handed him her file with names of Los Angeles bankers and real estate brokers, maps, sketches of possible land sites, building cost projections, addresses of empty warehouses, utility rates, railroad shipping fees, even temperature charts.

"Interesting how much information you can get when you're 'just a girl' and no one takes you seriously," she'd said.

Robert tapped the folder. "Looks like they took you seriously here." He had been mightily impressed, but Felicia's shrewd eyes probed her.

"I spent time in Albuquerque," Clarice said, "but came up empty." She'd turned away from her. "And I don't want to talk about it."

She thought about Mrs. Lopez, her jiggling hips when she'd asked about Mrs. Howe. *"She in Chicago . . . she has people there; she goes all the time go all the time."*

Clarice felt like she had swallowed a handful of dust. "So how could she not come and see me?" She yanked a mirror out of her bottom drawer and studied the spatter of freckles across her nose, touched her crooked lower tooth, yanked a curl. *How could that scarecrow of a girl turn into a goddess?* She threw the mirror against the wall; glass shards tinkled on the floor. "And how dare she look like Clay!"

Seven years of bad luck, a small voice chided.

"Bull," Clarice said. "I'm in charge now."

CHAPTER FIFTEEN

Kathleen spread her money out on her bed: three stacks of ten-dollar bills, five stacks of ones, and assorted change in Bea's marmalade jar. A year's savings. Her last raise had helped, plus the extra money Mr. Wendell promised today for working her afternoon off while he and Mrs. Wendell went shopping.

She counted the piles and tallied figures in her head. *Enough for my train ticket to Chicago and almost enough for a room at the YWCA. But I'll need more for food and new clothes, so I can greet my sister and brother in style.*

She thought of the plaid skirt and green sweater she saw in J.C. Penney's window last week. *Maybe I should put them on layaway now, maybe even a jacket and purse to match and high-heeled shoes.* She counted forward from today's date into the new decade. *Silly me, it will be almost spring when I get there, and I won't need a jacket or a sweater.*

She recalled the box of clothes that used to arrive each year from Grandmother Sybil. Pantaloons and wool jackets and boots. *As if we had Chicago winters.* She smiled remembering the morning her grandmother dressed her in black pantaloons and a jacket and sent her off to school. Mortified the kids would make fun of her, she hid the pantaloons in an old shed, but when she went back that afternoon to retrieve them—they were gone. She shrank remembering her grandmother's scolding, then smiled. *But those clothes, plus the dresses Bea made me, got me through childhood.*

She pictured Bea's long neck bent over her old Singer, feet peddling in perfect rhythm, while her skilled fingers guided rickrack as it climbed up from her lap. And she felt a touch of tenderness. That was long before Bea was her stepmother, yet she saw Kathleen's need for clothes way back then. She looked at her stacks of money. *To think I might actually afford to buy a new outfit.*

There was a knock on her door. Kathleen cracked it open.

"There is a lady on the telephone," Maria said. "She says she is your sister." Maria's eyes widened. "I did not know you have a sister."

Kathleen winced. Jill had never called at work before.

"She says to hurry," Maria said.

"I'll be right there." She closed the door and stuffed her stacks of bills into an envelope, dropped her change into the Mason jar, and tucked them in the back of her closet.

In the living room, Maria balanced Sarah on her hip. When she saw Kathleen, her chubby arms reached out to her.

Kathleen put Sarah over one shoulder, cradled the telephone between her ear and other shoulder and said, "Hi, Jill, what's up?"

"Henry's on his way to your place!"

Kathleen squeezed Sarah and the baby wailed in protest. "Hang on, Jill." She set the receiver down and handed Sarah to Maria. "Change her diaper, please," and then called for the housekeeper. "Carmen, get Sarah's bottle out of the icebox and heat it. Now!"

The two women left, and Kathleen picked up the receiver. "But Henry's off in the army."

"Not anymore," Jill said. "He showed up at home this morning. He seemed okay at first, but this afternoon he started acting weird like he does. He kept saying you killed Miriam, and he was going to make you pay."

"How does he know where I am?"

"One of the Lopez boys. Eduardo, I think. His big mouth mother must have said something. I tried calling Hartley, but he's out in the shops where they don't have a telephone. They said they'd give him the message."

"How long ago did Henry leave?"

"About thirty minutes. I called and called you, but your party line was busy, so I got the operator to break in. Should I call the police?"

Kathleen trembled. "Not after what happened with my last job." Then speaking calmer than she felt, "I can handle him, Jill."

"Not this time you can't. Get out, now."

"Try Dad again," Kathleen said and hung up.

She glanced at the clock. *I've got to get Sarah out, and Maria and Carmen too.* Her heart thumped against her chest. *Please, Lord, don't let Henry make me lose this job, too.*

She ran to the nursery and grabbed Sarah. "Get the diaper bag, Maria. Carmen, bring the bottle, and let's go." The two startled women followed Kathleen across the back yard and out a side gate to the next-door neighbor.

Mrs. Dickson opened the door. "Sorry to trouble you," Kathleen said. "I need Sarah to stay here for a while. Maria and Carmen too, please. Lock all your doors and windows and don't let anyone in. *Nobody.* Do you understand?"

With an astonished look on her face, Mrs. Dickson ushered Maria and Carmen through the door.

Kathleen turned to leave and heard the bolt slide into place. With the baby safe, she ran back to the courtyard. *I should have told the Wendell's about Henry. I should have called the police. I should have . . .*

"Where are you going, Sis?"

Kathleen whirled around to face Henry.

Dressed in army fatigues and hat, he raised his chin. "I'm a soldier now." He tugged the bottom of his jacket. "See, I'm official."

An earthquake rumbled through Kathleen's chest. "Then why are you here?"

Henry dropped his hand. "I ran away."

"They'll come get you. They'll throw you in the stockade."

Henry stammered. "They, they tried to kill me."

Kathleen backed away from him. "Who's trying to kill you?"

"The Sergeant and the others. They shot at me, but the bullets bounced off the radio waves. Then I saw the mess hall cook stir poison into my eggs." He reached for her hand. "Don't let them hurt me."

Kathleen's voice quavered. "No one's going to hurt you."

"Watch me, Sis." Smiling, he changed from a frightened man to a playful boy. The boy Kathleen once knew. He hoisted an imaginary gun over his shoulder, clicked his heels together, then marched back and forth to a murmured cadence.

The rumble in Kathleen's chest eased. "I'm proud of you," she said. "We're all proud of you."

He marched up to her and saluted.

Kathleen saluted back. "You'll make a fine soldier."

Henry relaxed his stance, then grabbed Kathleen's upper arms and shook her. "Why did you kill her?"

"Kill who?"

"Miriam; our mother."

"Miriam was not our mother."

"She tried to be, but you wouldn't let her."

"Miriam was our stepmother. And she wasn't even nice to us."

"She was nice to me."

Kathleen spoke softly. "No one killed her, Henry. She died from the stroke."

Henry crossed his arms. "You were sitting in the pew next to her. You must have done something to her."

Kathleen recalled how devastated Henry was that Sunday morning when Miriam fell over dead in church. How devastated they all were.

"They told me you poisoned her."

Kathleen shook her fists. "Who are, *They?*"

Henry's eyes glazed over. His lips moved silently.

"You need to go back," Kathleen said.

"They'll shoot me."

Kathleen screamed, "You're out of your mind, Henry," and she ran toward the gate.

Henry caught up with her, grabbed her wrist and yanked her back.

She shook him off, snatched a rake propped against the fence, and thrust it at arm's length in front of her like a shield.

"Think you're smart, eh?" Henry clasped his hands over the rake handle and twisted. "They taught me this in infantry school."

Both of their hands locked around the rake handle. They turned, twisted, whirled around the yard in a frightening dance until Henry caught his boot on the wooden cross and stumbled over the cactus.

Kathleen scrambled up and sprinted across the yard.

Henry chased her.

Backed up to the fence, with no escape, Kathleen's terror paled when compared to the anger that held her in place. "Go back to the army," she said, "before you get in trouble."

Henry's eyes blazed. "Trouble? Here's trouble." He drew back his boot and kicked her in the stomach.

Kathleen grabbed her groin. Her legs folded. Lying on the ground, she thought about the neighbor's hog her dad helped butcher last winter, it's horror-stricken face as the ax pierced his head. She looked at Henry standing over her now, and terror returned.

* * *

"I should have stopped him," Jill muttered, as she stood at the end of La Vega Road. "I should have called the police. I should have . . . dear God. I should wring Edwardo's neck."

She had called Hartley again, but a gruff-voiced man said Hartley had already left. "Message? What message? Ah, you mean the one about Henry going to Kathleen's. Nah, we don't deliver silly girl messages like that."

"How could you not give him my message?" she'd screamed.

A car approached. Jill waved. But the driver turned the corner and sped away. She brushed tears with the back of her hand. "Where are you, Hartley?"

She ran toward the house. Her foot caught in a gopher hole, and she fell on a rock. Blood oozed from her hands and knees. She pushed herself up and limped back to the house just as Hartley drove up.

"Hartley, thank God. You've got to save Kathleen!"

* * *

Kathleen lay sprawled on the ground, her skirt split up the side, her blouse in shreds.

Henry loomed over her, jeering, "I've got you now," and he drew back his fist.

"Henry! Stop!" Kathleen screamed.

Henry's fist froze.

Kathleen rolled over, pushed herself up, and sprinted toward the gate where Hartley stood on the other side, frantically jiggling the latch.

She held her open palm in the air. "I have to fight him myself, Dad, or I'll never be free of him."

On seeing Hartley, Henry knelt and pressed his hands together as if in prayer. "Make them go away, Dad. Please make them go."

A siren ripped the air.

Henry's face contorted like a frightened child; he grabbed Kathleen's hand. "Let's go, Sis." He dragged her across the brick pathway, whipped her back and forth, and threw her onto the fence.

Two officers burst through the gate and landed on top of Henry as he screamed, "She killed my mother! She killed my—"

One officer flipped Henry over, thrust his knee onto his back, and handcuffed him.

Hartley knelt beside Kathleen, pulled hair off her face, and placed his hand over her forehead. He gently lifted her legs, then her arms. "I don't think you have any broken bones."

Mr. and Mrs. Wendell rushed up. "Where's Sarah?" she said.

Kathleen whispered. "At the Dickson's. Maria and Carmen are with her. I'm sorry—"

"Not now," Mrs. Wendell said, and she ran toward the neighbor's house.

"Shall I radio for an ambulance?" an officer asked.

Kathleen groaned. "No. No ambulance. Just help me up, please."

They spoke to the officers a few moments. On their way back to Kathleen, Mr. Wendell picked up the wooden cross, stuck it back in the ground, and pressed dirt around it. He and Hartley lifted Kathleen to her feet, walked her slowly to the house, and lay her on the sofa.

Hartley took an Indian blanket off the back of a chair and tucked it over her, and then felt the back of her head. "You've already got a knot," he said. "Lie still while I go chip some ice."

Pain cut up Kathleen's neck like a knife. Her shoulders throbbed. Her head pulsed.

Hushed voices drifted from the kitchen. Mr. Wendell's, "It's over, dear . . . yes, she's in shock I think; you can come home now." Then Hartley's, "She'll be alright, Jill. He beat her up, but . . . yes, you did the right thing. Yes, I'll tell her."

Mr. Wendell came back to the living room, and Hartley followed with an ice-filled bag and placed it under her head.

Mrs. Wendell came through the front door with Sarah in her arms.

On seeing Kathleen, Sarah waved her tiny arms and kicked. "Kaka, Kaka."

Kathleen tried to lift herself up, but her shoulders collapsed. Her voice was barely audible. "I'm so sorry."

"Don't apologize," Mr. Wendell said.

Baby Sarah squirmed. "Kaka, Kaka."

Kathleen closed her eyes and saw the faces of the Blount children. Lonnie, and little Janie with her jam-smeared mouth. Mrs. Blount's tight face when she fired her. Then strangely, the Lopez boy, Eduardo, who had sealed her fate. She rubbed her temples. *Everything comes back to Henry. Why don't I know that by now?*

Mr. Wendell's voice boomed. "I want you to go home with your father."

Kathleen sat up and looked longingly at Sarah. "I will miss you, little one." She looked at Hartley. "I need you to help pack my things."

"Don't take too much," Mrs. Wendell said.

Kathleen blinked. "I, I don't understand."

"We want you back as soon as you're ready."

Tears welled. "But I thought that, after this, you wouldn't want me."

Mr. Wendell took charge. "I called the Blount's before we hired you," he said. "Mr. Blount told me what happened and how you handled the, ah, situation. His children told him how you protected them. He said he wished he had you back. That they've had three different sitters since you left." He cleared his throat. "That's why we hired you. You know how to handle the unexpected. Not everyone so young does." He hesitated. "There were other reasons, of course."

"And I'm so grateful," Mrs. Wendell said.

"Grateful?" Kathleen's voice quavered.

"Maria told me how you made sure Sarah was safe first. How you made her and Carmen stay with her. You even took a warm bottle and diapers."

Then the three of them, Mr. and Mrs. Wendell and her dad, told her that Henry was on his way to Presbyterian Hospital, and that he would probably go on to New Mexico State Hospital in Las Vegas.

"The Asylum?" Kathleen gulped. At the look on her dad's face, she felt immediately sorry.

Mr. Wendell said, "The officer told us that Henry probably hears voices. That they've seen this kind of thing before. And the doctors will know what to do when they get him to the hospital."

Hartley sat next to Kathleen and buried his face in his hands.

Kathleen put her arm around his shoulder. "Dad, I'm sorry." Then feeling his nakedness before these people that he barely knew, she pulled his head to her aching shoulder and sheltered him while he sobbed.

CHAPTER SIXTEEN

Walter's face still stung from the icy October morning as he hung his coat on a hanger and brushed it smooth. *Funny how most people dread winter coming, but I don't mind it.* He rubbed his hands together. *Reminds me of Alaska.*

He sat at his desk, and his thoughts drifted to panning gold in icy streams, the snowy mountains above Skagway, plank sidewalks, muddy streets, and noisy saloons. *I'm too civilized for that now.* He smiled. *But I'm also rich and successful.*

He leaned back and crossed his hands behind his neck. *I even donated to that Jane Addams's Hull House where Laura taught piano and art to those poor immigrants. She used to beg me to give a donation. But hell, they should work for what they get, like I did.* He sat up. *But giving money to Hull House is good politics now; shows I'm civic minded. Imagine, me a benefactor. Wonder what Laura would think of that?*

He picked up the front page of the *Tribune,* and the latest article on Marshall Field's new Merchandise Mart caught his eye. It was supposed to be the largest building in the world. He frowned. *Field's has the carriage trade for sure. But my new store will carry gowns from Paris, suits from London, top of the line everything. Hell, the City Treasurer's wife even shopped in my State Street store last week and complimented my line of women's wear.* He slapped his fist into his hand. *I'm going to give Marshall Field's a run for their money, and I'll topple them in the process.*

His intercom buzzed. "Miss Pruitt is on the line, sir."

He picked up the telephone.

"Something's gone wrong on Wall Street," Clarice said. "Downtown Merchants have called a meeting tonight at six."

"Ah, yes," Walter said, "that drop in the stock market. Last night's paper was full of it."

"People are in a panic to sell. They even closed the visitor's gallery."

"Don't worry. I'll go. But this will blow over. We'll get through today and have the weekend to cool off."

Walter scribbled "D T Merchants" on his calendar. *Waste of my time meeting with that bunch of stuffed shirts. Bet most of 'em lost a bundle yesterday.* Then picturing the long faces of his fellow merchants one by one, he relished the thought of meeting with them. *Bet their starch has wilted now.* He tapped his foot. *Businessmen; investing profits in the market instead of plowing them back into their stores, buying stocks on margin, gambling for sure.* He'd learned his lesson from Big Jake at the Faro table in St. Louis.

On Thursday, Clarice burst into his office. "The Market's hit bottom, Father. They say people are jumping off roofs on Wall Street."

Walter waved his hand in dismissal. "Don't panic. You know I don't have money in the stock market. This won't impact us."

"I'm not panicking," Clarice said, "but everybody else is. Most of our salesclerks are on the telephone with their brokers. Even the janitor is on the phone."

"Good gosh. Did everyone in the world buy stocks on margin?"

"How else would they buy them?"

"Don't they know that what goes up must come down?"

"Apparently not."

The following Monday, Clarice said, "I just heard Rosenwald might cover the first round of margin calls for his Sears and Roebuck employees."

"Ours don't expect the same, do they?"

"I've had lots of questions."

"Only fools put money in nothing but a piece of paper."

"Well, Potter, J. P. Morgan and those other New York bankers aren't fools, and they just put in forty million each."

"They made enough when the market was strong. Seems to me they owe it."

"Maybe. But it's going to be bad, Father, really bad."

"It will be for the speculator. But since we don't have money in the market, it's not going to hurt us."

"I wish I could believe you."

"Didn't we talk about this over the weekend?"

"Yes, but—"

"I have calls to make, Clarice. Try to calm those clerks down. We'll talk later."

Disturbed by the urgency in Clarice's voice, Walter took out a sheet of paper and listed his finances: own home outright, notes paid-off on State Street store and warehouse, forty thousand left on note for the Madison Street store, construction on new store over half-complete.

He chewed his knuckles. He had a checking account for the house bills, savings account for emergencies, and enough money set aside with the lawyer for Clarice and Clayton's care should something happen to him. *Bought into that partnership of westside apartment buildings last year; shouldn't have maybe, but a man must take some risks. Land. Brick and mortar. That's where I put my money.*

He glanced at his safe. Clarice's college money was in a hidden compartment where only he could find it. He had to deal with banks to finance his stores, but after T. L. Guthrie and First Bank of Fairbanks, he didn't put any more money in banks than he had to.

Walter felt the warm glow of a job well done, the pride of a man with superior foresight.

"Let the fools go down," he said. "I'm all set."

***

In early February, the bank called in Walter's note for the Madison Street store. He pulled forty thousand dollars from his savings account and paid it off.

Spring orders arrived.

Shelves were still packed with marked-down fall and winter merchandise, so they moved it all to backrooms and stocked the new spring finery. He slashed prices and ran super specials in the *Tribune*.

In early summer, Walter called his managers together. Yes, they had completed their markdowns. Yes, their salesclerks were friendly. Yes, their displays were in good order. And no, they did not know how else to bring in customers other than at gunpoint.

"Then go back to your departments and get rid of your highest paid employees," Walter ordered.

"But Mrs. Bonner has been with me for fifteen years . . . Mr. Tate has never had a complaint in his file . . . Mr. Hauser's wife is sick, and they have a new baby."

Walter took a deep breath. "It's them or you."

He left his coat and tie in his office now, while he and Clarice closed checkout counters, moved displays, consolidated merchandise, and laid-off more salesclerks.

In late March, the loan company called. "There's a problem with financing on that new store, Mr. Pruitt."

Walter scrambled, but found no money for new building loans anywhere, so he drew enough out of his store account to pay the contractor for another thirty days. His partnership with the apartments folded, but instead of his earlier anguish, he felt relief. He would not have to pour more money into half-finished buildings.

He called in his highest performing mangers, increased their workload, and then fired the rest. *Dear God, some of those men were with me from the beginning, but I had to do it.* He tightened. *Didn't I?*

Salesclerks clamored at his door. "Can you see your way to give me an advance on my paycheck, Mr. Pruitt? The bank is calling in my house note . . . I have three little girls, Mr. Pruitt, and I'm their only means of support . . . my husband lost his job at the stockyards, Mr. Pruitt, so might you find him a spot at the warehouse? He can move boxes, sweep, clean, anything."

Walter's heart beat fast all the time.

In April, his bank closed its doors for good. His contractor demanded full payment. Walter balked. The contractor walked. And with no money to hire a new one, his entire investment become a steel forest of posts and beams.

Clarice cornered him in his office. "Swimsuits are here, and our shelves are still full of spring mark-downs. They're unloading them now."

"Move the spring merchandise to the back room."

"It's already packed with fall and winter clothes."

"Then move them all to the warehouse."

"And when the warehouse is full?"

Walter shook his head at the enormity of his next decision. "Don't place any new orders. We'll bring out last year's mark-downs and put them back on the floor."

"I've laid-off so many people I hardly have enough left to do it," Clarice said.

"I know, I know. But this is temporary. We'll get back on track."

"Have you seen the tarpaper shacks on Randolph Street and the lake? And those men sleeping on the lower level of Wacker Drive?"

Walter rubbed his temples. *I turn the other way when Tom drives past, so I don't have to look at them. But I'm not going to tell you that.*

"What about the lines at the soup kitchens?" Clarice said.

Walter waved her away. "Damn it! I can't be bothered by soup kitchens now."

Clarice's eyes blazed. "Well, you better be bothered, Father. Because hungry people don't shop."

By late September, vendors demanded payments, raggedy men begged at the front door, priests sought donations for their charities. Frightened salesclerks turned pale when Walter walked by, so he hid in his office and let Clarice deal with the people.

Well-dressed people peddled their belongings on the streets. Wedding dresses, cloth coats, dishes, toys, went for a pittance if anyone bought them at all.

Children cried.

Walter let his driver, Tom, go, then the gardener, then the housekeeper. He kept Esther on to cook. Dust lay thick over the dim house, and no one cared.

Clarice finally said it. "We can't keep both stores open, Father. We've got to shut one of them down."

Walter pressed his hands on the sides of his head like a vise. "I can't . . . can't."

"Then we'll lose both stores."

The next month, they closed the Madison Street store, consolidated everything into the State Street store, and laid-off more employees. Walter hid in his office by day and left Clarice to handle the people. Back to his old habit of sleeping at his office, he'd paced the floor; searching. Searching for what? He threw up his hands. "For answers, damn it!"

He had planned so carefully. Did not borrow any more money than he had to; did not put money into the stock market; never placed his stores at the mercy of stockholders. He shook his fist in the air. "And what damn good did it do me?"

CHAPTER SEVENTEEN

Clarice sat on the edge of her bed and arched her back. Sales were down. Profits had dropped to record lows, and she felt helpless to do anything about it. She rubbed her neck. *So much for our great marketing plan.* After long weeks of climbing stairs, building displays, moving boxes, settling disputes, and laying people off, weariness washed over her like an ocean wave. Her shoulders throbbed. Her body ached as if she'd been in a fist fight and lost. She lay down like a tired child, and darkness welcomed her with instant sleep . . .

* * *

She can't move. She tries to breathe, but she can't, and she knows she's buried in an avalanche.

"I'm digging, Clarice, I'm digging," her father cries as his shovel scrapes against the snow.

Hurry Father, hurry. I can't breathe!

The snow shifts, her arms break free, and she claws her way out of the snow. She takes a deep breath, and icy air pierces her lungs like arrows. She grasps her chest, but there is no warmth in her.

Her father's shovel stands stuck in the snow. She sees the outline of his footprints walking away from her, and she screams, "Why did you abandon me, Father?"

Chill winds rip her shoulders and tear her neck. She looks around for her coat, and then remembers she left it at home. Father is going to be furious. She shivers. But Father said it was not going to snow.

Across the street, another man is shoveling.

The man drops his shovel. "I'm Kathleen's father," he cries. "She's trapped!"

"Keep digging; keep digging," Clarice shouts.

Up the littered street, she sees ragged human shapes huddling over a fire like prisoners of war. She tries to wedge into the warmth, but a gnarled man pushes her back. It's Mr. Long from Men's Wear. He has the same look on his face when she laid him off last spring.

She shivers again and shakes. Her icy hands ache. "It's me, Mr. Long, Clarice Pruitt, please let me in."

His face is a maze of cuts and scratches; his eyes are dark circles. "Get out," he cries. "You don't belong here."

Other faces look up at her: Mr. Agan, from Men's Shoes; Mrs. Walton, from Children's Wear; Mr. Jackson, from down in Bookkeeping; old Bradley, the Custodian. They were all let go when she closed the Madison Street store.

"Look what you've done to us," they shout.

Clarice runs. She stumbles and skids face first across the snow. Her face is raw; ice shards pierce her hands. She raises her head and sees a lone figure in a blue trench coat watching her from across the street. "Help me," she cries.

He turns and walks away.

"Don't leave me, Father; please don't leave me!"

* * *

Clarice woke with a jerk. Shivering, she rolled on her side, and in the dim light saw her ivory lace scarf draped over the sides of her dresser, her catch box of loose coins, sample bottles of Evening in Paris perfume, her coat and sweater stretched over a chair. She pulled her blanket up to her chin and tried to dissect her dream. *Those people looked so shattered. What will they do with all that anger?*

She hugged her chest. *Father left most of the layoffs to me, and I let him; otherwise, he would have just sent them a note. And the more I go out on the floor now, the more he stays in his office. How many times can he go over those ledgers?* She rocked back and forth. "I don't like what's happening either, but I'm facing it."

The clock chimed three. She threw off her covers, yanked her robe off the hook in her closet, and stepped into her slippers.

Downstairs, Esther sat at the kitchen table with a long notepad in her hand. "What are you doing up at this hour?" Clarice said.

Esther jumped and slapped her bony hand over her mouth. "You scared me, Miss Clarice."

"I'm sorry," Clarice said, then sat down across from her.

Esther frowned. "What are *you* doing up?"

"I had a bad dream," Clarice said.

"Then I'll make us some hot chocolate."

Clarice rubbed her stomach.

Esther poured the steaming chocolate. "Do you want to take it in the dining room?" she asked.

"I'll stay here with you, if you don't mind."

"No, ma'am. I don't mind."

Clarice wrapped her hands around the warm cup and nodded toward Esther's notepad. "What are you doing?"

"Taking inventory."

"Of what?"

Esther's face clouded. "Something's wrong around here, Miss Clarice."

"You've got that right," Clarice snapped. Then not meaning to put her troubles on Esther, added, "Forget I said that." And as Clarice had done in her childhood, she blew bubbles in her cup, and they both giggled.

"So, why are you taking inventory?" Clarice asked.

"Well, I tried to make toast this morning and the bread box was empty. Yesterday, I went to cook a pudding and there wasn't any sugar in the tin." Her soft gray eyes looked troubled. "I bought a pound of sugar last week, and I made two loaves of bread the day before yesterday and put them in the box myself."

Clarice frowned. *A cup of sugar? A loaf of bread? If that were my only worry.* Then trying to hide her annoyance, she said, "Can't you just go back to the store and buy more sugar? Bake more bread?"

"I did," Esther said. "But things keep disappearing. I've tried to tell Mr. Walter, but he doesn't want to hear it. I'm glad you came down here, so I can tell you." Her mouth trembled. "I don't want Mr. Pruitt to think I'm stealing. I can't lose this job."

"How could you even think that?" Clarice said. And then, *Why wouldn't she? We let everybody else go.* She leaned toward Esther. "You've been here since before I was born. You know everything about this house, while I know very little."

Esther sighed. "It's just that things have been bad since my daughter died. And my son-in-law got laid off two months ago." Her eyes glistened. "He don't have enough groceries to make lunches for school. All four children need shoes, and the little one has outgrown her coat. I help when I can, but my son-in-law seems so down in the dumps he's just given up, I think, and he sleeps most all day." Her face puffed. "He's not even caring for the children, Miss Clarice."

Clarice squeezed her eyes shut. She'd had sent a sympathy card and flowers when Esther's daughter died, but no further action was needed—or so she thought. She recalled the desperate people in her dream huddling over the fire. *They must have families, too.*

She looked at Esther. "I'll give you money every week for the children's lunches. Let me know what size shoes they wear and the coat size for the little one, and I'll bring some from the store."

"How can you afford it, with you closing the Madison Street store?"

"We're managing," Clarice said. She rubbed her forehead. "And I can't sell those damn shoes anyway!"

"I won't take charity for myself," Esther said. "But I will take it for my grandchildren."

Clarice's face burned. "There's still plenty of food in this country, but nobody has money to buy it. I have double-breasted suits and fur coats, house dresses with butterfly sleeves, and straw hats rotting on shelves and racks, and people can't buy them either."

"What's going to happen to us if this depression don't let up?"

"I wish I knew," Clarice said. "But things have got to get better." She scooted her chair next to Esther. "Now let me see your inventory."

* * *

Clarice headed back to her room, then saw Clay's door ajar, and stuck her head through the crack. "Late to be hitting the books, Brother."

"And late to be prowling the hallway," he said and motioned her in.

"I couldn't sleep. Esther made me hot chocolate."

"Esther's up, too?"

"Taking inventory. She's all worried about some missing food."

Clay walked to his desk.

Clarice came up behind him and yanked the soft golden hair on his neck. "You need a haircut."

"Maybe next year."

She peered over his shoulder. "How long have you been studying Russian history?"

"A while," Clay said. "I'm on the last of the tsars now."

Clarice pulled up a chair and sat next to him. "Aren't those people Communists or something?"

"They are since the Revolution, yes."

"Father calls them Reds. He says they want to take rich people's money away and give it to poor people. That they have secret cells here in the states, and they're planning to take over our country."

"Well, now might be the right time to do it."

Clarice squinted her eyes. "Why do you say that?"

"Because people are sick of this depression."

"Father says the Reds don't believe in God."

"That from a man who never sets a foot in church?"

"Well, I don't go to church, either. And neither do you."

"You're too influenced by what Father thinks."

131

Clarice wiped her forehead. "He's on my mind all the time. He's hurting."

"*He's* hurting? What about the six-hundred thousand people out of work in Chicago alone?"

Clarice winced. "I've had to lay some of them off myself."

"And do you know that a child died of starvation at Children's Memorial last week?"

"Well, Father had to close the Madison Street Store. He never even opened the new one, and the State Street Store is barely making it. I don't know how much longer we can hang on."

Clay glared at her. "You're comparing your stores to a dead child?"

"Of course not. But what can I do about it?"

"Communism postulates that everyone shares the wealth; not just a few at the top."

"Postulates? When did you start talking like a professor?"

"Do you know that J.P. Morgan did not pay any income tax last year? And McCormick at the *Tribune* and Florsheim hardly paid any."

Clarice shrugged.

"Try to understand the enormity of what's happening, Sis."

"But we're not hungry. And I feel bad for the children, but there's nothing I can do about it."

Clay slammed his book shut. "All you care about is that damn store."

"It's our life, Clay. You'll find that out when we lose it. Then what will you do?"

"Don't you know how desperate hungry people can be?"

"They have the soup kitchens. They're eating at least."

"Families are living in tar paper shacks in the snow. Families are breaking up. Parents can't feed their children, so they're putting them on trains hoping some family will adopt them."

She brushed a tear off her cheek. "You're scaring me, Clay."

Clay opened his palms in the air. "Clarice, the fearless. Afraid of her puny brother?"

"It's your voice. You've never talked to me like that before."

Clay spoke gently now. "Can't you see how blinded we are by our wealth? How much others are suffering?"

"I dreamed about some of those people I laid off. They were huddled over a fire. I was freezing, but they wouldn't let me in." Her lips trembled. "They hated me, but I had to lay them off. I had no other choice."

"We all have choices, Clarice."

"Choices?" Her voice squeaked. "Like you choose to stay in this room all the time."

"I read newspapers. I know what's happening. It's you and Father who live in a cocoon."

Clay's eyes darted to the ceiling, and Clarice found herself looking at the whites of his eyes. His way of avoiding she knew, and she waited.

He rubbed his forehead. "I'm sorry, Sis. I know you're trying to keep us going. I just wish you might feel more for others."

Tears streamed down her face. "I have you, Clay, and Father. You're the only ones I care about. Can you understand that?"

"I can," Clay said. "I just feel sad for you."

Sad for me? Clarice sighed. For her tears were not for the suffering people but were for her beautiful brother who shuts himself in his room all day and only knows the world through newspapers and books. *What's going to happen to him?*

CHAPTER EIGHTEEN

Walter stared at the pile of unopened mail on his desk. His shirt was creased with sweat, and his hair lay in greasy strings. He ignored the ringing telephone. It could only be Clarice, and he did not want to talk to her now. He walked to the window. Sleet and snow lay over the city like a fluffy white blanket while crews cleared the streets. *Useless. It'll ice over again tonight.*

He paced from the window to his desk to the window again and back. He had called on every banker he knew who had survived the crash and closures, inquired of every acquaintance, even loan sharks. He was deep into his accounts for Clarice and Clay, and his household fund would be empty after next month's expenses. The house was up for sale, but no one had money to buy it. He stopped in front of his safe. Clarice's college money was inside, nearly the last of his cash, but it would not even begin to pull him out of the hole he was in.

He went back to his desk and picked up the front page of the *Tribune* and read the headline. "Robert Bradford Chairs Relief Committee." In smaller print, "Local financier assembles business leaders to address needs of the homeless."

He slammed the newspaper down. "Some people still have money!" He thought of Felicia, and his jaws tightened. *How could she have met, much less married, a man like Robert Bradford?* He wrinkled his forehead. *And how in hell did she engineer herself into my daughter's life?*

An eerie quiet settled over him. He looked around his office that had been his home as if he were a bum who had stumbled in and wasn't sure what to do. He picked up the front page and reread the article. Newspaper in hand, he paced back and forth again with thoughts of Felicia swirling in his head. He wiped his brow.

Back at his desk, he stared at the headline again for a long while. He closed his eyes and rubbed the middle of his forehead. He couldn't do it . . . wouldn't . . . and yet, what choice did he have? He opened his eyes, pulled a white card out of his wallet, and dialed Felicia.

* * *

"Sorry about your table, Mr. Pruitt," the Maître d' said, "It's been a long time since we've seen you, and the young waiter is new, you see."

Walter pointed to a table at the far corner. "That one will do. And Mrs. Bradford will be joining me." He followed the Maître d' across the dining room and admired the long flowing dresses. *The latest style flatters a woman's figure . . . it's about time.* He recognized a Chanel and other brands he carried and wished he could sell what he had left of them.

He sat down and glanced at his "old table" where a silver-haired man in a dark blue Frederick Scholte suit sat across from a younger man in a two-piece brown tweed. The younger man looked grave as they sparred back and forth. Walter smiled. He had negotiated some pretty good deals at that table himself.

Felicia walked toward him. Her auburn hair puffed above her head like a crown, and her soft green dress draped her body like thin leaves of spring.

How does she always know exactly what to wear? He stood and pulled out her chair.

The waiter brought menus.

"Just soup, please," Felicia said. "French onion."

"Just soup?" Walter said.

"I have another appointment at one-thirty."

He nodded to the waiter. "Then French onion for the lady, and I'll have the stroganoff." The waiter jotted their orders on a pad, and then went on to the next table.

Walter frowned. "I was looking forward to a leisurely lunch."

Felicia looked at her watch, a magnificent gold timepiece sparkling with diamonds and emeralds. "You have something to discuss with me?" she said.

Walter had planned to take the soft approach, engage her with compliments, weave her through this distasteful task, but she had already disarmed him. He swirled his glass of water. "I was hoping we could talk first. Old times maybe, catch up on things."

Felicia raised her eyebrows. "We have no 'old times' remember?"

Walter grinned. "My, but we're sharp today." He took a sip of water then set the glass down. "Well, since you want to get down to business, I have a proposition for you." He winced. *Damn. A fool's choice of a word.* He opened his mouth to apologize, but the waiter appeared with her soup.

Felicia edged her spoon through sticky cheese, and steam rose with a faint smell of sweet onions. She ate a few spoonsful and set her spoon down. "So, Patrick, what do you want from me this time?"

Walter seethed. "I thought we agreed to stick to the present."

"If we have no 'past' then we have no 'present' either."

Despite himself, he smiled.

Felicia glanced at her watch again. "I don't have time to banter with you, Walter."

He dabbed his mouth with his napkin and placed it back on his lap. "All right then, I want you to make me an appointment with your husband."

"Robert is accessible. You can make your own appointment."

"Perhaps, but as you know, I have not had business dealings with him before. And I, well, I might need your assistance."

Felicia looked at him coolly. "What kind of assistance?"

"Well, to be frank, I need a loan."

"Well, you won't get it from Robert."

"I will with *your* help."

"And why should I help you?"

Walter leaned toward her. "Because, it will be in your best interest to do so."

The waiter appeared with Walter's stroganoff and set it on the table in front of him. "Will there be anything else, sir?"

Walter shook his head.

"Ma'am?"

"No, thank you," Felicia said. The waiter left, and she looked at Walter. "Robert is funding soup kitchens. He's chairman of the Mayor's committee to help the homeless. He's not financing businesses now."

"So I read in yesterday's *Tribune*. But you can persuade him, I'm sure. And if everything goes as I expect, you will have nothing to worry about."

Felicia raised her eyebrows. "And if it doesn't?"

Walter studied her for a long moment. "Then we'll both go down."

Felicia picked up her spoon and swirled it in the lukewarm brown liquid of her abandoned soup. "So, Patrick, here we are again. You need me to help you get money."

Pain shot across Walter's forehead. *Damn woman.* He shoved his stroganoff from one side of his plate to the other. *Stay calm, Walter . . . she has more to lose than you do.* He took another sip of water and set his glass down. "It's simple this time, my dear. I need money, yes, unfortunately. And you need me to keep quiet."

Felicia stood. Her white napkin clung to her green velvet dress, and she peeled it off.

Walter glanced around the dining room. "People are looking."

Felicia placed her napkin on the table and sat down.

"It's Clarice's future," he said. "If I don't get some money and fast, I'll lose my State Street store, and she'll be ruined, too."

"So, you're linking your daughter's future with mine now. Interesting turn of events, don't you think?"

Walter waved his fork. "It's one thing to consider."

Felicia folded her napkin. "Call me tomorrow morning at eight," she said, "and I'll give you a time."

Walter lowered his eyes. "I'm sorry. I didn't want to ask this of you, but I have no choice."

Felicia glanced at her watch. "I have just enough time to make my one-thirty appointment with Clarice."

Walter dropped his fork. "With Clarice?"

"Our monthly tea, you know."

"No, I didn't know. You won't—"

"Won't what?"

"Say anything to her."

Felicia stood, pulled a five-dollar bill out of her purse, and dropped it on the table. "Maybe this will help."

CHAPTER NINETEEN

Walter waited in the outer office on the twelfth floor of the London Guarantee Building and twisted his watch. His heart pounded as he bounced his curled knuckle against his mouth. *Lord; don't let me sound like a pleading child.* The door opened, and he stood.

"Come in," Felicia's husband said. He shook Walter's hand, ushered him into his office, and motioned toward a chair in front of his desk. "Please, have a seat."

Walter's stomach churned. He had forgotten what a powerful combination Bradford's black eyes made with his silver hair and olive skin. *And he's the only thing left between me and disaster.*

Bradford extended his open cigar box.

"No, thank you," Walter said, "I'm a pipe man."

"I'm a pipe man, too, but I like the taste of these Cuban cigars."

While Robert seemed to make a production of lighting his cigar, Walter admired his wall of books, Persian rug, mahogany desk, old oak paneling, and he shriveled on this man's turf.

"You're admiring my office?" Robert said.

Walter smiled. "You read my thoughts."

"My wife is the decorator. But then, you know my wife, don't you?"

"I, well, she . . ."

Robert waved his hand in dismissal. "Of course, foolish of me, your wife and mine were friends." He leaned back. "Interesting how they met at that charity dinner and became inseparable . . . but that was a long time ago. You and I have been intent on running our businesses, and our paths haven't crossed much." He sat up straight. "But Felicia and I both think a lot of Clarice. She's a smart young woman, and she did an excellent job for me in Los Angeles. I'm glad for this opportunity to tell you."

I shouldn't have let Clarice go on that blasted trip.

"I see why you put her in charge of your stores."

"Yes, but it's only for now. I'm sending her to college after this depression is over."

Robert's eyes locked on Walter's. "My wife, well, she never had a daughter. I think she fancies Clarice that way."

Walter's stomach churned. "So, it seems." Then wanting to appear relaxed, he tried to settle into the high-backed chair. He glanced at Robert leaning back in his soft leather, and his jaws tightened. *The man planned it this way.*

Robert rested his cigar on a crystal ashtray. Smoke rose in a noxious cloud. "Well, Mr. Pruitt, your time is as valuable as mine, but before we begin, let me say that I admire the way you built your stores. You chose good locations, stocked quality merchandise, and displayed it to advantage. While I'm not in retail myself, I know a sound operation when I see one."

"I built slowly," Walter said. "Didn't carry unnecessary debt. Paid off everything early and own it all outright."

"Sound," Robert said, "I congratulate you." He picked up a pencil and tapped it on his desk. "Well, Pruitt," he hummed, "Pruitt? It's of German derivation, is it not?"

Walter forced a nod.

"Where did your people originate?"

"Germany."

"But what city, or a small town, perhaps?"

Walter felt like a third-grader sitting in a corner wearing a dunce's cap. "I, well, I'm not sure."

Robert tilted his hand back and forth in the air. "Ah, yes, America the melting pot. Forget about the old country. My mother and father were from Germany is why I asked. Weimar, home of Johann Wolfgang Goethe, the poet. They took me back to visit once.

It was beautiful and rich with history." He took another puff of his cigar, let it out slowly, and looked at Walter. "But I was born here. My Father and mother worked at a processing plant, and somehow they managed to put me through the University of Chicago." He leaned toward Walter. "I *know* Chicago and everything about it, including the murk and mess of its politics."

Walter stiffened. "I know something about politics, too."

Robert took a puff of his cigar. "My wife was born in Kansas City, but her father chased after gold to Alaska when she was a young girl." He took another puff, then ground it out in the ashtray. "Have you ever been to Alaska, Pruitt?"

Beads of sweat popped on Walter's forehead. "No, I mean, yes."

Robert leaned back. "I don't mean to waste your valuable time with idle talk, Pruitt. You have something to discuss with me, I understand."

Walter made a steeple with his hands. *Felicia, I hope you did your job.* "Well, you said you've followed the progress of my stores."

"I have."

"Then you know that I'm down to only my State Street store and my warehouse."

"This depression's hit everyone. They say it can't last much longer, but—"

"We've weathered these slumps before," Walter said. "And the businesses that survived were ahead of the game."

"And a lot of well-run businesses went down."

Walter reared his shoulders. "I'm confident that my State Street Store will prosper again. And when business picks up, I will reopen my Madison Street Store."

Robert picked up his pencil and tapped it in a drum roll.

Walter gritted his teeth. *I should grab that damn pencil and shove it down his throat.* "It's just that I have a cash flow problem right now; I need new capital to keep the doors open. I've put my house up for sale, but no one seems able to buy it. I'll keep it for collateral, if necessary. Down the road it will be worth a fortune."

"You're asking me for a loan?" Robert said.

"Just enough to get me over the hump. You'll get it all back with interest."

"You just said you don't believe in carrying unnecessary debt."

"In normal times, not, but—"

"And if this depression doesn't end soon like you predict, and you can't pay me back?"

"Then you'll have a valuable building in a downtown location and a warehouse. Perhaps a beautiful home should you require it."

"Useless tax liabilities are what I would have."

Walter's head jerked back. "But Felicia said . . ."

"So, you've spoken to my wife?"

Walter's face burned. *This man holds my life in balance; he can tip the scales at his will.* "It will be a strict business loan," he said. "You'll get your money back with interest."

"I asked have you spoken to my wife."

"We, well, we had lunch."

"That was a mistake."

Walter stammered. "I, I don't understand."

"I said that lunch with my wife was a mistake."

"I, I meant her no harm, I . . ."

Robert leaned over his desk toward Walter. "You threatened my wife, Pruitt."

Walter's voice quavered. "Are you turning me down?"

"I'm turning you down."

"But my buildings would more than cover your loss should the worst happen."

"The worst?" Robert's eyes protruded. "You've not seen it yet."

"But it's not just me I'm asking for. I have an army of people who'll lose their jobs. And there's Clarice, of course."

"So, you'll use your daughter to get what you want?"

Sensing disaster, Walter took a deep breath. *I'm sorry, Felicia.* "I won't use my daughter," he said. "But I will use your wife."

Robert raised his eyebrows.

"I met Felicia in a saloon in Fairbanks. Her name was Annie Parsons then. She was a—"

"And Annie met an Irishman named Patrick Roark," Robert added. "He asked for her help with a certain task he was working on. In return, he promised to take her to Kansas City."

Walter's throat felt like cardboard.

Robert went on. "It seemed there was a timely withdrawal of funds from the First Bank of Fairbanks. And this fellow, Roark, well, he left town right after. Forgot all about his promise to Annie, I guess."

Walter perched on the edge of his chair.

"Relax, Roark, I'm glad you did. Run, that is. Because I met Annie on a train to Chicago. She was coming to look for you, by the way. She was lovely and vulnerable. And she was with child."

Walter jumped up. "Child? Did you say with child?"

Robert waved him down. "Don't worry, man. You did me the biggest favor of my life. I fell in love with Annie before we got to Minneapolis; talked her into marrying me as we pulled into Wisconsin; and I've never been able to thank you properly until now." He poured water from a silver pitcher and handed a glass to Walter. "You look a little pale, Pruitt."

Walter gripped the glass with both hands.

"Felicia was her mother's name by the way. But then it's easy to change a name, isn't it? And there was the little matter of a miscarriage. A baby girl, nearly fully formed, the doctor said. And there would be no more children for Annie, ever."

Walter dropped the glass. Water streamed down his legs and puddled on the polished oak floor. *A baby girl . . . my baby girl?* He dug his fingernails into the sides of his forehead. "Dear God—oh, good God!"

Robert's eyes looked slick as oil. "If you ever try to blackmail me or my wife again, or if you ever say an unkind word about my wife to anyone. And that includes your daughter. I will personally see that funny business in Fairbanks is opened for review, and the guilty party who got off free be held to account."

Walter grabbed his stomach.

Robert stood. "And that earlier business with your father. Stolen money, however gotten, and then your father was killed. Suspicious, I'd say. Patricide?"

Walter shot up. "You can't know anything about that."

"Enough money," Robert said coolly, "the right connections, and you can dig up anything." He raised his eyebrows. "I wonder what Clarice might say if she found out her 'honorable German father' is only a thieving Irishman?"

Walter's arms flailed. "You leave Clarice out of this!"

"That, Pruitt, will be up to you." Robert pointed to the door. "Now get out!"

CHAPTER TWENTY

Driving home, into the setting sun, Hartley looked past the soft brown sand and ragged slopes to scruffy low juniper trees and sighed. *How simple life is in the desert. Creatures fend for themselves or they die, while we humans live in a jumble, not knowing what to do half the time.*

It had been six months since the police took Henry to the mental asylum in Las Vegas. He had always liked the little New Mexico town, but not now, since seeing his son strapped to a chair crying out for someone Hartley couldn't even see.

The grinding road, the squeaks and rattles of his touring car could not blot out the painful thoughts of the dimly lit hospital with its gray, cracked tile, screams echoing down the long hallway, metal doors clanging shut behind him, the doctor's grim words: "There's nothing more we can do for him. We tried the ice baths and isolation and restraints. We even injected him with insulin, but he stayed in a coma too long. We won't try that again. They're experimenting with something called electro-shock, but it is likely years away."

Hartley looked across the sand to an outcrop of jagged rocks and fought back tears. *Henry was so smart. He did pat-a-cake at five months, said "mama" before he could sit up, won the school spelling bee every year.* He recalled the fort Henry had built in their backyard. *The little fellow worked for three days and begged me to sleep in the fort that night. "Just you and me Daddy, please."* He chewed his lower lip. *And I told him I was too tired. Dear God, too tired for an eight-year-old boy?* "Did I lose him then, Lord? If not, then when? How?"

His chest ached. *All the pain Laura went through to have that boy after her loss of those two in Chicago. There was no more wanted child in the world. What would she think if she knew?* He shook his fist. "It's your fault, Laura! How could you leave me with this?"

Miles passed. His anger eased as his mind drifted back to his desperate wedding to Miriam with her pale, gray eyes set deep in her solemn face, her pleated white dress. His hands had trembled as the congregation looked on. "Do you, Hartley, take Miriam to . . .?" Tears rolled down his cheeks. Those were the same promises he'd made less than three years before with Laura. He would have folded right then if Henry hadn't gripped his leg and held firm.

Hartley shook his head to clear it. *And how Henry loved Miriam. Transferred his love from his mother to her without a whimper until Miriam fell dead in church.* "Was that my fault, too, Lord? Should I have known she was sick?"

A honk from behind startled him as a pickup truck pulled out to pass. Two Indians dressed in buckskin sat in the bed, their leathered faces firm against the wind. A second pickup passed pulling a horse trailer. Hay blew out both sides while a golden horsetail streamed out the back as if waving goodbye.

Vultures circled. Black wings flapped as they swooped down on a carcass. A dirt road veered off to the left, and Hartley's eyes followed as it disappeared over a distant hill. His mouth felt like cotton. *I could drive to the end of that road and let the desert take me.*

He lifted his foot off the gas pedal, pulled to the side of the road, and draped his arms over the steering wheel. He closed his eyes, and a light desert breeze glided over the side of his face. *Sweet death . . . not to have to hurt anymore . . . not to hurt anyone else.* He lifted his head. His face tingled. The gripping pressure in his chest lifted like a feather in the wind. He sat for a long while gazing at the barren hills, the swarming vultures, the lifeless sky.

He shifted his car into reverse, backed up, and started up the endless dirt road.

* * *

Bea stood over the bubbling pot stirring as the smell of beef stew filled the house.

Sybil tapped her boot on the new yellow and blue linoleum. "Nothing smells better than a pot of stew, does it, Dear?"

"Your welcoming present," Bea said.

Sybil groaned. "That train ride from Chicago gets harder every time I make it. I'm getting old and crotchety, I guess."

Adrift in her private rhythm of home and food, Bea ladled stew into a small bowl, blew, tasted, nodded, tasted again, then added salt and a sprig of rosemary. She nodded satisfaction, then filled her cup with steaming coffee and sat across from Sybil.

"You know, Dear, I'm not a nosy mother-in-law who wants to know everything that goes on in her children's lives, but what was Hartley thinking to let Kathleen work as a common servant?"

"Kathleen is a Nanny," Bea said. "She's in charge of the child."

Sybil's face scrunched. "Changing nasty diapers, wiping baby drool, sounds like a common babysitter to me."

"Kathleen loves that baby, and Mr. and Mrs. Wendell are good to her."

"Well, she should have stayed home and finished high school."

Bea went back to the stove and picked up the pot. "Another cup of coffee?"

Sybil waved. "Oh no, don't worry about me." She glanced at the wall. "My, that teapot clock I gave Hartley still keeps time, doesn't it? And the wall would be completely bare without it."

"Well, we've still got to paint yet—"

"Speaking of time, shouldn't Hartley be home by now? I barely saw him last night, and he left before daylight this morning."

"I don't know."

"You said he had business to tend to east of Santa Fe?"

Bea glanced toward the window. "Some business, yes."

"That old touring car. I bet it broke down in that wretched desert."

"It still runs good," Bea said, "despite the rattles." She brushed scattered crumbs off the blue checkered oilcloth, caught them in her hand, and dumped them in the nearby trashcan.

"You've been working all day. You must be tired."

"I'm fine," Bea said.

"And speaking of tired, Hartley looked like a wet dog when he met me at the train last night. He could hardly lift my bag."

"Well, he does a lot around here."

"Oh, I know that. Before he married you, I came every summer to help out."

"So I heard."

"And Hartley hardly touched his supper last night. When he was home with me, he ate two helpings of everything and then some." Sybil's face contorted. "Oh dear, I didn't mean to suggest that you're not taking good care of him. You always fix hot sturdy meals." She glanced around the kitchen. "And this house is spotless. Laura never cleaned house or cooked for him, you know."

"But Laura couldn't—"

"I know I shouldn't say this, but Kathleen being a servant, well, I should have expected as much from *Laura's* daughter."

"That was so long ago," Bea said. "How could Laura influence the choices Kathleen makes now?"

Sybil tapped her fingers on the table in rhythm with her tapping foot. "Worst day of my life was when Hartley took up with that Irish girl. She stayed in bed most of the time and wouldn't even take care of her husband and children. He begged money from me to pay a housekeeper." She stirred her coffee. "I hate to say it, but Hartley ignored these children's early breeding. If there had been enough love in that family . . ."

Bea dropped her cup. China shattered as copper liquid spread over the oilcloth. She pushed her chair back and let coffee puddle into her hands.

Sybil's head bobbed. Her bun bounced. "Oh dear, I didn't mean to upset you."

Using her hands as a vessel, Bea walked to the counter and

dumped the coffee into the sink. Back at the table, she folded the tablecloth and dumped the broken china into the trashcan.

Sybil rummaged through her purse and pulled out a lace handkerchief. "As I was saying, Laura didn't . . ."

Bea whirled around. "Hartley loved Laura!"

Sybil jiggled. "Well of course, of course."

Bea gazed out the open window. *Oh God, how he loved her.*

Sybil twisted her handkerchief. "But then I was so happy when Hartley married Miriam. She was such a lovely German girl, and Henry adored her. Poor Hartley, and Henry too, they didn't know what to do after Miriam died." She took Bea's hand and held tight. "But you've been a good influence on Henry too, and you take wonderful care of my son."

"Thank you," Bea said and withdrew her hand.

"Speaking of Henry, I haven't received a letter from him in a long time."

Bea glanced toward the window again. "He's not very good at writing."

"When will he finish his training?"

"Maybe next month," Bea said.

"Well, tell him to write his grandmother."

"He hasn't even written to us," Bea said.

Sybil looked at the teapot clock. "My word, it's after seven o'clock. What kind of business would keep Hartley this long?"

* * *

Baby Sarah's cry pierced the late afternoon air. Kathleen dropped her dishtowel and hurried to the nursery. Sarah kicked, and Kathleen smiled. *Chubby little legs, walking now, and getting into everything.* She draped Sarah over her shoulder and swayed side to side. *And with your daddy on the road all the time, and your mother shut up in her room, you feel sad too, don't you little one?* Sarah grew limp. Kathleen lowered her into the crib and touched her fuzzy head. *And with the dishes, the wash, scrubbing floors and cooking, I don't have time for you either, little one.*

The Wendell's had let the gardener go, then the housekeeper, Carmen, and finally, Maria. She remembered Maria's tears; later, Mrs. Wendell saying, "Maria's mother needs her at home," though they both knew that wasn't the real reason. Kathleen wandered from room to room. *It doesn't take long for silver to tarnish and dust to cling.* She rubbed her hands over a crystal vase wiping away a dull film. *And fine things to lose their polish.* She dropped on the sofa and punched a loose pillow. With her wages cut twice and her workload doubled, it hadn't taken long for her dream of finding Clarice and Clayton to get pushed aside, too.

Why did that stock market have to crash anyway?

Mr. Wendell had explained it. "People bought shares in companies and were given pieces of paper called stocks. The stocks went up in value, so they bought more stocks on credit and sold them, and everyone made money. But then lots of people started selling, prices went down, everyone got scared and sold at the same time, and they all lost their money."

Kathleen sighed. *Something like that.*

She'd told him she didn't know anyone with money in the stock market, and he said it didn't matter, because companies lost money too and laid off their employees, him being among them. He had been Director of Sales. But after the market crashed, he'd scrambled just to find a job as a traveling salesman making less than a third of what he made last year. But he seemed glad to have any kind of a job. He'd looked at her with sad eyes. "We're putting a lot on you I know, with your pay cuts and the extra work, but that's the only way we can keep you on. And we need you."

Kathleen picked up the pillow and squeezed it. *They, need me? When all I know for sure is that Mrs. Wendell stays shut in her room most days, and I'm too busy to give Sarah the attention she deserves.* She glanced around the room. *And this house is a mess.*

She tucked the pillow behind her head and leaned back. But her dad was still working at the railroad, and Henry has a bed and three meals a day at that place. She thought of Maria and Carmen. *At least I still have a job.*

There was a knock at the door. She opened it to find her father clinging to the door frame.

"What's wrong, Dad?"

"I'm all right now," Hartley said. "But I wasn't a while ago."

Kathleen guided him to a chair. "Sit still while I get a wet rag." She returned shortly and lay a cool cloth over his forehead.

Hartley's mouth quivered. "I went to the asylum and saw your brother, and he didn't even know me." He peeled the rag off his forehead and dropped it on the red tile floor. "The doctor said there's nothing more they can do for him. That they've tried the ice baths, isolation and restraints—everything." He took her hand. "There must be something else they can do. God couldn't be that cruel."

Kathleen squeezed his hand. "I don't think God did this to Henry."

Hartley's nostrils flared. "Well, who then, or what?"

"I don't know either, Dad." She noted his rumpled shirt and pants. "But what happened to you? You're white as a ghost."

Hartley held up his hands. "I almost was one." Then, as if reciting words memorized for a play: ". . . and I drove to the end of the road, climbed up a rock, and stared at that desert for a long, long time." He sighed. "Sand ripples like water, Kats. The wind scatters our fate like sand, and we're helpless to do anything about it."

"You're not helpless, Dad. You might feel that way, but you keep going, you and me."

As if not hearing her, "I don't know how long I sat there," he said, "but I wanted the desert to take me; let the vultures strip my flesh and scatter my bones over those rocks."

Acid boiled up Kathleen's throat. *And leave it all to me!* She opened her mouth to say so, but he touched her hand, and she stopped. She looked at his knotted fingers and thought of his long years at the Santa Fe machine shop, struggling to keep his family together. "Sometimes I used to wish Henry would go away, so it would just be you and me."

Hartley smiled. "You were such an easy child."

Kathleen lifted her eyebrows. "Easy? What choice did I have when you were so consumed with Henry?"

"You were my heart. But Henry defied me no matter what I did. Then just when I was ready to give up, he would do better, and I'd try again."

"Ah, Dad, you're torturing yourself."

"Henry could have done anything he wanted; been anything."

Kathleen bit her lip. *Henry's life is over. He'll rot away in that asylum, while I . . .*

"You wouldn't know him, Kats. Even that ornery look in his eyes was gone. He's gone."

Kathleen winced. She was ashamed of Henry and shamed herself for feeling that way. Yet she could not help it. She looked at her dad. "Henry inflicts pain even when he's locked up."

Hartley paced back and forth in front of her. "My nerves are all tangled."

Kathleen eased her head on the pillow and drank in the soft browns and greens, muted orange in this high desert room. *The wind scatters our fate like sand . . .* she looked at Hartley. "Maybe God wants us to be still, so he can untangle us."

Hartley tossed a pillow aside and sat next to her.

"So, why didn't you just let the desert take you?" she said.

He took her hand and squeezed it. "I thought about you, and I couldn't. You're the only bright spot in my life."

Gentle waves of warmth washed over her. "You blame yourself for everything where Henry is concerned."

"Yep. I take credit for it all."

"You don't deserve credit or blame. Henry can't help the way he is, and neither can you."

Hartley dropped her hand, leaned back, and let out a long sigh. "Somehow, I don't know why, but I feel better."

Kathleen patted his leg.

He looked at the clock and jumped up. "Uh oh, I better get home. Bea's going to be furious."

"Worried," Kathleen said. "There's a difference, you know."

Hartley grinned. "I know."

He rubbed his right hand over the top of his head. "Where's my hat?"

"You weren't wearing it when you came in, Dad."

"Hope I didn't leave it on that darn rock." He took her hands, pulled her up, then gave her a quick peck on the cheek. "Thanks, Kats." He kissed her other cheek then walked toward the door.

"Dad . . ."

Hartley turned around.

"Be careful, Dad. And no more desert roads!"

CHAPTER TWENTY-ONE

Still reeling from shock from his meeting with Robert Bradford, Walter drove to the street where he'd once lived as Patrick Roark, thirty-six years ago. His pants were still wrinkled from the water he'd spilled in Bradford's office. His damp belt swelled around his waist. His blue, silk tie lay twisted like a wrung rag.

Robert's face still taunted him. *"The matter of a miscarriage, a baby girl."* He slammed his fist into his open hand. "And she was mine, damn it!" *How the man must have enjoyed himself, casting his line, hooking, then reeling me in. And Felicia set me up, scripted the whole thing herself. How she must hate me.*

He stood in front of the apartment building he'd once called home and noted the old stairs were recently repaired but unpainted, the front door had rotted, the old cracks in the sidewalk were now gaping holes. In his old flat, a gray rag plugged a hole in the window. He thought of his mother, her sunken silhouette in the rocking chair. *Another life. Another person. Yet here I am back.*

Let me be sick, Lord; let those boys beat me again and leave me on this stinking sidewalk to die. He recalled his long-ago vow: *I won't die on a cold hard sidewalk where people walk on my blood as if I were never here.* Pain ripped through his chest like broken glass. "Dear God, I'm going to lose everything. Be a nobody again."

A small boy brushed past him, ran up the steps, and opened the front door to the hallway. The stench of cooked cabbage, rancid grease, stale sweat choked him. Acid boiled in his throat. He ran to the curb and threw up on the street. *Purging my past?* he wondered.

People stared. Those walking by turned around. An old woman offered help, but he motioned her away. He wondered if she knew him. He winced. It's been over thirty years. *No one knows you, fool.*

Gloom pressed like a hundred-pound weight on his shoulders. *A man builds a life, and then that life is taken away from him.* A peddler pushed his cart up the street. *Will I be like him? Will I be Patrick Roark again?* He clenched his fists. "If it comes to that, I'll go west again." He sniffed a laugh. *Sure, Pruitt, hop freights, fight off bums, and make your way on horseback? Hell, I'm not the man Patrick Roark was. But who am I?*

He walked back to his car hoping to find it in one piece. In the old days, he would have left his driver, Tom, at the wheel with instructions. And he wondered where Tom was now, and what he was doing. *Broke like me, I suppose.* He turned the corner, and a man stood by his Packard Eight Sedan with his foot braced on the running board. Walter's stomach lurched. *Are they going to take my car?*

The man wore a double-breasted suit with pinstripes and polished black shoes. Walter sighed in relief. *He's wearing one of my line of suits at least.* He walked closer, and the man extended his hand. "Hello, Patrick. I'm Ferris McKenzie."

Walter stared. The man had the same thin face but without freckles now, and his thin red hair lay plastered above his narrow forehead. He reached out and shook the hand of the man who had rescued him from so many beatings during his childhood. "Ferris McKenzie," he said. "Well, damn!"

* * *

Walter looked around at the red velvet chairs, the marble bar, and Tiffany lamps. "Not the usual speakeasy," he said.

McKenzie leaned back. "There's plenty more like this down the alley. You have to know the password to get your nose through the door."

"I've had access," Walter said. "Just didn't take the time. I was too busy working." He glanced around the room again. "All these women, you didn't used to see that."

"Everybody's still buying and drinking," McKenzie said. "There's over a hundred places like this on the north side alone raking in over five million a year." He crossed himself. "Best thing that ever happened, this prohibition."

Walter sank into his chair and savored the warm bourbon gliding down his throat. "Never drank much," he said, "but I could develop a taste for this."

McKenzie raised his glass. "A drop o' the creature, as my old man used to say."

Walter raised his. "A drop o' the creature," he said and wondered how many years since he had thought of himself as Irish.

"I saw your picture in the *Tribune* for the grand opening of your Madison Street store. Your name was different and your stature, but your face was the same."

Walter snickered. "I thought about changing it, too."

"You had two successful department stores, a third one under construction, a fourth on the books before the bottom dropped out." He opened his suitcoat. "I bought this at your Madison store. You carried good lines."

Walter wondered how his old rescuer knew *good lines*. "I still do," he said. "But I'm down to just my State Street store now."

McKenzie pulled a pack of Chesterfields out of his pocket and held it out.

"No, thanks. I'm a pipe man." He recalled Robert's words, *"I'm a pipe man, too* . . . he winced. *Damn that Bradford. Damn his soul to hell and back.*

McKenzie lit his cigarette from a silver monogrammed lighter.

Walter noted his gold watch, diamond tie tack, and gold cufflinks. Suddenly conscious of his own disheveled appearance, he sunk into his chair. "You seem to know a lot about me," he said.

McKenzie snapped his lighter shut and dropped it into his pocket. "It's my business to know about people. But with you, it was personal."

"Personal?"

"I come home every Wednesday to see my mother. She told me yer old man got gunned down on the street. 'A real shoot out,' she said," and he made the sign of the cross. "God rest his soul. Then I heard about your mother." He crossed himself again. "God rest her soul, too. I used to wonder what happened to you. Then after I saw your photograph in the *Tribune* of your store opening, I started checking."

"So you could rescue me again?"

"You had guts."

Walter snickered. "All I remember was panic." *Funny, how Ferris McKenzie is the only face I remember; blocked out the others, I guess.* And he could hardly believe he was sharing a drink with his former rescuer and feeling kinship with the man.

"You ran like hell," McKenzie said, "but when caught, you took it with the best of 'em."

"Is that why you offered me your hand?"

"And you refused it. I respected that."

Walter nodded. "I went out west after my folks died. Made some money, then came back and invested it in my State Street store." He searched McKenzie's face. "You seem to know what happened after that." He took another sip of bourbon. "But most everything's gone now, thanks to this depression or whatever they call it."

"And some of this city's shrewdest businessmen are already out of business."

"Even the shrewd can run out of capital." Walter tilted his glass, and bourbon swirled in bronze circles. "You know about me," he said, "while I know nothing about you."

McKenzie stubbed out his cigarette and leaned toward Walter. "If you're interested in knowing about me, I'll tell you."

Walter squinted. "And if I'm *not* interested?"

"Then we'll have another round of bourbon, talk about old times and part friends. If we meet again in public, you don't know me."

"And if I *am* interested?"

"Then your past and mine will stay where they belong. How you got your money and lost it would be not be my business." McKenzie's keen eyes met Walter's in an ironclad stare. "But what you do from now on will be my business."

Walter glanced across the speakeasy at a woman wearing a green felt hat, her biased-cut skirt swirled gracefully to the floor. *Those skirts and hats were my lifeblood until that damn stock market crashed, and I had to go begging to that son of a . . .*

"Shall I go on?" McKenzie said.

I can keep trying, but I'll go down and leave Clarice penniless. And what would become of Clayton? Mucus stuck in the back of his throat. *Run, Patrick, run!* He cleared his throat, took another slow sip of bourbon, and set his glass down. "Go on," he said.

McKenzie smiled. "Even as a dumb kid you were smart. You ran, but when cornered you swung like the best of 'em. Good credentials for my line of work."

Walter shook his head at the irony. "My running away was an asset?"

"Use your brains is my motto. If that doesn't work, then knock the hell out of 'em."

Walter chuckled. "Well then, I qualify."

"I like to know what makes people tick. Have a knack for it, they tell me. Anybody even tries to put something over on me, I know it before they begin." His eyes locked on Walter's. "Do you understand what I'm saying?"

Walter shifted in his chair and tried to smooth his wrinkled tie. He took a quick breath, leaned toward McKenzie and nodded. "I understand."

McKenzie nodded back. "Well then, Pruitt, like I told you, I've followed your progress. You have influence. You know the right people. You socialize in the right places. And you have a warehouse."

CHAPTER TWENTY-TWO

Clarice tapped her fingers on her desk. "These figures don't make sense!" She had searched each column, gone over sales reports, checked every bank statement, yet nothing balanced. She pressed her lips tightly together. *And I'm to going to find out why.*

Her intercom buzzed. "Mr. Beale is here, Miss Pruitt."

"Beale?"

"The new accountant Mr. Pruitt hired. You asked to see him."

"Oh, right, send him in, please."

Beale strode into her office and looked around as if evaluating a piece of real estate. His shoes were custom-made, and his three-piece, Italian tweed suit was top of the line. He took off his hat and a black curl dangled over his forehead.

Clarice watched him carefully. *He doesn't look like our other accountants, and he acts as if he owns the place.* She stood and extended her hand. "I don't believe we've met, Mr. Beale."

He shook her hand and held it a little too long. "No, ma'am, but I wish we had. Met a lot earlier, I mean." His eyes darted toward the bookshelf, the Roman numeral clock on the wall, and then to Clarice.

He's like a fox sniffing out his territory. Who does he think he is? Clarice motioned him to the chair across from her. "Let's get right to business," she said and opened her ledger book. "Have we had an increase in collections I'm not aware of, Mr. Beale?"

"No, ma'am."

"Did you make any changes in our billing procedures?"

"No, ma'am."

"Then will you please explain these extra deposits?"

"I can't," Beale said.

"You can't? Or you won't?"

"I reconcile my side of the books."

Clarice lifted her eyebrows. "What do you mean, *your side of the books?*"

"Just following your father's orders, ma'am."

Clarice leaned toward him. "Who is charge of this store?"

"You are, Miss Pruitt."

"And I can fire you, Mr. Beale, if you won't give me the information I want."

Beale leaned back in his chair and crossed one leg over the other. "Like I said, I answer to your father."

Clarice studied his piercing blue eyes, his finely cut nose, and strong cheekbones . . . the way he tilted his head.

As if sensing her thoughts, Beale smiled. "Pardon me for saying so, ma'am, but I find your intelligence most attractive." He leaned toward her. "I find *you* most attractive."

Clarice had seen this look from other men, but it had never made her heart race. Her cheeks grew hot. The stirring in her groin surprised her.

"I'd like to take you to dinner tonight. The Congress Hotel perhaps, then maybe a drink at a speakeasy, and we can discuss this further."

Clarice glanced at the ceiling. *Those blue eyes . . .that curl dangling over his forehead.* She thought of her long night ahead in the gloomy house, and she was tempted. She looked at Beale. *Clever, coming on to me, stalling. Why?*

"Thank you for your interest," she said. "But if you can't answer my questions, we don't have anything to discuss." She stood. "I'll speak to my father about this."

Eyes dancing, Beale brushed the curl off his forehead and stood. "Maybe another time then, ma'am."

After Beale left, Clarice dialed the warehouse. One of the new hands answered. "Twill be a pleasure to find ye father, Miss Pruitt. Just hold on." She pursed her lips. *Those Irishmen . . . why did Father hire them?*

After a few moments, "Yer father's workin' a delivery, Miss Pruitt. Might I be telling him what ye want?"

"I'll be telling him myself," Clarice said and slammed the receiver down.

Hours later, Clarice's intercom buzzed. "Mr. Pruitt is on the line, ma'am."

Clarice grabbed the telephone. "Father, thank goodness. I've been trying to reach you all day. We've got to talk."

"About what?" Walter said.

"Well, the store, of course. You remember the store, it's on State Street."

"I don't have time for sarcasm, Clarice."

"Nor do I, Father, but you're always at the warehouse."

"Working to keep the store afloat."

"So am I. Only I've discovered deposits that I can't account for, and nobody will explain where they came from. Not even, Beale, that new accountant you hired. I'm running the store, but—"

"Isn't that what you've always wanted?"

"But I've always been able to walk into your office and talk when I needed to." She shuffled a piece of paper from one side of her desk to the other. "Listen, I have a meeting later this evening. Why don't you come home tonight, and we can talk in the morning? Esther said she'll have breakfast ready by six."

"If you insist."

"I insist," Clarice said, and she reared her shoulders. *He's the one who taught me. And I won't run an operation that I can't control.*

* * *

It was almost midnight when Clarice let herself in through the side door and found Esther at the kitchen table.

Esther chided her. "You shouldn't be out this time of night. There might be a robber out there."

"A robber?"

"Somebody's stealing our food again, and some bed clothes went missing last week."

"Are you sure you're not imagining all this?"

Esther waved her index finger. "Six blankets are missing and four pillows. I'm not sure how many sheets they were packed so tight on the shelf, but at least five or six are gone. I checked the shed to see if there's a bum sleeping out there, but nothing was out of place."

Clarice sighed. "All right. I'll talk to Father in the morning, but now I have work to do."

Esther pointed at her briefcase. "That's all you do. You should be out with boys, going to parties, dancing the Charleston like other young girls."

Clarice chuckled. "I detest parties. And can you see me dancing the Charleston with my knobby knees?"

"But you don't even have any women friends except for Mrs. Bradford."

Clarice lifted her briefcase to the table. "Even if I wanted friends, I don't know anyone outside the store."

Esther harrumphed. "Well, it's not natural." She picked up her notebook. "I'm going to check the pantry to see if anything else is missing."

Clarice spread her reports over the dining room table. *Out with boys, dancing, women friends?* She counted their age difference and wondered why Felicia even bothered with her.

A half-hour passed. An hour? Her pencil squiggled as she lined up figures in neat rows. *Numbers don't lie; they're either right or wrong.*

Esther cracked the door. "Somebody's outside," she whispered. "I shut out the light like I was going to bed."

Clarice groaned. Then seeing the alarm on Esther's face, she cut off the dining room light, followed her into the darkened kitchen, and peered out the window. "I don't see anything."

Esther shushed her. "Listen."

Footsteps pounded on the walkway.

Esther grabbed her arm.

Clarice shrugged her off. "Go get Father," she said. "Tell him to call the cops." She looked wildly around the kitchen, grabbed a carving knife off the counter, and slipped behind the door.

The lock turned. *A thief with a key?* Clarice wondered. Her heart pounded as she raised the knife over her shoulder.

The door creaked open, and a boot crossed the threshold.

"No!" Esther screamed

And Clay shot through the doorway.

Esther crossed herself. "Mister Clay! We could of killed you!"

Clarice froze with the knife over her shoulder.

Clay held his open palms in the air. "Easy, Sis," and he took a careful step toward her. He took another step, wrapped his hands around her wrist, and the knife dropped to the floor with a clang. He braced her arm and guided her onto a kitchen chair.

Clarice's hands shook. "Dear God, Clay. What were you doing?"

Clay grasped her hand, and the trembling young woman, the slender man, and the robe-clad housekeeper huddled together as if they were lone survivors of a deadly storm.

"What's going on here?" Walter's deep voice jarred the silence. He turned on the light switch.

Esther rubbed her eyes. "We thought we caught a robber, but it was only Mr. Clay."

Walter looked at the knife by Clarice's feet. "What were you going to do with that?"

"Stop him," Clarice said.

"And get yourself killed in the process." He turned to Clay. "What were you doing out this time of night?"

"Taking food and blankets to the people on Randolph Street."

Esther's eyes widened. "The bed clothes; my groceries."

Walter shook his head as if to clear it. "You took our belongings to those bums?"

"They're not bums, Father. They're honest people who lost their jobs and now they're hungry."

"Stealing? From your own home?"

"I call it sharing," Clay said. "I've been doing it for a while now."

Walter shook his head again. "What the hell?"

Clay stepped toward him. "Is it right for us to live in this house with food and clothes to spare while others are hungry and cold?"

Walter's chest puffed. "Why not? I've worked hard for everything we have. Everything *you* have."

"They worked hard too, Father, but they lost their jobs, then their homes and possessions, and now their pride."

"Pride? They can't have any pride to live in those hovels. And neither can you if you associate with that ilk!"

"Have you ever been hungry, Father? Have you ever had to wrap yourself in newspapers to stay warm?"

Walter's eyes blazed. "You bet I have! And I didn't expect another man to feed me." He waved his finger at Clay. "Look at you. Twenty-three years old and never worked a day in your life. Couldn't make your own way if you tried."

Clarice's eyes darted back and forth between her father and brother. *After all their years of silence.*

Clay's voice softened. "Go out there with me, Father. I think you might see—"

"They're trouble makers. Reds. I hear the Communist Party holds regular meetings out there."

Communist? Clarice recalled her earlier conversation with Clay about the *Reds.*

Walter flipped his hands in the air. "My son, the great learned one, and he's nothing more than a common thief. I should call the cops right now."

"Go ahead," Clay said. "Who do you think they'll arrest?"

Walter waved his hand in dismissal. "You don't know what you're talking about."

"The cops know your name, Father, along with McKenzie and the rest: payoffs, extortion, running liquor out of the warehouse." Clay turned to Clarice. "We've been living on mob money, Sis."

Clarice grabbed her stomach. *No, it can't be true.* Then she thought of Beale in his custom-made suit, those Irish thugs at the warehouse, the extra deposits. She searched her father's face and saw that it was true. "So, that's why the books don't add up!"

Walter pleaded, "We had exhausted our money. I was down to your college money, and I couldn't touch that."

"My college money?" Clarice's voice squeaked. "You sold us out to save my college money?"

Walter's mouth quivered. "I tried everything. Everyone. I even went to that son of a bitch—"

"The Mob?" Clarice shouted. "North side or south, Father? Capone or Moran? How many men have you killed?"

"Don't be ridiculous. It's only liquor."

"And liquor is illegal!" Clarice hands flew to her hips. "I can't believe you threw your integrity out the door—"

"He never had integrity," Clay said.

Walter backed Clay to the wall. "When I kicked your mother out, I should have sent you with her!"

Esther gasped.

Clarice's hand flew to her mouth.

Clay and Walter stared at each other as silence enclosed them like an ancient tomb.

Esther's shrill voice pierced the silence. "It's true!" She crossed herself again. "God forgive me, but it's true."

Walter raised a threatening hand toward her. "Be quiet, fool. You weren't even there."

"I was there," Esther said. "Yes, you sent me away, but you acted so strange, I knew something was wrong, so I came back early." She looked at Clarice. "Your mother was rocking you in the parlor, so I slipped upstairs. No one knew I was up there."

Walter started toward Esther. "I said, be quiet!"

But the words poured out of her. "I heard you yelling, accusing her. Then little Clarice cried, and Miss Laura laid her in the bassinet." Esther looked at Clay with tear-filled eyes. "She tried to get up the stairs to you, but he pulled her down. I heard her scream when he pushed her out the door."

Walter's voice shook. "She lied to me."

Clarice looked frantically back and forth between Esther and Walter. "Who lied?"

"Your mother," Walter said. "She told me her father was dead, but I found him."

Esther waved her finger in his face, "You planned it. You already had her bag packed when you pushed her out the door."

Walter took another threatening step. "I said be quiet."

Esther stepped aside and turned to Clay. "Your mother came back for you children, but he took you away. She didn't have money for a lawyer, and he blocked her at every turn. She tried to get in to see you, but he called the cops." She reached her hand out toward Clarice. "She never would have left her babies."

Clarice felt as if the earth had dropped out of the sun's orbit leaving her in total darkness. Her knees buckled. Clay caught her and helped her onto a chair.

Walter pleaded again. "You were better off without her."

Clarice gripped the table. "Who was better off?"

"You were!" He pointed to Clay. "She had already ruined him."

Clarice shot up. "You're the one who treated Clay like a leper!"

Walter drew back his fist, but Clay stepped between them and slammed Walter to the wall.

Esther screamed. A terrified mouse scampered across the gray tile floor.

Walter's face contorted. "Look at you, young pup. I'll cut you off and see how long you last."

Clay slugged him.

Blood spurted from Walter's nose as he slid down the kitchen wall to the floor.

Clay towered over him. "You already cut me off, Father, a long time ago." He turned to Clarice. "Leave him to his dirty business, Sis. We don't need him anymore!"

* * *

More pain came when Clay stood in Clarice's bedroom doorway with his suitcase in hand.

"Don't leave me, Clay."

"I should have left a long time ago, Sis."

"But not now. Not like this."

Clay lowered his suitcase to the floor and walked to the window.

Clarice stood beside him.

He parted the curtain and pointed to the dark rectangle of a picnic table below. "My last memory of Mother was eating supper at that table, just you and me and her. There was snow on the ground, and she wrapped you in your blanket and set you in the highchair. You were just learning to eat with a spoon . . . she tucked me in bed and kissed me that night, and that was the last time I ever saw her."

"I used to watch you stare at that table. Why didn't you tell me?"

"You didn't want to hear. Remember?"

Clarice felt her innocence slip away. "I based my whole life on his lies." Her lips trembled. "And Esther, she knew the whole time, yet she never said a word."

"I looked in on her," Clay said. "Her bag was packed, and she was praying."

"Esther lived with us all of my life, yet when her daughter died I barely acknowledged it. No wonder she kept quiet." Her hands swept the room. "I've always hated this house. Like I knew something bad happened here."

"While I clung to it," Clay said. "And my memories."

"I should have listened to you instead of Father. But I was so angry at our mother for leaving, and now . . ."

Clay put a comforting hand on her shoulder. "Your anger kept you going, Sis. Look how capable you are. And you kept me going, too."

"Where is Father?"

Clay glanced down at his suitcase. "He's gone."

Clarice looked at Clay with tear-filled eyes. "Father's gone, and now you're leaving, too."

"I have to find my own way now. Father was right about that."

"But where will you go? How will I find you?"

He held her out at arm's length sternly as a teacher might a disobedient child. "I don't know, Sis, but I feel free for the first time."

Clarice's eye glistened. "Why did he send our mother away? And what about that business with her father. What did he mean?"

Clay shrugged. "It doesn't matter anymore."

Anger shot through Clarice like hot lava. "It matters to me," she said. "And I'm going to find out. You can bet on it!"

CHAPTER TWENTY-THREE

In Albuquerque, Clarice stared out the window at the skeletal shrubs, dried cacti, and overgrown juniper.

"Is this the right place?" the taxi driver asked.

"This is the correct address," Clarice said, "but it doesn't look like the right house." She squinted. *What happened to this place since I was here last?* Exhausted from the train ride from Chicago, Clarice had wanted to see Kathleen alone. But now she wished Felicia were by her side instead of in that Alvarado Hotel room.

The driver grumbled. "What are you going to do, ma'am?"

Clarice jerked to attention. "Find my mother!" she said. "You wait here." She stepped out, unlatched the front gate, and walked to the front door. She was about to knock when a young woman came from the side of the house, shading her eyes with her hand.

"May I help you?" she said.

"I'm Clarice Pruitt."

"You . . . you're my sister." Kathleen's voice quavered.

"I saw your classified ad in the *Chicago Tribune*." Clarice clenched her fists. *How dare she look like Clay.*

"But that was almost two years ago. I thought—"

There was a sharp cry from the rear of the house. "I need to check on the baby," Kathleen said, and then motioned for Clarice to follow. "We can talk in back."

Clarice walked the same brick pathway she'd walked before and watched Kathleen pick up a pink teddy bear, a string of jingle bells, a red and yellow striped ball and put them in a playpen. Then she lifted a fuzzy haired toddler to her shoulder and murmured in her ear.

Clarice felt a hollow ache in her chest, such longing, yet she could not turn away.

Kathleen kissed the baby on the forehead, set her back in the playpen, then walked back to Clarice.

"I found your names in my mother's cookbook when I was nine."

"I learned about you when I was twelve, when I snooped through my father's trunk."

Kathleen's face brightened. "I've been saving my money to find you. I have enough for my train fare to Chicago, but I need more to stay at the Y."

Clarice gestured toward the house. "It looks like you should have plenty."

"Well, it's been harder with this depression and cuts in my salary."

The screen door squeaked, and Mrs. Wendell came out on the back step. "Is everything all right, Kathleen?"

"Sarah's all right," Kathleen said. "She keeps throwing her toys out of the playpen, and I keep putting them back."

Mrs. Wendell stood quietly.

"This is Clarice," Kathleen said. "She's . . ."

Clarice extended her hand. "I'm Clarice Pruitt."

Mrs. Wendell shook it cautiously. "I'm Lorena Wendell," she said and looked Clarice up and down. She looked at Kathleen. "Would you like some time alone to visit?"

Kathleen glanced at Clarice. "I think so; yes."

"Then I'll take Sarah. I just need you to have supper ready by five."

"The beans are already cooked," Kathleen said. "I only have to make the cornbread."

Mrs. Wendell reached into the playpen. "Come to mama," she said. As they passed Kathleen, chubby arms reached out to her, "Kaka."

Kathleen picked up the teddy bear and handed it to Sarah. The baby clutched it to her chest as they disappeared into the house.

Clarice blinked. "That's not your baby?"

"Well no, I—"

"And this isn't your house?"

"I work here," Kathleen said.

"But your neighbor told me you live here."

"I'm the nanny," Kathleen said. "I care for the child and a lot more."

Clarice stifled a laugh. "You're just the nanny?"

"Sure. What did you think?"

Clarice brushed a curl off her forehead. "Obviously, I didn't think at all."

Kathleen reached for her hand. "I've wanted so much to find you. You can't know . . ."

"I came to find my mother," Clarice snapped.

Kathleen wrinkled her brow. "Your mother?"

"That's the only reason I'm here."

Kathleen gazed toward the mountains. "I don't remember much," she said. "I was only four when she went, and my dad, well, he won't talk about her."

Warmth, a sense of order rippled through Clarice's chest. "So, she left you, too." Her voice oozed with sarcasm.

"She, well, she didn't have a choice."

Clarice waved her hand impatiently. "Where is my mother?"

"She's at Niles Cemetery, just north of Chicago. She made my father promise to bury her there."

Icy fingers grabbed Clarice's throat. "Bury her?"

Kathleen's face paled. "You don't know?"

"Know what?"

"Our mother died of tuberculosis when I was four."

Pain ripped through Clarice's chest. "You're lying. I saw her in Chicago at your grandmother's store. You were there too, and Henry."

Kathleen looked at her for a long moment. "I don't know who you saw, but my mother died when I was four."

"But Henry called her mother, he said she was an angel."

Kathleen's forehead wrinkled. "That must have been my stepmother, Miriam. She's dead, too."

Shaking inside, "I don't understand," Clarice said.

Kathleen reached for her hand again. "Please, let's sit down."

Clarice shook her head in annoyance. "I want to know what happened to my mother!"

Kathleen rubbed her temples. After a moment, she said, "One of Mother's lungs collapsed when we lived in Chicago. My dad brought her here for the cure, but she died nine months later." She sighed. "I thought you knew."

"How? How could I know?" Clarice waved her finger in the air. "I came here last year. Your neighbor, Mrs. Lopez, said my mother was in Chicago."

"She was talking about Beatrice, my newest stepmother. She has people in Chicago, too."

Clarice felt like she'd been hit by a fist. Shaking inside, she braced her legs to steady herself. "Then I want to see Henry."

"That's, well, it's not possible."

"Why? Is Henry dead too?"

Kathleen hung her head. "He's just not here."

Everything seemed to blur in front of Clarice. *Is anything like it seems?* "You just don't want me to see him. You're afraid he'll tell me the truth."

"The truth?" Kathleen squeezed her eyes shut, then opened them. "The truth is that Henry is in the New Mexico State Insane Asylum. He's in a bad way, I'm afraid. My dad went to see him last week, and Henry didn't even know him."

Clarice stared at the lone blooming cactus, bright yellow flowers among wicked thorns. Her mouth felt like sandpaper. "What other secrets are you hiding in this gosh awful place?"

"We need to talk," Kathleen said.

Clarice shook her head again. "If my mother is dead, then we have nothing to talk about."

Kathleen's voice shook. "I've been searching for you all my life. Finding you and Clayton is the only thing that's kept me going."

Rage, painful as a deep cut shot through Clarice's chest. "Clay is *my* brother. You stay away from him!" She turned and ran toward the gate.

Kathleen followed her. "Don't go; please, not again."

Clarice tore through the gate, jumped into the taxi, and ordered the driver to step on it. She looked over her shoulder and she saw Kathleen, the last link to her mother, standing in the road with her arms open. *My mother is dead. Henry's in a lunatic asylum.* She brushed her wet cheeks. *What am I going to do now?*

CHAPTER TWENTY-FOUR

Kathleen blinked against the dull ache that throbbed behind her eyes. Without thinking, she went about her work like a puppet on a string washing dishes, sweeping the kitchen floor, moving dust around the living room.

Mrs. Wendell watched her like a silent mourner. "Shall I call your father?" she said.

"No, don't call Dad."

"Your sister then?"

"I have no sister."

"The one at the telephone company."

"No, don't call, Jill."

Near tears, Mrs. Wendell handed Kathleen a bottle. "You feed Sarah while l finish dusting."

Holding Sarah close, Kathleen watched the milk from the bottle disappear, and then laid her in her crib.

She trudged to her room, dropped on her bed, and stared at the scrolled ceiling. She felt empty, splintered like the feathers of a faraway cloud. She looked at the lace doily Mrs. Wendell had crocheted for her dresser, the sweater tossed over her chair. *I don't belong here. I don't belong anywhere.*

There was a soft knock on her door, and she opened it to Mrs. Wendell.

"There's someone here to see you."

Kathleen shook her head. "I don't want to see anyone."

Mrs. Wendell raised her eyebrows. "It's a lady, kind of fancy, her dress and all, and she's wearing white gloves."

"I'll be there in a moment," Kathleen murmured. She splashed water on her face, ran a comb through her hair, then walked cautiously into the living room.

The woman extended her gloved hand. "I'm Felicia Bradford," she said. "I was your mother's best friend." She hesitated. "I'm also Clarice's friend."

"What do you want?" Kathleen said, ignoring her hand.

"To get to know you some too, I hope."

Felicia pulled off her gloves, folded them into her shiny, black purse, and glanced around. "This room is lovely, rich with warm colors."

She looks like an eastern lady who just arrived on the frontier and not found it as rough as she had imagined. "Thank you," Kathleen said.

"May I sit down?"

Kathleen motioned toward a chair, then sat across from her.

"I saw your classified ad in the *Chicago Tribune* to find Clarice and Clay. Very courageous of you."

Kathleen sighed. "Desperate was more like it."

"Clarice grew up thinking her, and your, mother abandoned her because of you. Your ad really jolted her."

"I've dreamed of finding Clarice and Clayton for so long."

"Clarice thought your ad might be a crude attempt by your mother to find her. She didn't know Laura had died, you see. It was a great shock to her."

"And to me," Kathleen said. "Clarice showing up without warning then running away." She winced. "Twice." She searched Felicia's face. "Why?"

"She was in shock, I think."

"Why did she come if she didn't want anything to do with me?"

"Good question," Felicia said. "You'll have to ask her."

"She hates me. I saw it in her eyes."

"Clarice hates everyone right now. She's in a very bad way, I'm afraid."

Kathleen picked up a pillow and fluffed it. "It was all about her. *Her* mother and Henry. She wouldn't even acknowledge me."

"Perhaps," Felicia said. "But there's a lot more to her than that."

Kathleen clasped her hands together. "I felt so sorry for her. To think her mother was alive, and then to find out she died years ago. I tried to talk to her, but she didn't want to; didn't want me."

"It will take some time, I think."

Kathleen shrugged. "Well, I can't help her. Don't want to, is more like it."

"Clarice has to help herself."

Kathleen studied her. "You were my mother's best friend?"

"The closest thing to it, I think. Your mother was very private."

"She's been a mystery my whole life. There were times when I hated her for leaving me. As if it were her fault she died."

"Do you have any memories of her?"

"Only a vague one. And then sometimes I think I imagined it." She gazed at the window. "I remember her dark room. She was lying on her bed watching me and Henry cutting pictures out of magazines." She looked at Felicia. "I felt like love was flowing from her to me. It's hard to describe. Her cheeks were bright red, and I thought she was happy. Now I know that red cheeks were a sign of her tuberculosis."

"I wish I had known," Felicia said.

Kathleen shook her head. "Dad never told me about Clarice and Clay, and I guess nobody told Clarice, either." A tear formed in the corner of her eye. She brushed it with her index finger. "I'm sorry," she said. "It's not your fault."

"I'm sorry, too," Felicia said.

Kathleen grabbed another pillow. "What was my mother like?"

"Solemn," Felicia said. "Like you, I imagine. Her voice was mellow, soft like velvet. She didn't talk much, but when she did, you wanted to listen." She smiled. "You sound a little like her, I think. And she liked to read the Bronte sisters, *Wuthering Heights* and

Jane Eyre, I remember, and Shakespeare's, *Othello*. She seemed sad that Othello did not trust Desdemona. Like someone had hurt her once."

Kathleen tucked her hair behind her ears. "I read *Jane Eyre* my first year in high school. I couldn't put it down, yet I never thought I might experience it."

Felicia smiled. "You have your mother's mouth and square chin, I see."

Kathleen touched her chin.

"She played the piano, beautifully. She was beautiful; like you only different."

Warmth flowed through Kathleen, like when Sarah fell asleep on her chest.

"Her favorite color was turquoise blue. She wore a blue dress that was stunning with her bright blue eyes, and she always wore an ivory brooch. She said it belonged to her mother."

Kathleen closed her eyes. *Pieces of my mother . . . will I ever put them together?* It helped to know she liked turquoise blue. She looked at Felicia. "I only have one picture of her, taken at the train station before we boarded for Albuquerque. The doctor told Dad her only chance to live was to move her to a dry, arid climate. They had never even been out of Chicago."

"A sad trip, I imagine."

"Two small children and a dying wife," Kathleen said. "I think about it a lot." And with the telling now, she felt the drama of her sickly mother she never knew and her dad facing an unknown future, or no future at all. The courage it took to leave their home for this faraway high desert town. She crossed her hands over her chest, and warmth seeped into the holes of her wounded heart. Taut muscles at the back of her neck eased. She shook her head. "I never told my dad about finding Clarice and Clayton's names in her cookbook. Every time I asked him about Mother, he teared up, so I finally quit asking." She reared her shoulders. "So, I decided to find them myself."

"And Clarice ran away."

"Why does she hate me?"

"She thought you had *her* mother. That was part of the misunderstanding, you see."

"Some misunderstanding."

"Well, Walter, that's Clarice's father, told her that Laura abandoned them when Clarice was a baby. She was rather bitter about it. It's all very complicated."

"Well, it's not simple here, either."

"Clarice told me about your brother, I'm sorry. It was a lot for Clarice to find out all at once. It's been too much for her. And for you, too, I suspect."

Kathleen looked deep into her eyes. "How could she have left those two children?"

"Ah . . ." Felicia said. "Now we're at the heart of the matter."

"If you were my mother's best friend, you should know."

"Clarice just learned that Walter, that's her and Clayton's father, he kicked Laura out in the middle of the night. Clarice was just a baby and Clayton not much older. It was a great shock to her and to Clayton, too."

"Why did he kick her out?"

"That's what Clarice wants to know. Her father said Laura lied to him about her father. He would be your and Clarice's grandfather."

Kathleen shrugged. "I don't even know his name, nor anything about him."

"Clarice and Clayton don't know anything, either. Walter just blurted it all out in the middle of a family argument. Clay slugged him, then they both took off. You'll have to ask Clarice for details."

Kathleen sniffed. "She only wanted Henry and my mother; not me."

"And now she doesn't have any of you."

"She made her choice."

Felicia's sharp eyes seemed to appraise her. "And now you must make yours."

The thin desert air seemed to thicken. "Clarice leaving was like losing my mother all over again."

Felicia tilted her head. "I was only fourteen when my mother died. I felt sorry for myself, too."

Kathleen's eyes flashed. "You've known me for ten minutes, and you accuse me of feeling sorry for myself!"

"I don't see any difference between you and Clarice. You're a little softer maybe, but you're both mourning a mother you never knew."

Kathleen stiffened. "What do you want from me?"

"To finish what you started when you placed your classified ad."

"Things were different then. I was different."

"Nothing has changed," Felicia said. "And despite Clarice's behavior, I think she wants to see you." She pulled a white card from her purse and handed it to Kathleen. "Clarice and I will be at the Alvarado Hotel until Tuesday. Come, so we can talk, have a bite of dinner at least."

"What good will it do to talk?"

Felicia looked at her steadily. "The pain I see here is from *not* talking."

"And if we talk, then what?"

"You can go back to Chicago in my private railroad car. We have room enough for three."

A private railroad car? Kathleen had seen one once at the Santa Fe yard and stolen a peek inside. Velvet and leather, thick carpet, and brocade curtains. It might as well have been from Mars. "I've saved enough money for my own train ticket," she said, "and almost enough for a room at the YWCA."

"You can stay with me," Felicia said. Her voice gathered momentum. "And the three of us, if we have to dig up half of Chicago, we'll find out the truth."

Kathleen stiffened. "I can't just leave. I have a job, obligations."

Felicia picked up her purse, stood, and looked at her for a long moment. "The only obligation you have, Kathleen, is to yourself."

CHAPTER TWENTY-FIVE

Kathleen stood over her cowering father and showed him no mercy. "Why didn't you tell me I have a sister and brother?"

Hartley grasped the edge of the kitchen table.

Kathleen sat down across from him. "Why wouldn't you tell me about my mother? Why didn't you—" Paralyzed with fury, her mouth opened again, but the words locked in her throat.

"How did you find out?"

"I found their names in Mother's cookbook when I was nine. Why did you keep them a secret?"

He looked down at his gnarled hands. "You don't understand how it was then."

"I know how it was for me. And for Henry too, I'm sure. Only we didn't talk about it either. Did you and mother have an affair or something, and that's why she left her children in Chicago?"

Hartley looked up. "It wasn't like that."

"Then what was it like?" She taunted him and felt immense pleasure in doing so.

Hartley's face reddened. "That was a long time ago. You have no right to ask these things."

Kathleen reared her shoulders. "Well, I have the right now. The girl showed up at the Wendell's door last week and demanded to see 'her' mother!"

Hartley's mouth fell open.

"Her name is Clarice, Dad, and the boy is Clayton. Do you know that?"

"Yes, of course I know."

"And if you think I'm angry, you should have seen Clarice. She didn't even know Mother was dead. How could you do that to her?"

Hartley jumped up like a startled cat. "I told that man, Pruitt!" He paced across the room and back. "Your mother begged me to tell the children myself. To tell them that she loved them, that she did not want to leave them, and she was sorry. I went to that house, but Pruitt refused to let me in. He said he would tell the children himself."

"Well, he didn't," Kathleen said. "You should have seen Clarice's face when I told her Mother was dead."

Hartley's face drained of color. "It was my fault. She didn't want to leave Chicago. But in my desperation to save her life, I forced her to come." Tears filled his eyes. "I never saw her desperation . . . or didn't want to see it." He wiped his brow. "And she died, anyway."

Kathleen's voice softened. "Ah, Dad, you keep punishing yourself for the wrong things."

He pressed his hands to the sides of his face. "After your mother died, I just wanted to keep my family together. Take care of you and your brother and keep you safe." He pulled his knotted fists to his chest. "And now Henry is in that place. And you won't even live at home anymore."

Kathleen's voice quavered. "Couldn't you see how miserable I was?"

Hartley sighed. "It was easier not to." He rubbed his temples. "I'm a coward, you see. Everything I touch turns to ashes."

Heat flushed through Kathleen. "Ashes, Dad. You're saying I'm ashes!"

Hartley shriveled like a withered weed. "I promised your mother I'd take care of you children. I tried."

"It was all about you, Dad. You and your memories of Mother, and Henry. There was nothing left over for me, or those poor children in Chicago who didn't even know their mother had died."

"She felt like a failure for not raising them. She adored Clayton, and Clarice was only a baby. She wanted to make it up by raising you and Henry, but she never got the chance." His voice shook. "But most of all, Kats, she wanted you to think well of her."

"I may think well of her when I know what happened."

Hartley walked to the open window. Kathleen studied his balding head, seasoned brown from sand and sun; the taut lines in his neck like twisted rope.

"These Mountains," he said. "This sky . . . I knew this is where I wanted to be the first time I got off the train." He looked at Kathleen. "I came here to live; and your mother came to die."

He came back to the table. "You said you found their names in her cookbook?"

Kathleen walked to the bookshelf, pulled the cookbook off the shelf, and set it on the table.

Hartley rubbed his hand over the cover. "This one was her favorite. I could never bring myself to use it." He stood over Kathleen's shoulder while she opened it to the fateful page.

She felt his hot breath on her neck, smelled grease on his overalls, and his sweat. She pointed to her mother's writing. "Just two names," she said. "A record of her lost children, and it changed my life."

"I didn't know she did it," he said.

"She should have written their names in her Bible like she did mine and Henry's."

"She did what she thought was best."

"She did what was easiest, Dad, and so did you. But we all deserve the truth now."

Hartley gathered cups and saucers and carried them to the counter, swished them in the dishpan, rinsed, and then spread them over a towel and dried his hands. He came back to table, picked up the cookbook, and handed it to Kathleen. "Take safe care of it."

She pressed it to her cheek. "Thank you, Dad."

His eyes looked hollow as an endless cave. "What are you going to do?"

"Maybe I'll go to Chicago."

Hartley's face turned ashen. "You be careful, Kats."

"Careful of what?"

Hartley's mouth quivered. "Don't go digging stuff up. Leave her soul at rest."

Fury deep within her raged. "And what about my soul, Dad? And Clarice and Clayton's? Or are they just ashes too?

* * *

Later that afternoon, gloom hung like an ominous cloud as she sat across the kitchen table from Mr. Wendell. *He looks like that man in the newspaper last week who lost three sons in a house fire.* The grief-stricken face had stayed with her.

"I found the empty pill bottle by her bedside table. The doctor said if I'd been a half-hour later, she would have died."

Kathleen started. "Gosh! I knew she was feeling bad, but I didn't know she would do something like that."

"Melancholia, the doctor called it. It's like a long sadness. She'll be in the hospital a while. A long while, I'm afraid."

Kathleen bit her lower lip. *What's going to happen to me? What about my job?* Sudden remorse gripped her. *Selfish, selfish, when poor Mrs. Wendell . . .* she circled her spoon in her steaming coffee and recalled Mrs. Wendell staring into space; shutting herself in her room. Her "quiet times," she'd called them. She looked at Mr. Wendell. "She seemed fine this morning, full of smiles even, when she urged me to go to my dad's."

"She called me at the motor court to check what time I'd be home. She sounded happier than she'd been in a long time. The doctor said she probably felt relieved at finally making her decision; that she'd likely been thinking about it for a long time. It's just lucky I came home early."

"But why would she try to kill herself?"

He cracked his knuckles. "I should have known."

"Known what?"

"It was three years ago yesterday that we lost the baby."

Kathleen jerked her head back. "Baby! What baby?"

He brushed a tear off his cheek. "We had a baby boy before Sarah. His name was Daniel." His eyes brightened. "We called him Danny. She found him dead in his crib one morning, and the doctors couldn't tell us why. He was only twelve weeks old."

Memories flashed: Mrs. Wendell checking on Sarah, more often than needed; searching Sarah's mouth for scraps of paper she might choke on; the two of them scrubbing Sarah's bottles, boiling them, and then doing it all over again. "You should have told me," she said.

"We decided not to. You were a stranger then."

"You trusted me with Sarah. You should have trusted me with that, too."

He rubbed his forehead. "It hurt too much to talk about him."

Was it only this morning I was in Dad's kitchen talking about not talking?

"We sensed you were strong, Kathleen. We saw how you dealt with your brother. How you protected Sarah at your own peril. That's why we kept you on and let the others go, frankly."

Kathleen stared into her cup. *Strong?* She felt like a limp noodle after the boiling water was poured off.

Mr. Wendell got up and straightened a counter that did not need straightening, went to the sink and rinsed cups. *Like Dad,* she thought again.

Back at the table, he was an angry child with his plans quashed, his hopes ruined. "To be honest, it was a matter of *my* pride. Be strong. Don't talk about it." He looked at her shyly. "You understand that, don't you?"

Meaning Henry, she knew. *They've been so good to me, never probed for information, treated me like family or a trusted friend.* "I understand," she said, and then glanced toward the window. "The white cross; it's for him?"

"It's for Danny."

Kathleen felt herself sinking, the weight of it all pulling her down like an anchor. *Secrets . . . and the energy it takes to hide them.* Yet, she persisted. "But you should have told me."

"I know that now. And a lot of other things too," he added. "I should not have taken this job on the road, but it was all I could get with this depression we're in. And I didn't want to lose this house."

"So you left them with me."

His mouth twisted. "I built the house to protect them." He pointed toward the window to the courtyard. "Enclosed it even, but it didn't help."

"You protected them by hiding the truth?"

"That was wrong. I'm sorry."

Kathleen sighed. "So, what's going to happen now?"

"The doctor told me to lock up her pills. That she can't be left alone for a while, for a long while." He nodded decisively. "I'll put a lock on the medicine cabinet and give you the key. I'll tell my banker that you're in charge of the house account, so you can pay the bills."

Kathleen gazed at the pie safe. She could not believe he was talking about Mrs. Wendell as if she were a wayward child. Her Mrs. Wendell, who smelled of lemon soap, taught her how to tame her flyaway hair, and to choose the right lipstick. Never offering hand-me-downs, she gave her a new wool skirt for Christmas, a shirtwaist dress for her birthday, glass beads and a scarf in an Easter Basket. She looked at Mr. Wendell. "And what will you do?"

"I have to go back on the road. I'll put this house up for sale, but who knows how long it will take. Once I get out from under it, I'll move us to a smaller place." He rocked back and forth. "I'll do whatever it takes to stay close to them."

"Is there family that might help?"

"Only her mother in Milwaukee, but, well, she doesn't want her to know."

Kathleen wrinkled her brow. "But wouldn't her mother want to know?"

Mr. Wendell sighed. "I suppose she would. But to tell the truth, it's a matter of my pride now. She wasn't happy with me when I moved her daughter to this 'godforsaken place."

Kathleen's hand flew to her mouth to stifle her chuckle. "That's what my grandmother calls it."

Mr. Wendell put his hand on his throat, seeming to stifle his, and then they both burst out laughing.

And the laughter lifted them. The ominous cloud disappeared.

Mr. Wendell's eyes looked hopeful. "We're depending on you, Kathleen. Sarah needs you. We all need you."

Kathleen gazed out the window and remembered how she always took a long last look at the mountains before going to sleep at night. The one thing that will never change, she'd thought. Then she learned in school that the mountains were eroding, slipping away from her bit by bit.

She looked at Mr. Wendell. "So, I would be a guard in a locked fortress?"

"It might seem so for a while. But she cares a great deal about you, Kathleen. She will respond to you."

To oversee this beautiful woman, who treated her so kindly? Unthinkable. But how can she leave her and Sarah with a stranger? Kathleen felt robbed, as if something precious had been stolen from her. *It's be an enforcer here or go home and live in fear of Henry's return, or I could live in a cardboard box like those people in the newspaper.* She reached into her pocket and fingered the card Felicia gave her. *And what about Clarice and Clayton? My dream.* Kathleen looked in Mr. Wendell's stricken eyes and felt them slipping away from her no matter what choice she made.

CHAPTER TWENTY-SIX

Walter guided the delivery truck into the loading dock and record-ed time of arrival on his clipboard. Two more trucks were due to-day but scheduled to arrive at separate times to avoid attention.

A patrol car pulled up. An officer got out of the dusty cruiser, yanked his pants over his lumpy belly, adjusted his gun belt, then sprayed a glob of spit on the driveway. He looked in the side-view mirror and tucked strings of brassy hair under his hat, then strode up to Walter. "I gotta' look inside, Mr. Pruitt."

Walter nodded to his assistant. "Open it up, Toby."

The officer made a production of poking his nightstick into the boxes yet stopped four rows back, not five, where the bedding pad-ded cases of liquor. He walked back to Walter. "Everything looks on the up and up, Mister P."

Walter slipped the officer a thick envelope, it quickly disap-peared into his pants pocket, and he lumbered back to his patrol car and drove away.

With this weekly scene played out, Walter shook his head. He hated dealing with this sloppy, red headed Irishman who is happy with peanuts while the rest get rich. He pressed his lips tightly to-gether. *And I'm stuck with this crummy booze run.*

His men unloaded the truck, and Walter checked off each box on his clipboard. One column for cotton "pillowcases" and another for "sheets" which held twelve bottles each of uncut liquor. The crew stacked the boxes of sheets in the assigned space, then the pillowcases surrounding the hard stuff in the middle. With everything in order, Walter walked the warehouse floor. *Looks like any other warehouse, just like before.*

Back at his desk, he recorded the number of liquor boxes in his ledger book then calculated his percentage. The next shipment would be "shirts" and "pants". He stretched his back. *It's so easy . . . crooked cops, precinct captains, politicians, informants, Detective Braddock. Everyone gets their cut.* A chill wind blew through the open window. *Easy enough . . . a little too easy?*

There was a knock on his door, and Toby stood in the doorway.

"Next delivery is on the way, sir. Should be about forty minutes."

"Everything ready?"

"Ready," Toby said.

Walter motioned toward the cracked leather chair across from him.

Toby took off his cap and sat down.

"It's been hectic this week since Rudy quit," Walter said.

"You got that right. Two more deliveries today and four pickups tonight."

"You do excellent work, Toby. I keep you on for a reason."

"Yea, like my wife and four kids and sick mother-in-law."

"Most of the other men have families too, but I can't trust them for this level of work."

A buzzing fly landed on Toby's red cheeks and he flicked it off. "If it wasn't for this job, well, I've watched the neighbor's kids scratchin' through trash for food." He stiffened. "That's not going to happen with mine."

Walter's eyes hardened. "A man takes care of his family."

Toby fingered his cap. "That's the reason I stay on, sir, and take my chances of maybe goin' to jail if I get caught."

"You'd be out by the end of the day."

"Yeah, but my wife and mother-in-law, well, they think this is an ordinary warehouse."

Walter thought of Clarice. "They wouldn't understand, huh?"

"My wife might, but not my mother-in-law."

Walter leaned back. "But things are changing. The north side with Moran fighting to take over Capone's territory. More shootings with the O'Donnell's on the south and west sides. Everybody's on guard since that massacre on Valentine's Day"

"They would of got Moran too, if he hadn't spotted the squad car and doubled back to the coffee shop with his guards. He's the smart one, but some of his men paid the price."

"Capone's behind it for sure, but they'll never get him." Walter sat up straight. "And he gets too much press for me. Those damn reporters nearly trip over themselves for an interview. It's going to come back on him someday."

"And on us?" Toby said.

Walter cracked his knuckles. "Not if we're careful."

Toby picked up his cap, smoothed the bill, and set it back on his lap. "Speaking of Rudy, uh . . . what if he talks?"

"If Rudy talks, a goon will work him over, and they'll just pay off another politician." He looked hard at Toby. "You and I know the full operation, the suppliers, and the higher-ups. If one of us double-crosses them, well . . . your wife will be a widow and Clarice an orphan."

"Don't you have a son, sir?"

"He'd be an orphan, too."

"My kids will not go hungry. I'll take my chances."

Walter nodded. "But this prohibition can't last much longer. Our beer used to come from the Heights, and now we're getting hard stuff from Canada. Capone's already moved into the labor unions and gambling, even businesses. I give it two, maybe three more years."

A delivery truck groaned up the driveway.

Toby hopped up. "I'll get this one, sir." He headed toward the door, then turned around. "Uh, thanks, Boss."

Walter walked to the window and watched his men gather as Toby guided the backing truck into the loading dock. He looked up the trash-littered street to Mike's Pawn Shop, a second-hand furniture store, and a boarded-up corner grocery. *Nobody pays much attention to this place. A goon shows up every week to snoop but hav-*

en't seen Ferris McKenzie since we met at that speakeasy. He cracked his knuckles again. *Guess he's too good to come to this dump.*

He recalled McKenzie's words as he'd extended his silver cigarette lighter. "It's my business to know about people, but with you it was personal." Walter looked at the deserted warehouse across the street. *How personal was it, McKenzie? Am I still just a scared kid to you? Are you using me to make millions while I'm stuck with a mere percentage?* He banged his fist into his open hand. "I make it happen, damn it."

Back at his desk, Walter picked up the front page of the *Tribune* and stared at the photograph of Robert Bradford handing a check to a matronly lady in front of Jane Addams Hull House. *Damn man with a whore for a wife, and he turned me down for a loan. Threatened me.* He dropped the newspaper in the trash. *It should be me on the front page, but I'm stuck in this hole in the wall.* He felt his years of hard work drifting away like tumbleweeds on the Texas panhandle. He flexed his hand as if trying to grasp the years back. "Hell! I succeeded because of my smarts and the shrewd moves I made."

He crossed his hands behind his neck. *I could get my own sources from one of those counties in Virginia. They say the night hills light up like Christmas trees from the whisky stills. Or, I can siphon off more here to keep Clarice afloat, work out legalities with the house, and go west again. Maybe start up a general store.* He closed his eyes and felt his energy ooze back like a long-lost friend.

He grabbed his pencil, scribbled notes on a long pad, then stopped. *But that accountant says Clarice hasn't touched the money I put into her account. Damn, she's stubborn. Sees things in black and white.* He recalled Clarice walking the floors of Pruitt's with him at night, supervising inventory, training employees, going over the books. *Guess I taught her that.* He tapped his pencil on the desk. *But if it comes to taking the money or losing the store—she'll take it. And when she does, I'm out of here. And I won't go away empty.*

He thought of Ferris McKenzie again as they downed bourbon in the speakeasy: *"How you got your money and lost it is no business of mine but what you do from now on, will be my business. If you understand what I'm saying?"* Walter snapped his pencil; it broke into two splintered halves. *He's making millions while I'm stuck in this backstreet warehouse."* He clasped his hands behind his neck and stared at the water-stained ceiling. "I understand, McKenzie. But I'm smarter than you are."

CHAPTER TWENTY-SEVEN

Clarice looked across the tarpaper tent to her brother and barely noticed his ragged clothes and chopped hair. "How did you get so handsome?" she said.

"Hey," Clay threw up his hands. "It's all this fresh air."

Clarice stepped into his open arms. *I've got to tell him about our mother. But will it destroy him?* She squeezed him hard. "I've missed you, Clay."

He held her out in front of him. "And I you, Sis, but how did you find me?"

"I figured you were on Randolph Street since that's where you took our food. But nobody in this place knows your name."

"We're not the same people here. We go mostly by description or somebody's whim."

"Yeah, like Shorty, Red, Pretzel. After I described you, this old woman said, 'Ah, the Smart One.'" Clarice grimaced. "She didn't have any teeth, Clay. How can she eat without teeth?"

"No problem at the soup kitchen."

Clarice looked around at his cot, two wooden crates, a rope, and a cardboard box. "Nice place," she said.

"It's all I need for now."

Clarice's mouth trembled. "We can go home, Clay."

He opened his palms in the air. "And leave all this?"

"You're not safe here. Winter's coming, and you'll freeze to death."

"I'll be all right, Sis. But where have you been? I tried to telephone but the operator said the line was disconnected. I figured you were sleeping at the office."

"I did for a while but didn't like it much, so I'm staying at the Bradford's."

Clay squinted his eyes. "Bradford? The Capitalist? He's part of the greedy mess this country is in."

Clarice stiffened. "Robert is head of the Governor's Joint Relief Fund. He donates to soup kitchens."

"While he's tucked away in his mansion and others go hungry."

"They're my friends, Clay, and besides; I don't have any place else to go."

"Why aren't you staying at the house?"

"I don't have enough money to heat it or take care of it even, so I closed it up."

"No money?" he said.

"I'm sinking every penny, and I mean *every* penny I make back into the store."

"And how are things at the store?"

"I didn't think you'd care."

"I care what might happen to you with those mobsters around."

Clarice brightened. "The store is surviving without mob money. Just barely, but we might make it."

"What about Father?"

"He shows up at the store now and then to look legit, but he avoids me, and I avoid him. I rented a small warehouse in Northlake, so I don't have to deal with him and his illegal liquor."

"Be careful, Sis. The three of us are still business partners, on paper at least, so we can't be clean."

"Father created a special account for the store. He said it was a loan, but it's mob money, must be, and I won't touch it. His trucks show up with deliveries occasionally, but I just stack the merchandise in a corner of the backroom and don't put it out on the floor. So, technically we're clean, and we'll stay that way or go down."

Clay motioned her to a crate, and then sat on one across from her. "Something's different," he said. "You're different."

How well he knows me, the moods of my face, each tug of my hair. She twisted her finger around a curl. "I have something to tell you."

Clay stretched out his legs. "I'm ready."

Clarice winced. *Maybe not for this.* She touched her throat. "Well, when I was little, I went through Father's trunk and found an old obituary for our grandmother showing our mother as her next of kin. It listed Mother in Albuquerque, along with her husband and a girl and boy. The girl's name is Kathleen, and the boy is Henry."

She twisted her hands.

"Go on," Clay said.

"Well, on my way home from Los Angeles, I got off the train in Albuquerque and found the house where they lived. Nobody was home, but I found Kathleen, and then lost my nerve and ran away without talking to her."

"What were you afraid of."

Tears welled. "I don't know . . . myself, I guess." She sniffed. "Doesn't it sound stupid to be afraid of myself?"

Clay's eyes softened. "And then what?"

Clarice's mouth quivered. "Our mother is dead, Clay. "

Clay looked deep into her eyes. "I've always known our mother was dead."

As if captured in a still photograph, Clarice froze. And then, "How? She demanded. "How did you know?

"The man, the husband, he came to our door. Back then, whenever I heard the doorbell, I always thought it was Mother. I lived for it until that night when my hopes were dashed."

Clarice twisted her collar.

"The man told Father that Mother died of tuberculosis. He asked if he might tell us himself, but Father refused. Then he asked Father to tell us that she was sorry and that she loved us both until the end."

Clarice pulled her sweater up over her shoulders and gripped it under her chin.

"Father stayed home the next day and I waited for him to tell us, but he never said a word." Clay's nostrils flared. "And I could not abide him after that."

"So, you retreated to your room."

Clay stood. His cap scraped the side of the patched tar tent. The whole side of his cap was black. "It was a coward's way out, I know. But I could not be his son after that."

Clarice balled her fists. "I could kill him."

"Don't, Sis. Things have a way of coming back."

"But look what he did to you."

"And to you," Clay said.

"My stomach's been in knots since Albuquerque. Why did you just now tell me?"

Clay's eyes sought hers and held. "Because I knew her love. But the only thing you knew was his. I couldn't take that away from you. Even now I don't want to."

"You could have."

"Not without hurting you I couldn't."

Tears slithered down Clarice's cheeks. "Ah, Clay, if only we had talked instead of trying to protect each other."

"We survived, Sis." His face brightened. "Look how smart you are and strong. You have no idea how strong."

"But I'm filled with hate. Our mother, then the girl because I thought she had our mother, when all that time Mother was dead, and now I hate Father."

Clay opened his hands. "The only thing stronger than hate is love. You'll see your way through it someday."

Clarice let out a long sigh. "I don't see how."

"There's something ticking inside you. It's your energy, I think."

She wiped her brow. "And I'm exhausted." She looked at him through narrowed eyes. "You said I was different. But so are you. It's your voice, the way you're looking at me, the way you're standing."

"I've found somewhere where I belong."

"You belong to me, Clay."

"That won't change."

Clarice tucked her hair behind her ears. "Everything changes. Maybe that's why I was afraid to face Kathleen."

The corners of Clay's mouth curved up.

"Come to Felicia's with me." Clarice begged. "You'll have food at least, and we can figure out what to do next."

Clay gave her a fierce look. "I won't stay at Robert Bradford's house. And you shouldn't either."

"Felicia took me to Albuquerque in her private railroad car, she—"

"And for the cost of that ride in her private railroad car, I could feed a hundred people for a week!"

"What good would a week do?"

"They might have meat to eat instead of watered down soup; mothers might have enough milk, so their babies won't cry."

"And then what?"

"We were part of the problem, you and me, wanting for nothing in our mansion with plenty to eat and warm beds."

Clarice shot up.

Clay stood and grasped her hand. "I'm sorry, Sis. That wasn't fair."

"Then let's go back to our house. Father isn't there anymore. We can close off the upper floors and live downstairs to save heat."

"I belong here."

"In this horrible place where you don't have enough food."

"I'm doing something. Just like you always wanted."

"What are you doing?"

His eyes danced. "We have a printing press and are publishing pamphlets. We're planning a hunger march through the stockyards to Federal Street. We—"

"Who are 'we'?"

"A collection of laid-off workers, some old union leaders, socialists, even a few mob men hiding out."

"Socialists? Unions? The Mob? How can you associate with them?"

"Somebody has to fight this poverty, this destruction, or we'll all starve to death."

Clarice's stomach churned. "You go upsetting things with your pamphlets and marches, and they will arrest you."

Clay opened hands to shush her. "Listen, Sis. A fellow here still has mob connections, and he knows Father." His eyes narrowed. "If Father ever crosses them, well . . ."

"Father can take care of himself. But don't you get into trouble, because I might not be able to bail you out."

He shuffled his feet. "I wouldn't want you to."

Clarice sat down and thought of their isolated childhood, clinging together in the void left by the mother they never knew. *Clay and I, we don't know who we are.* She looked at Clay with his stringy hair tucked behind his ears, his soft eyes and square chin. *He looks so much like Kathleen.* She flicked her tongue over bottom lip. *But I'm not going to share him.*

"What's going on in your smart head?"

She glanced around the tent again. "I'm wondering what you do without your books?"

"I'm hoping you'll bring them to me." He reached into his shirt pocket and pulled out a sheet of paper. "These are the ones I want for now. Maybe later you'll bring more."

Clarice pointed an accusing finger at him. "You knew I'd come."

"Of course." He took her hands and pulled her up. "Come on, Sis. I want you to meet my friends."

* * *

Clarice parked in the circular driveway and looked at the house she had lived in all her life. *What happened here to make Father push my mother out the door?* She pulled an empty cardboard box out of her trunk and walked to the front door. As she turned the key, she noticed a long sheet of paper nailed to the side of the door, and she ripped it off. "Thirty-day Notice . . . Delinquent . . . Cook County Tax Office." She waved it in the air. "Father, you didn't even pay the damn taxes!"

She walked through the silent rooms and wrote her name in dust on the oak dining table, straightened a limp doily over the back of the blue velvet sofa and nearly stumbled over its bulbous legs. The kitchen counter where Esther rolled puffy dough for noodles and made cinnamon buns was empty and cold. The rusted icebox door gaped open. The monstrous black stove stood desolate in the corner. Pantry shelves, once crammed with food, held a half-empty bottle of maple syrup, a dusty flour sack, and a lonely can of chicken noodle soup. A rat scurried past her feet, and she jumped. *It all started over Esther's missing food.*

Upstairs, cobwebs drooped from the corners of her bedroom ceiling. Dust lay like thick fog over her empty dresser. *It's only been three months, but it looks like I've been gone for a year.* In Clay's room, she pulled out his list: Karl Marx, Nikolai Bukharin, Lenin, Charles Darwin, *On the Origin of Species,* Upton Sinclair's, *The Jungle, The Canadian Rockies, History of Western Civilization.* She shook her head. *Socialists, Darwin, Marx; Clay's turning against everything we've been taught. And what does he think he can change with pamphlets and marches?*

She carried the box to the foot of the stairs, took a last look around, and waves of loneliness washed over her. *Everything changed when Kathleen put that classified ad in the Tribune. Why couldn't she have left us alone?* Outside, she dropped the box of books into the trunk, got in her car, and squeezed the steering wheel. *Kathleen wants me in her life, but I don't have room for her.* She pushed in the clutch, punched the starter, and headed toward Felicia's.

As she pulled into the driveway, she glanced across the autumn lawn to the remains of Robert's vegetable garden. Spring and summer mornings, he worked the garden, stuffed ripe vegetables into burlap sacks, then dropped them at the soup kitchen on his way to the office. *Why would a man like Robert do that?* She rubbed her temples. *Because he cares about other people—while I only care about myself.*

She looked at the rambling farm house. *Maybe Clay's right. I don't belong here. But where?* She bit her lower lip. *I could sleep at the store like Father did. Or make a bed behind boxes in the back room, and nobody would know I'd slept there.* She sniffed a laugh. *But this place looks pretty good right now.* She got out of her car with a spring in her step.

The maid, Margaret, showed her into the living room where Felicia greeted her with a smile and said, "Look who's here."

Kathleen stepped toward her and extended her hand. "Hello, Clarice."

Clarice froze. "Well, damn!"

CHAPTER TWENTY-EIGHT

Clarice stood in Felicia's living room with her hands on her hips, glaring at Kathleen. "Why did you come here?" she said. "And why now?"

Kathleen backed away from her. *She's like a festering boil ready to burst.*

"I invited her," Felicia said.

"You invited her? With everything that's going on in my life?"

"She's your sister."

"We may have the same mother," Clarice hissed, "but that does not make us sisters."

"I came to find out about our mother," Kathleen said. "Some pieces of the puzzle, some fragment of who she was, and why she abandoned you and Clayton."

"Abandoned? Ha! We agree on that at least. But I don't care anymore."

Kathleen crossed her arms over her chest. "Then why did you come to Albuquerque?"

Clarice smirked. "Because I wanted to face my mother just once. Ask her why she never came back to see me." She tossed her hands in the air. "But I didn't get to because she was dead. Dead, damn it!"

"That's enough drama, Clarice." Felicia reached for her hand. "Come sit with us, so we can sort this out."

Clarice's eyes blazed. "There is no 'us' where she is concerned." She turned and stomped toward the door. Her knees buckled, and she grasped the back of the wingback chair.

Kathleen reached out to steady her, but Clarice waved her away.

Felicia came up behind her and helped her to the sofa. "You haven't eaten all day, I suppose."

"Not enough time," Clarice mumbled.

"Then I'll make you a sandwich. We can talk later."

"You two talk," Clarice said. "I'm going to bed."

Felicia nodded toward the stairs. "Well, the heater in your upstairs bedrooms went out this morning. You'll have to share the guest room with Kathleen."

Clarice's face reddened. "Forget that!" Her legs seemed to spring to life as she stomped out the front door and slammed it.

"Sorry," Felicia said. "Things aren't exactly working for her right now with the store and her father and brother."

"Why is she taking it out on me?"

Felicia shrugged. "What did you expect?"

"I thought she might be willing to talk at least."

"I hoped so too."

"She was so full of rage in Albuquerque. But I thought by now she might . . ."

"Might what?"

"Well, maybe not be so angry."

"Clarice stays angry."

Kathleen's eyes widened her. "How could my mother have a daughter like her?"

Felicia looked her in the eye. "You knew what she was like before you came here. So, deal with it."

"Deal with her?"

"I can't do it for you, dear."

Kathleen blinked back tears. "I would go home to Albuquerque tomorrow, but I don't have a job."

Felicia leaned into her. "What happened with your job?"

"Well, Mrs. Wendell got sick suddenly, and her mother came from Milwaukee to help out." Her voice quavered. "They begged me to stay, and I miss little Sarah, but I can't spend the rest of my life taking care of other people."

Felicia fingered her chin. "What *do* you want for the rest of your life?"

Kathleen glanced across the room to a framed picture of a young girl with golden hair standing in a field of clover. *Why can't my life be simple?* She looked at Felicia. "I want to find out what happened to my mother. I want Clarice to talk to me. I want to see Clayton. And I want to find peace with my brother, Henry, for what he did."

"Whew!" Felicia brushed her forehead. "A tall order there."

Kathleen chuckled. "Right now, I'd settle for one decent conversation with Clarice. Maybe we could be friends at least."

"Clarice doesn't have any friends."

Kathleen shook her head. "Neither do I."

* * *

The next morning, Kathleen sat across the kitchen table from Felicia and munched raisin muffins topped with orange marmalade. Sunshine streamed through the bay window as she pointed to a building across a carpet of brown grass. "That looks like a barn," she said."

"It was a barn. But Robert made it into a carriage house. The previous owner fancied himself a farmer. Only the land didn't cooperate."

"And this house, it's, well, different."

Felicia's eyes lit up. "Robert bought it long before he met me. Our living room was part of the old farm house, this nook part of the original kitchen, and he just wrapped the rest of the house around it. After we married, he added the second story, enlarged the kitchen, and added his den."

The little breakfast nook was enveloped in sky blue wallpaper dotted with orange and yellow daisies. The round table with its bright yellow cloth, flowered china and matching placemats and napkins, lent a sense of order. "This is my favorite spot," Felicia said. "I like to think the farmer's wife might have looked out this window while she chopped vegetables for supper or mended a shirt, perhaps."

"Maybe she looked out at the flowers," Kathleen said.

Felicia laughed. "She probably looked out at the chicken coop. I tore down the wire cage myself and put in the flowerbeds. You should see them in spring."

"You love it here, don't you?"

"Most people seem surprised. Like we should have something more extravagant I guess, but its simplicity suits me. Especially now when so many people are hurting."

"What about Robert?"

"He grew up on the north side with German immigrant parents. He knows what poverty is."

"My dad's parents brought him over from Germany when he was four. His mother still tries to run our family like she did in the old country. She never forgave Dad for moving us to Albuquerque."

"I found Albuquerque interesting. I loved the Spanish architecture at the train station and the Alvarado Hotel next door where Clarice and I stayed. I liked the happy music, and the people seemed to have their own ways. Quiet, not grinding and noisy like here."

"It started as a Spanish outpost in 1706 and was named for a Spanish Viceroy. There are petroglyphs carved in the volcanic rocks on the west mesa." She grinned. "I got A's in history."

Felicia flashed her turquoise ring. "I loved the Indian jewelry, and you probably saw the pottery in the living room. I really had to bargain for it."

"Albuquerque's home," Kathleen said. She took another bite of muffin and thought of Clarice. "Will she come back, do you think?"

"Do you want her to?"

Tired, from her restless night, Kathleen sipped the last of her coffee. "I'm not sure."

Felicia carried the dirty dishes to the sink while Kathleen wiped the table. The doorbell rang and moments later, Clarice stood in the kitchen doorway. Her hair lay plastered on one side, frizzy on the other, and she wore the same wrinkled green skirt she'd worn the day before. She looked at Felicia and then Kathleen. "You invaded my life," she said, "and now my best friend's."

Felicia put a muffin on a plate and set it on the table. "I'll pour you some coffee."

Clarice dropped into the chair and tore into the muffin.

Felicia set another muffin on her plate, and she ate it with equal relish between gulps of coffee. "You slept at the store, didn't you?"

"I didn't have anywhere else to go."

Kathleen studied Clarice's pale face and sunken eyes and recognized the same fear she'd felt the night she'd slept in Morningside Park after her own flight from home. Warmth seeped up from deep within. "I don't have anywhere else to go either," she said.

Clarice's face reddened. "You just couldn't leave this alone, could you?"

"And why do you keep running away?"

"I don't answer to you!"

Felicia looked anxiously back and forth between them. "Good gosh, you two. Can't you see that all you have is each other? What do you have to lose?"

"What do we have to gain?" Clarice snapped.

Kathleen looked at Clarice with tear filled eyes. "The mother we never knew. Who she was and some piece of the puzzle of what happened to her." Her lips trembled. "And to fill this giant hole in our hearts."

"My father still hates her," Clarice said. "But he won't tell me why."

"My father still loves her," Kathleen said. "But he won't talk about her, either."

Clarice looked at Kathleen with tearful eyes. "Was she a bad woman like my father says? Or was she the woman your father still loves?"

"I'd like to know," Kathleen said.

Clarice rested her chin in her hands. "I'm tired."

Kathleen sighed. "I'm tired, too."

"So am I," Felicia said. The three women glanced back and forth to each other, and they all burst into laughter.

Long minutes later, "It's funny," Clarice said, "but I feel better."

Kathleen gathered her hair and tucked it behind her ears, "I feel better, too."

Felicia walked to the stove, picked up the pot, and held it in the air triumphantly. "Let's have another cup of coffee, ladies. We have some talking to do."

CHAPTER TWENTY-NINE

True to Clarice's habit, they made a list: Cook County courthouse records, old neighbors, places Kathleen remembered from her childhood visits to Chicago, Niles Cemetery . . . anything that might help them find out information about their mother. Kathleen rolled her eyes. "Let's go see my grandmother first. She never liked Mother; maybe now she'll tell us why."

Clarice rubbed her hands together. "Ah yes, your grandmother." Then she'd told Kathleen about finding the store when she was fourteen, and Sybil had accused her of stealing hair ribbons; how she'd hid behind the bakery just to get a glimpse of her mother; and how Henry had chased her down the street.

Kathleen listened with admiration, wishing she had been so brave at fourteen.

Bells jingled as they slipped through the front door of the Howe's Grocery. A tall man in a blue flannel shirt waited while Sybil pushed jars, cans, sacks of beans and flour with one hand, while her other hand danced over an adding machine. Without glancing up, she said, "I'll be with you ladies in a minute."

Clarice whispered, "It still smells like old salami in here."

Kathleen sniffed, "And dust and mold and old paper sacks."

Kathleen waited in the corner while Clarice slipped down the side aisle toward the ribbons.

Sybil bid her customer goodbye, looked at Kathleen, and her eyes widened. "What are you doing here? Is something wrong with your father? Henry?"

Kathleen crossed her fingers. "They're fine," she said. *Not so true with Henry, but that's all she'll get from me.*

"Well, your father didn't write me you were coming. You'll have to wash your own bed sheets."

"I won't be staying here, Grandmother."

Clarice came up the side aisle and stood next to Kathleen.

Sybil's face twisted as if she had just caught a mouse in the flour bin. "Who *are* you, young lady?"

Clarice extended her hand. "I'm Clarice Pruitt."

Sybil nodded.

Kathleen slipped her arm around Clarice's shoulder. "Clarice is my half sister. Mother's daughter from her first marriage."

"I figured as much. You look just like her only your hair is frizzy. And wasn't there a boy?"

"You know about us?" Clarice said.

"Of course, I know. I figured out who you were that day I caught you sneaking through my ribbons. Why didn't you say who you were back then?"

Kathleen winced. "She was just a child."

"An abandoned child, I'd say."

"Something happened to make my mother leave," Clarice said. "We're hoping you can help us."

Sybil snorted. "Well, maybe your father was smarter than my son."

Kathleen's mouth quivered. "Why did you dislike her when Dad loved her so?"

"I never said a word to you children."

"And that's how we knew."

Sybil picked up a feather duster, walked to the end of the counter, and danced it over bottles of Karo Syrup and soda cracker tins.

Kathleen caught Clarice's smile. "I do the same thing in my store," she whispered, "we just can't help it."

Sybil walked to the other side and dusted the jars of peppermint candy, lollipops, and licorice. She put her feather duster under the counter and looked back and forth between Kathleen and

Clarice. "You girls were raised by your fathers," she said. "So why do you care about her?"

"We have a right to know what happened," Kathleen said."

"You girls don't have any rights."

Clarice's eyes flashed. She flattened her hands on the counter and leaned menacingly toward Sybil.

Sybil's back stiffened like a broomstick. "She was Irish." Her hands clawed the air. "They grubbed so long in those potato fields, they're only good for the dirty jobs here. And their pint," she added.

"I know what you think of the Irish," Kathleen said, "but surely there was more."

"She was Catholic."

"Catholic?" Kathleen said. "That's it?"

"Your mother fingered those rosary beads like they were some kind of voodoo magic."

"She was dying!" Kathleen made a choking noise in her throat. "Those beads are all I have left of her, except for her cookbook."

Purple veins pulsed on Sybil's forehead. Her nostrils flared. "What kind of a woman would leave two little children?"

"That's what we're trying to find out," Kathleen said.

Sybil flinched. "She tricked my son into marrying her, but she paid. God gave her the consumption!"

"You hateful old hag," Clarice shouted. "Just wait till God finishes with you."

"She jinxed him, and my poor son is still paying. Miriam found that out, and so will Beatrice, mark my word."

Kathleen's eyes burned. "The stroke killed Miriam!"

Sybil reared her shoulders. "Your mother was Irish, she was Catholic, and she took my son away from me. What more do you want to know?"

Clarice leaned over the counter again. "I'm glad you're not *my* grandmother."

Sybil backed into the corner and curled into a ball.

She looks like one of those potato bugs I used to roll in my hands.
"We've come as adults," Kathleen said, "wanting to know about our mother."

Sybil uncurled. "Well, your mother was not worthy of my son."

"And did you treat her like you treat me?"

"I own the house you lived in. I bought your clothes, I cooked your meals, I cleaned your floors."

"You did it for Dad and Henry. Not me."

Sybil mouth twisted. "Girls don't matter."

Kathleen's face grew hot. "Since I don't matter, Grandmother; I never want to see you again."

Sybil flipped her hand in the air as if batting a fly. "You just lost your inheritance, young lady!"

"I never had one," Kathleen said. "It was all going to Henry, anyway. That's your way."

CHAPTER THIRTY

Two days later, they gazed at the weed filled lot. Kathleen pointed to the square scar where Hartley and Laura's home once stood. "It was about there," she said. "A blue house facing Archy Avenue. Dad told the people that we used to live there so they invited us in. It burned down shortly after."

"What was it like?" Clarice said.

Kathleen recalled her feelings as a ten-year-old standing in the house where her mother once stood, seeing the wood stove where she'd cooked, the corner where she rocked Henry's cradle. *Did she know she was going to die?*

A cool breeze licked their faces as they walked down the slope toward the empty lot.

"It was just one room," Kathleen said, "and they had Henry and me both." She walked a few steps and blocked off the imaginary house with her hands. "The back porch was about here. Dad told me Mother was happiest when she sat on the steps and 'let the breeze wash her face'. That's how he said it, anyway. And that she never liked Albuquerque because it was too dry."

"But your dad's house is close to a river."

Kathleen winced. *She knows nothing about us.* "We didn't move to the house by the Rio Grande until after Mother died. Grandmother bought the house, and Dad pays her back every month." Her eyes darted to a faraway cloud, then to Clarice. "You heard her, she likes to hold it over his head."

"Why doesn't your dad just pay the house off and be done with her?"

"He tried to once, but she tore up his check and mailed it back. Holding Dad's mortgage is a way of maintaining control." Kathleen kicked a pile of dirt, then bent down and picked up a rusty nail and turned it over in her hand. "Everything about them has been destroyed."

"You're here," Clarice said.

Kathleen's heart fluttered. She dropped the nail and ground it into the dirt.

Clarice pointed to a house on an adjacent lot. "It looks pretty old. Maybe someone there knew her."

They walked to the house, Kathleen knocked, and a silver-haired woman in a blue flowered dress invited them in.

"They didn't live there long," the woman said. "The lady got the consumption and they moved out west. They had two little ones, as I recall."

"I was one of them," Kathleen said. She nodded toward Clarice "And she's my sister. Our mother died about a year after she moved to Albuquerque."

"I figured as much. She was awful sick."

"We don't remember her," Clarice said. "We're trying to find someone who does."

The woman gazed out the window toward the empty lot. "She didn't talk much, him either, but she had a lovely voice. My side window faced hers, and I could hear her singing even as sick as she was." A faint smile crossed her face. "I borrowed a cup of sugar once, and she invited me in. You children were playing on the floor." She stroked her chin. "I can't recall what we talked about, but she didn't want me to leave. No one ever come to see them except Mrs. Dooley."

Kathleen lifted her eyebrows. "Mrs. Dooley? My dad has mentioned her."

"She was my son, Derry's, piano teacher. A jolly soul one doesn't forget. She must have taught your mother, too, because she always walked over to your house as soon as she finished here." She gazed at the blue streaked sky. "The consumption took Derry too . . . he was only twelve. Three years later, it took my husband."

"I'm sorry," Kathleen said.

As if her losses were long-ago reckoned with, the woman nodded. "Mrs. Dooley still lives on Thirty-Sixth Street last I heard."

* * *

Mrs. Dooley's eyes looked like murky gray fog. "You're who?" she said.

"We're Laura Howe's daughters," Kathleen repeated. "You may have known her as Laura Pruitt."

"*My* Laura's daughters?"

"I'm Kathleen Howe." She nodded toward Clarice. "And she's Clarice Pruitt. You were her piano teacher I understand."

Mrs. Dooley's legs wobbled. They braced her arms and guided her onto a chair where her shoulders collapsed over her stomach like a squashed accordion. Yet her strong voice defied the frailty of her body. "Laura was like a daughter to me. My husband died young, you see, and we never had children." She motioned toward a faded green sofa. "You girls sit down."

Across from the sofa stood a bookcase crammed with dusty books and a statue of the Virgin Mary. On the side wall, darkened with the patina of age, was an upright piano with sheet music stacked almost to the ceiling and an old metronome squeezed into the leftover space.

Mrs. Dooley looked back and forth between them. "How did you find me after all this time?"

"Our old neighbor on Archy Avenue," Kathleen said. "We're trying to find out what happened to our mother, and we hope you can help us."

Mrs. Dooley pulled a green knit shawl off the back of her chair and settled it over her shoulders. "Carlin hired me to give your mother piano and voice lessons."

"Carlin?" they both said at once.

"He was Laura's stepfather."

Kathleen looked at Clarice. "I've never heard that name before."

Mrs. Dooley gazed at the ceiling. As if pulling out memories, she said, "Carlin told me that Laura had the voice of an angel." She harrumphed. "That was the only thing we agreed on. He hired me to teach her piano, so she could perform." She looked at Kathleen. "Laura learned faster than any student I taught. With a voice that beautiful, she didn't need voice lessons, so mostly I listened to her sing." Her eyes brightened. "After her lessons, I taught her the Irish reels, slip jigs, and hornpipe, and we danced and danced."

Soothing warmth flowed through Kathleen to know her mother danced.

"Tell us about this Carlin," Clarice said.

"Well, Laura's own father died when she was twelve or so, I'm not sure. But you girls must know that."

"My father won't tell me anything," Clarice said.

Mrs. Dooley frowned. "From what I know of your father, child, I don't doubt it." She looked at Kathleen. "But surely Hartley has told you."

"I don't know much more than she does. Dad teared up every time I mentioned Mother, so I finally quit asking."

"Well, Hartley adored Laura from the moment he saw her. After her daddy died—"

"What did he die from?" Clarice asked.

"Laura told me that she came home from school one day, and her daddy had gone to the hospital. Now Laura adored her daddy, mind you, and she didn't even know he was sick. She went to the hospital herself but couldn't find him, and no one would tell her where he was. A few weeks later, her mama told Laura he died."

Clarice sat on the edge of the sofa. "That doesn't sound right."

"There was no wake, no funeral, nothing. Laura never even got to tell her daddy goodbye."

"Do you know which hospital?" Clarice said.

"I didn't know them then. But times got hard after that. Laura was smart, and she loved school, but she had to drop out to help her mama survive."

Kathleen recalled her own exit from Albuquerque High School: the principal's desk, ringed with stains of morning coffee, paper clips askew, piles of paper everywhere.

"Laura and her mama baked sweet rolls at home, and Laura sold them door to door. That's how she met Hartley."

Clarice raised her eyebrows. "So, she knew him before."

"Hartley fell in love the first time Laura pushed her cart through their door. But his mother refused to trade with the Irish."

"Her being Irish," Clarice said, "it drove everything."

"And Hartley was German, so neither told their parents about the other."

Clarice tucked a curl behind her ear and leaned back. "How did my father come into the picture?"

"Mr. Pruitt saw Laura delivering rolls to a store near his warehouse. She was tall, and she had a regal manner about her that drew people." She looked at Clarice. "You remind me of her some."

A twinge of anger surprised Kathleen. *She can't be like my mother.*

"Well, Laura's mother had married Carlin by then, and he worked at the warehouse. When your father asked around about Laura, that old weasel must have smelled opportunity."

"My father is German," Clarice said. "Why would he marry an Irish girl?"

"Laura wondered the same thing. But then, she was never aware of her own beauty. Carlin arranged the marriage, just like in the old country. Laura didn't want to marry, but she was too young to do anything about it. And that mother of hers, well, she agreed to whatever Carlin wanted." She fingered her chin. "It must have looked like a good marriage though, with Pruitt's money, that big house, and a nice promotion for Carlin. But it broke Hartley's heart."

"Were they happy together?" Clarice said. "My mother and father, I mean."

"I saw little of Laura after her marriage. I went to that fancy house a few times, but when Mr. Pruitt hired an instructor from the university, he showed me the door. I don't think he wanted Laura reminded she was Irish and that included me."

"Did she see my dad after her marriage?" Kathleen asked. "Them being good friends, I mean."

"I don't think she left the house much, not even to visit her mother. And Clayton was sickly." She grabbed her stomach. "Her boys! Dear God. What about Laura's boys?"

"Henry's not well," Kathleen said. "I haven't met Clay yet."

Clarice's eyes looked like two black seeds. "Tell us what happened to our mother, please."

Mrs. Dooley's mouth trembled. "She banged on my door late one night and said Mr. Pruitt had kicked her out. She had already been to her own folks, but Carlin shut the door in her face while her mother just stood there."

Clarice's face reddened. "What kind of mother would do that?"

Mrs. Dooley clutched her shawl under her neck. "These old bones are drying up."

Kathleen knelt next to her. "This is too much for you. We can come back."

Mrs. Dooley crossed her hands over her chest. "I've held Laura's story in my heart for so long, it's aching to get out."

"Why did he kick her out?" Clarice said.

"Laura never told me. She kept things to herself mostly and never complained."

"Like my dad," Kathleen said.

"Laura went back the next day, but he had taken you babies away. She tried to get into that department store, but the security man had a police order, and he wouldn't let her in." Her face puffed. "Laura didn't stand a chance against your father and his high-priced lawyers."

Clarice let out a soft groan.

Hearing her anguish, Kathleen said, "This is too much."

Clarice's eyes challenged her. "Our mother is the one who lived it. We can sit here and listen at least."

"Well, I put your mother to bed. She wouldn't eat, and I had to practically pour water down her." Mrs. Dooley's voice gathered momentum. "The doctor wanted to put her in the hospital, but she refused. She lay in bed so long she could barely walk, but somehow she got to the piano in the middle of the night and played the old Irish tunes I taught her." The folds of her wrinkled face quivered as she looked at Clarice. "Laura didn't want to live without you babies."

Clarice squeezed her eyes shut.

Kathleen's stomach quivered. *What is she thinking?*

"And then, one day Laura got up and said she was going to find a job playing piano, so she could hire a lawyer to get her babies back. I gave her some of my students, and she got a night job playing piano at the theater."

Clarice opened her eyes. "What happened to Carlin and her mother?"

"Your father fired Carlin. He had set them up in a nice house, you see, so they had to move. I heard Carlin took off shortly after. Somebody told me later that Laura's mama died in the poor house."

"My father kept the newspaper clipping of her obituary in his trunk," Clarice said. "That's how I found out about Kathleen and Henry."

"Dear me. That's no way for a child to learn something like that."

"Then what happened?" Clarice said.

"Well, Laura helped pay for groceries, but she saved everything else. I begged her to tell Hartley what happened, but she said she wouldn't put her troubles on him. I worried about her riding the Elevated and walking alone at night, but she wouldn't listen. Then one night she didn't come home."

Mrs. Dooley's arms jerked wildly as if reliving her panic. "I went to the theater the next morning, but nobody knew where she was, so I went to the tractor store." She looked at Kathleen. "Hartley worked there during the week and at his mother's store on Saturdays."

Kathleen shook her head imperceptibly. *Something else I didn't know.*

"Hartley found Laura at Cook County charity ward. She'd been beaten and robbed. Raped, too, I imagine, Hartley wouldn't say, but she had been left for dead in an alley."

Kathleen moaned.

Clarice's eyes locked on Mrs. Dooley.

"She was bad with pneumonia. The doctor said it nearly destroyed her lungs. Hartley took her home, but his mother refused her, so he moved her to the house on Archy Avenue."

Kathleen's face grew hot. "Grandmother!"

Mrs. Dooley's mouth quivered. "I helped, and we nursed her best as we could."

"What happened next?" Clarice said.

"Your father divorced her. The papers came to my house."

"I didn't know any of this," Clarice said.

Mrs. Dooley reached her hand out. "Your father was a hard man, dear. But I can see your goodness."

"He should have told me the truth."

Mrs. Dooley smiled. "And you have your mother's sense of responsibility, I see."

"My mother's been like a phantom. I didn't even know she'd died until I went to Albuquerque, and Kathleen told me."

"*My Laura* would have told you about each other. But then she came down with the consumption. One lung collapsed and after that, it was survival. "Hartley begged Father Michael to marry them. But with Hartley being a Lutheran and Laura divorced, the church wouldn't allow it."

"Father Michael's name is on my father and Laura's marriage certificate," Clarice said, "and my baptismal certificate." She glanced at Kathleen. "I found those in Father's trunk, too."

Mrs. Dooley nodded. "Then he must of felt something for her."

"How can love so easily turn to hate?" Kathleen said.

Clarice sat up straight. "That's what we're going to find out."

"The doctor said that Laura's only chance to live was to move her to a dry, arid climate. But Hartley didn't have enough money. I gave him what I had, but it wasn't near enough. He begged his mother for a loan, but she refused him. Poor Hartley sat in this room and cried like a baby."

Kathleen shook her head. "Grandmother, again."

"How did he get the money?" Clarice asked.

"Her doctor loaned it. He told Hartley he'd lost enough patients to the 'white plague' already." She crossed herself. "Dear God, I put Laura on that train, and I never saw her again."

Kathleen knelt and took Mrs. Dooley's gnarled hand in hers. "Thank you for loving our mother."

Mrs. Dooley blinked back tears. "She had some happiness, I think. Her music, Hartley, and you children. She didn't deserve the troubles she had."

Clarice's eyes blazed. "It was the men who controlled her! My father, Carlin, Hartley, Father Michael, and the monster who beat and raped her."

"And what about the God who took her?" Kathleen said.

CHAPTER THIRTY-ONE

That night at Felicia's, Kathleen pulled a photograph out of an envelope and handed it to Clarice. "This is the only picture I have of Mother. Dad took it right before we boarded the train to Albuquerque."

Kathleen watched carefully as Clarice held it up to the light. *What is she thinking, seeing a photograph of her mother for the first time?*

Clarice ran a hand through her hair. "I see where these blasted curls came from."

Blasted curls? Is that all she sees? Who is this sister I longed for? She chided herself. *What else could she say?* She looked at Clarice. "I'm sorry you thought she abandoned you. I'm not sure how I would have coped with that."

"I still can't shake it," Clarice said, then handed the photograph to Felicia.

"Your mother was pretty in her quiet sort of way."

"How did you two meet?" Clarice said.

"Your mother was ill at ease in your father's social circle, and so was I. We gravitated toward each other."

"I can't believe you were ill at ease anywhere."

"You didn't know me then."

Clarice looked at her for a long moment. "Do I know you now?"

"You'll have to decide," Felicia said. "But back then your father and mother attended the same social events that Robert and I did.

While those society snobs swirled martinis and flashed diamonds, your mother and I found a quiet corner to talk."

"You never told me," Clarice said, accusingly.

"You didn't want to hear. And I respected that, knowing that you might someday."

"I still don't." Clarice squeezed her eyes shut, sighed, then opened them. "Damn, I don't know anymore." She scratched her throat. "So, what were my mother and father like together?"

"She never discussed her marriage. But I picked up things, nuances. And I never thought they were very well-matched."

Clarice glanced around the living room. "Did my mother ever come here?"

Felicia shook her head.

"Did you ever go to our house?"

Felicia shook her head again.

"You were best friends, yet you never went to each other's homes? I don't get it."

"We met every Wednesday for lunch. Friday mornings we went to the park, so Clayton could play with other children."

"Was it because of my father?"

"Of course, it was your father, Clarice."

"So why won't you to tell me about you and him?"

Felicia looked at the curio cabinet. Blue and white colonial dolls in ball gowns frozen in porcelain curtsies. "There never really was a *me and him.* But I found your mother irresistible. We were very different, but we liked each other at once. I wish I could tell you more, but our friendship ended when she disappeared. And I never got over it either."

"Well, if you and our mother were such good friends, why didn't she go to you when Father kicked her out?"

Felicia touched her chest. "I've asked myself that same question. Maybe she was afraid your father might find out where she was, or maybe she didn't trust me after all." She shrugged. "I wish I knew."

Clarice eyed her warily. "You felt guilty. That's why you befriended me."

"That might be part of it, and yet I sensed your intelligence, your grit, even as a little girl." She hesitated. "And your goodness."

"Goodness? Ha! I was your project."

Felicia raised her eyebrows. "My project?"

Clarice's face puffed. "You were the only woman in my life, and I adored you. How could you use me like that?"

Kathleen stood, abruptly. "I wish I had been 'somebody's project.'" Her shoulders throbbed. Her chest felt heavy as lead, "I'm going to bed," she said, and she climbed the stairs to their room.

Lying on top of the spread, a collection of thoughts crowded her mind: Clarice's anger, Mrs. Dooley, Felicia. A flicker of pain shot through her forehead. *How could Felicia be such good friends with Clarice and invite me here? What was her motive?* And she recalled the wary look on her father's face when he handed her the cookbook. *"Be careful, Kats."*

She crept to the window seat where a full, newly risen moon cast gleaming light over Robert's carriage house. The same moon as in Albuquerque, the same stars, and yet . . . gazing at the moon, she felt the same wonder she'd felt when she found Clarice and Clayton's name in her mother's cookbook. *Clarice and I are talking at least.*

The door opened softly. Keys clinked, shoes dropped to the floor. Feeling a "presence" behind her, Kathleen smelled Evening in Paris. *Funny I never noticed before. Clarice never sits still long enough.* She scooted to the side, and Clarice sat next to her.

"Felicia and I talked," she said.

"I didn't realize how difficult this would be for you."

Clarice sniffed. "I was such a horrible child. I thought it was my fault my mother abandoned us. I tried to make it up to Clay and my father, but . . ."

"And I thought it was my fault. Mother got the tuberculosis while she was pregnant with me. I still carry the germ inside." Kathleen chewed on her bottom lip. "I used to pretend that she was just visiting Chicago; that she would be home soon, and Dad would be happy, and everything would be all right." She glanced at Clarice. "Foolish, huh? Especially because Dad remarried."

"No more foolish than me. Blaming myself, I mean."

Kathleen heaved a sigh. "Love, hate, both strong, yet so fragile."

Clarice let out a soft laugh. "I've hated you so long it's hard to get used to anything else. But I'm working on it."

"I feel different now," Kathleen said. She sat for a long while, listening to a still small voice easing her into the night. She felt Clarice scoot closer and hoped that she was listening too.

There was a knock on the door, and they both jumped.

Clarice got up and opened the door to Margaret.

"You have a telephone call, Miss Clarice."

"This late?"

"It's the police."

* * *

Clarice pulled into the alley behind the store and saw Clay standing next to her father. Behind them, a pudgy police officer and a leggy man in a baggy suit with his hat cocked to the side. *Like Laurel and Hardy.* She winced. *Only I don't think this is going to be funny.*

She approached the men and wrinkled her nose at the faint smell of garbage and long-dead skunk. A cat whooshed past her feet. Mice scattered.

"Why are *you* here?" Walter said, accusingly.

"Her name and number are on our records," the officer said.

Walter glared at the man in the baggy suit. "What is this, Braddock?"

"Sorry, Mr. Pruitt. He had already called her by the time I got here."

Walter's eyes narrowed. "You know how this works, Detective."

"What happened?" Clarice said.

The officer pointed to Clay. "We caught him carting off this box of clothes. An inside job usually. One of your employees leaves it outside like trash and another one carts it off."

"He's my brother," Clarice said. "He had my permission."

Walter bellowed. "Well, I'm the owner, and he didn't have mine."

"It's just merchandise that wouldn't sell," Clarice said.

Clay stepped forward. "I'm taking it to my friends on Randolph Street, so they won't freeze to death."

"That bunch of socialists!" Walter stomped. "Over my dead body."

"Will one of you please explain?" the officer said.

Detective Braddock took charge. "Mr. Pruitt owns this store—"

"But I run it," Clarice said. "And I put the merchandise out for Clay myself."

The officer addressed Walter. "We caught him red-handed, Mr. Pruitt; it looks like she's an accessory. What do you want to do?"

Walter glared at Clay. "It's time you learned what the real world is like."

"I know what the real world is like, Father, and unfortunately, it's a lot like you."

Walter drew back his hand, but Clarice stepped between them.

The officer waved his nightstick. "No family brawl here."

Walter pointed to Clay. "Arrest him. I'll deal with her myself."

The officer jerked Clay's hands behind his back.

Clarice winced at the cold click of the handcuffs.

He placed his hand on top of Clay's head, lowered him into the back seat of the patrol car, and drove off.

Detective Braddock shuffled his feet. "Sorry, Mr. Pruitt."

Walter lowered his brows. "Keep your officers in check, Braddock. I don't want any press. Understood?"

"Understood," Braddock said, and then strode back to an unmarked police car and drove off, too.

Clarice waved her finger in his face. "How could you put your own son in jail?"

"My *son* stole from me. And it seems that my in-charge daughter helped him."

"You haven't cared about the store in a long time, Father."

"From what I hear, neither do you."

Clarice snickered a laugh. "I'm taking some time off is all."

"Consorting with the likes of Bradford."

"What is it with you and Felicia? And now Robert, too?"

Walter's eyes glazed over. "Stay away from them, Clarice."

She gulped a breath. "I don't have anywhere else to stay. The tax office put a notice on the house. We have less than thirty days to pay the taxes."

"You and Clayton go home. I'll take care of the taxes."

"Clay won't go back to that house."

He mocked Clay, "He will when winter hits 'or he'll freeze to death.'"

"I can't afford to heat the damn house. And I can't keep it clean." Clarice's energy drained as if someone pulled a plug and it swirled down a drain hole. She braced herself on the side of her car and heard horns honking on State Street, the grinding clack of the Elevated, a cat screech. "The store is going under," she said. "I'll have to lay off more people."

"Then use the damn money I put into your account, and you won't have to."

"I won't use mob money."

Walter's mouth quivered. "It's the only way for now. After this depression is over, we can go back to the way we were and—"

"There is no 'going back' with the Mob, Father. You know that."

Walter's eyes narrowed into the icy look Clarice knew well. "Then get yourself back to the store, or you're fired."

A sharp pain shot like an arrow through her chest. "As your manager, Father? Or your daughter?"

"Your choice!" Walter snapped.

Heat flushed through her body. "You can fire me as your daughter. But you can't fire me as manager without board approval, which consists of me and you and Clay."

He turned, stomped to his car, and slammed the door shut.

Watching her father drive away, *out of my life?* she wondered. *How did it come to this?*

She unlocked the door, set the box of clothes on the floor, then walked the lonely aisles to her office and called Robert Bradford.

* * *

Clarice handed the legal papers to the jailer, and he gave her an appraising look. "What's a pretty girl like you doin' here?"

"Just release my brother, please."

The jailer pushed himself up with his arms and scooted his chair back. Dangling his key ring, he pointed to a wooden chair in the corner. "Wait here," he said, then opened the steel door and clanged it shut as voices echoed from the hallway.

The jailer came back and pushed the door shut behind him. "He says he ain't leaving, ma'am."

"Let me talk to him."

"It ain't pretty back there."

Clarice stood. "I'm not leaving until I talk to my brother."

He shrugged. "Your choice, lady, but stick close behind me and keep yer eyes straight ahead."

Clarice followed the jailer into a cacophony of male voices and clanging metal. Her nose stung from blended urine, mold, and rancid hair grease. Men whistled and yelled, "Hubba Hubba, girlie, girl, how 'bout—"

"Got a lady here!" The jailer shouted, then stopped at the last cell where Clay stood with his fingers wrapped around the bars.

"Who's paying my bail?" Clay said.

"Robert Bradford."

Clay's eyes blazed. "I won't accept Bradford's help."

The jailer rapped his fingers with his nightstick. "We've enough of yer ilk round here, wantin' a free meal and bed."

Clay's eyes hardened. "I won't go."

The jailer unlocked the cell, jerked Clay's arms behind his back and handcuffed him. Back in the front office, he took off the handcuffs and held his nightstick over Clays head. "Sign here," he ordered.

Clay shook his head.

The jailer yanked Clay's left arm and twisted it behind his back. "Be glad someone thought enough to get you outa' here."

Clay glared at Clarice as if she had broken out with a dreaded disease. The jailer tightened his grip. Clay grabbed a pen and signed the release papers.

Clarice followed him out to the sidewalk, and he turned on her. "I'd rather rot in jail than let Bradford bail me out."

"Robert only arranged your bail because I asked him to."

Clay pointed to the jail. "And those poor fellows will rot in their cells because they don't know anyone with money."

Clarice wiped her eyes. "You're the only one I care about."

Clay backed away from her. "Bradford buys influence just like Father does. You saw him with that detective. Bet he pays him off every week."

"Do you think Father would have you arrested if he hadn't lost his stores and the pride that went with them?"

"You're comparing Father's pride to people who lost everything? Who don't even know if they'll eat tomorrow."

Clarice pressed her hand over her stomach and thought back to the only full meal she'd had this week at Felicia's, the tax notice on their house, the people she'd laid off. "It's sad, Clay, of course it is, but Father—"

"I don't want to hear about Father."

"Then that leaves me to deal with this wreckage."

Clay's eyes softened. "I'm sorry, Sis."

"Then come out of hiding and help me."

Clay seemed to study her for a long moment. "Are you sure it's me who's hiding?"

Clarice took a quick breath. "We're going under, Clay. And when we do, all the people in the store will be out on the street like you. Is that what you want?"

Clay bent down and kissed her forehead. "You'll figure it out, Sis. You always do."

Clarice reached into her pocket and handed him her business card. "Keep this, damn it. The Bradford's home telephone number is on the back." She looked deep into his eyes. "And don't you *ever* lose touch with me."

Clay dropped her card in his pocket and gave her his lopsided smile. "Come see me, Sis."

Watching Clay walk away, her eyes glistened. *I've lost Father, and now maybe Clay. Is the store next?* She wiped her cheeks. *What do I have to live for?*

CHAPTER THIRTY-TWO

"Why didn't Clarice come back last night?" Kathleen said.

"She always sleeps at her office when there's a problem at the store."

"The police called her late last night. How can we find out what happened?"

Felicia set a plate of cinnamon rolls on the kitchen table, and then sat across from her. "She called Robert early this morning. He said something about bail money, and then he left, too. It had to do with Clay, I think."

Kathleen spread a pat of butter on her roll and watched it melt down the sides. "Every time I mention Clay, Clarice brushes me off. It's like she's hiding him. Is something wrong?"

"I'm not sure," Felicia said. "I know Clay had a tough time adjusting to school, so Walter hired a tutor to teach him at home. According to Clarice, he rarely left the house after that. And now I gather he's at that homeless place in Grant Park. Hooverville, they call it."

"I saw some of those shanty towns on my train trip here. Albuquerque has some homeless, but things aren't so bad there."

"Why is that, do you think?"

"Albuquerque advertised in northern newspapers to, 'Bring us your Sick', meaning those with tuberculosis like my mother." She rolled her eyes. "They marketed our sunshine. Anyway, bunches of sick people came, so there are hospitals and sanitariums where people can work, plus the railroad. Dad worked at a sanitarium when we first moved there so Mother could get care. But he said her only treatment was lying on a cot on the roof all day, alongside the other patients. Lots of houses still have screen porches for their tuberculars they call them."

"Didn't they spread their diseases?" Felicia said.

"Lots of Indians died because they didn't have immunity. Some Spanish and white people died, too. When Mother's time came, Dad brought her home to die." She stared at her limp hands. *Why does this still hurt?*

"How dreadful that must have been . . . for all of you."

"My dad's still in mourning," Kathleen said. "He'll never get over her loss." Finally taking a bite of her cinnamon roll, she washed it down with coffee. "Mother was pregnant with me when she got sick. The doctor said I'll always carry the germ inside me, but I probably won't ever get tuberculosis or give it to anyone else." She shrugged. "Albuquerque's sunshine cured some, but not my mother." She took a sip of her coffee. "Speaking about diseases, Mrs. Dooley mentioned Clay was sickly."

Felicia looked up for a moment as if in thought. "I don't recall Clay being sick," she said. "But Laura always seemed protective of him, much like Clarice is now."

"Protect him from what?"

"Clarice rarely talks about Clay. He, well, he's sort of a mystery."

Kathleen took another sip of coffee, scooted her chair back, and walked to the window. Shriveled brown leaves clung to a weathered trellis by the side of Robert's carriage house. Barren branches of an elm tree reached toward the murky sky. *Why won't Clarice let me see Clay? Is she afraid of him, like I 'm afraid of Henry? Should I just leave him alone?*

A reddish-brown squirrel hopped across the grass, stood, wiggled his nose in the air, and then scurried off in a different direction. *So, Clay's a mystery, huh?* She clasped her hands together. *I came to find my sister and my brother . . . and I'm not going to leave until I find Clay, too.*

* * *

Early the next morning, Kathleen stepped off the Elevated, wrapped Felicia's blue, wool coat tightly around her, and then headed south toward Randolph Street. Morning throbbed with people pushing past her, horns honking, the rumbling clack of the Elevated blending with mournful whistles from steamers on the lake. *Chicago's always so boisterous while Albuquerque barely stays awake.* She quickened her pace.

As she entered the outskirts of the Hooverville, she rubbed her gloved hands together. "And now to find Clay!" She walked past shacks made of tarpaper, wooden crates, scraps of cloth, and tin cans hammered flat. Farther in, some were made of wood, assorted bricks, and sheet iron wired together. Men sat with their heads down while mothers hugged babies to their breasts.

She walked up to an old woman with yellow, gray hair, bent over a stubby broom, sweeping her yard. "Do you know Clay Pruitt?" she asked.

"What does he look like?" she muttered.

"He has blondish hair, and he's tall, I think, I'm not sure."

The woman gave her a puzzled look. "Don't know nobody like that." She turned, dragged her broom behind her, and went into her cardboard shack.

Kathleen looked up at the gunmetal sky and bit her lip. *How am I going to find Clay when I don't even know what he looks like? How could I be so dumb?* She glanced toward the woman's shack. *But if I don't, my quest to find my brother will fail.*

Deeper into Hooverville, she passed human packrats dragging scraps of lumber and tin, cardboard boxes, canvas, and burlap sacks. Rats darted between trash boxes while children played tag. She passed a puddle that reeked of feces and urine and wrinkled her nose. *What kind of person could Clay be to live like this?*

She walked up to an old man dressed in overalls and a red flannel shirt. A knit cap covered his head. "Please, sir, I'm looking for Clay Pruitt."

He waved her away. "Don't know him. Wouldn't tell you if I did."

Families hovered around fires roaring in oil drums cut in half. Little girls clung to their mothers. Teenaged boys played marbles with rocks.

No one knew Clay Pruitt.

She collapsed on an abandoned apple crate.

A young man with red hair wearing a mud-sloshed trench coat touched her shoulder, and she jumped.

He stared at Felicia's coat. "Pardon me, ma'am, but what are you doing here?"

Tears dripped down her cheeks. "I'm trying to find my brother," she said.

He reached into his jacket pocket and handed her a torn sheet which reeked with sour food and sweat.

Kathleen wiped her cheeks.

He touched her shoulder again. "You need to get out of here before dark hits."

"But I've got to find him," she said, and then stared at his bearded chin, freckled nose and faded blue eyes. "He's about your age, I think. His name is Clayton Pruitt."

"People hide out here, ma'am. Maybe you should leave him alone."

"But I've come so far to find him."

After a long moment, "Ask the Mayor" he said, then pointed west. "Go two blocks past Depression Avenue, right on Prosperity Street, and it's the third house on the left. There's a sign in his yard."

"Thank you, oh, thank you," Kathleen said and handed him his handkerchief.

The mayor's house was an assortment of wooden crates, planks, and battered sides of an old railroad car with faded serial numbers still visible. Tin cans, crushed cigar butts, and assorted garbage littered a patch of brown grass and weeds. A large wooden box with "U.S. Mail" painted on the front, stood to the side.

Kathleen knocked on the railroad car door. It slid open, and a thin man in a dusty blue suit and a red-striped tie stepped out. "Are you the mayor?" she said.

He reared his shoulders. "I am the mayor, indeed. What can I do for you?"

"I'm looking for Clay Pruitt."

He straightened his tie. "Well, maybe he's here, lady, and maybe he's not. Who wants to know?"

"I'm his sister," Kathleen said and sighed with relief.

He squinted his eyes. "Sister, huh? Well, I've seen his sister, and you're not her."

"I'm Kathleen, his other sister. He doesn't know me yet, uh, it's a long story, but I've come all the way from Albuquerque to see him."

"Albuqu . . . what?" The mayor's voice boomed. "Where's that?" He leaned closer and slowly appraised her again, lingering on the one piece of fine jewelry she owned, her small gold wristwatch. "Yer quite a dish, you know."

Kathleen backed away from him.

"Don't be afraid, young lady. I don't bite." He walked closer and looked her up and down. "Well, yer Clayton's sister, by gosh! You look just like him."

Warmth wrapped Kathleen like a blanket. Her heart beat faster.

"I hear he used to be rich," the mayor said. "He has that air about him, so I put him in charge of clothes procurement. We're gathering warm clothes before the snow hits hard."

"Please," Kathleen's voice quavered. "I must find him."

The mayor held up his open palm. "If you're his sister, then there's things you need to know about him."

Recognizing his need for approval, Kathleen sighed. *Maybe I'll get more information if I let him talk.* She tilted her head to the side. "Why do they call you mayor?" she said. "Isn't Mr. Cermak mayor of Chicago?"

"Well, you can be sure that *Mayor Cermak* and his cronies don't bother with this place, except to try and get rid of us. So, we formed our own government. Some say it's sort of communistic 'cause we pool resources, look after each other's children, and share what we have. He snickered. "Ha! Construction has stopped everywhere else in Chicago, but it's boomin' here."

He waved his finger as if giving a lecture at City Hall. "We have our own water and sanitation committees, and our own commissary. When food gets low, we check hotels and restaurants for their leavings, and then sort through their trash for those who can't make it to the soup lines and churches. A few bright ones like your brother scavenge anything they can find. Without them, our people might starve to death."

Kathleen glanced at her watch. "Excuse me, Mr. Mayor, it's getting late and I need to find Clay."

"Hold yer horses, young lady." He gazed at the mailbox. "Me, I put in nearly twenty years as brakeman at Chicago and Milwaukee Railroad, and then got laid off. Moved my family in with the next-door neighbor, but then he lost his job, and we were all out on the street. My wife took the kids to her mother's in Detroit, but things are bad there, too." His eyes hardened. "I always took care of my family, until this damned depression hit." He shuffled his feet. "Lots of bitter feelings here."

Kathleen lowered her eyes. "I wish I could help."

"Well, you've helped by listening," he said. "Now, for Clayton." He pointed west. "Go two blocks that way, right on Hoover Heights, and left at Hard Times Street. Find the building that looks like a barn, and his place is three spaces down on the right."

Following the mayor's directions, Kathleen stood in front of a tarpaper shack with a green blanket draped over the doorway. The yard was swept clean. Crates and boxes of assorted sizes were stacked neatly to one side. Black socks and a long-sleeved blue shirt hung from a clothesline strung between two bushes. She thought of the young man in the trench coat. "People hide out here . . . maybe you should leave him alone." She twisted her watch. *What if he doesn't want to see me?*

The green blanket parted and a young man with copper hair stepped out. He held a book in his hand.

Kathleen glanced toward the street. *What if he hates me like Clarice did.* Her chest felt tight as a wound top ready to twirl as she watched the young man walking toward her. His face seemed to shine. *Dear God. He does look like me.*

He stopped in front of her, looked deep into her eyes, and reached for her hand. "I'm Clay," he said, and then nodded toward the wooden crates by the side of his house. "Come sit so we can talk."

CHAPTER THIRTY-THREE

Father Michael sat in his office and pulled what looked like his last string of white hair over his brown speckled head.

Clarice watched him with amusement. *He looks like Humpty Dumpty in a black cassock.*

An open Bible lay on a regal pedestal behind him. A crystal pitcher and glasses sat on a battered wooden table at his side. Piles of papers spilled over his desk, along with books and charts and Hershey Bar wrappers. Clarice shook her head imperceptibly. *No wonder he's so round.*

He tapped his fingers on his desk.

Clarice noted his manicured fingernails. *Strange for a man, a priest anyway.*

"So, you're Laura Pruitt's daughters," he said, then looked at Kathleen. "Or shall I say Laura Howe?"

"Kathleen came all the way from Albuquerque," Clarice said. "You were our mother's priest, we understand, and we're hoping you can answer some questions."

Father Michael took off his spectacles and wedged them on his desk between candy wrappers. "What kind of questions?"

Clarice shifted to the edge of her chair. "My father told me she abandoned us when I was a baby. In his eyes, she was a demon."

"And according to my father, she was practically a saint," Kathleen said.

Father Michael rubbed his chin. "It was such a long time ago. I don't know if I can help you girls."

Clarice's eyes begged him. "You may be our last chance, Father."

He twisted his ring. "I have served the Bridgeport Parish for over thirty years." He picked up his spectacles and settled them back over his nose. "I confess I had to look up some things after you called." He moved a pile of papers aside and thumbed through a thick, black leather book edged in gold. "I baptized you, Clarice, and Clayton too. It's right here."

Clarice got up and peered over his thick shoulders at her and Clayton's name in flourished black script along with their mother and fathers'. Her eyes stung. *We were a family once.*

Father Michael turned the pages again and turned the book toward Kathleen. "You and Henry were baptized together," he said. "Your mother was sickly, I remember." And with a note of surprise in his voice, "I baptized all four of Laura's children."

Back in her chair, Clarice said, "You knew her well then."

"I performed Laura's marriage to your father."

"Did they attend mass here? My father and mother, I mean."

"I know Laura came and brought you and Clayton with her. I Don't recall seeing your father there." He shifted his massive body, and the chair squeaked in protest. "After Laura, uh, left, I called on your father about your and Clayton's religious education, but he told me he would take care of your education himself." He paused. "I had never been to that house before. It was, well, a bit imposing."

"I still live there, or I did," Clarice said.

"My Dad told me that you refused to marry them," Kathleen said.

Father Michael cleared his throat. "The divorce from Pruitt, of course. After that, Laura could not marry in the church and could not receive the sacraments. But she did come to mass."

Kathleen raised her eyebrows. "My mother could not receive the sacraments, yet you baptized me and Henry?"

Father Michael stiffened. "The Church does not penalize children for their parents' sin."

Clarice clapped her hands together. "Well, whoopee for the church," she said, which earned her a stern look from Father Michael.

Kathleen's face puffed. "A priest finally married them by Mother's deathbed."

"That may have saved her soul," he said. "But the church holds to its beliefs all the same."

Clarice shot up. "It's the same God, isn't it?"

Father Michael waved her down in nervous dismissal, "Of course, of course." He cleared his throat again. "Now, how I can help you ladies?"

"We went to see Mrs. Dooley last week," Kathleen said. "She filled us in on some of what happened to our mother. We're hoping you can tell us more."

His eyes brightened. "Well, if anyone knew about Laura, it was Delora Dooley. The woman is a true saint. She gave free piano lessons to some our neediest choirboys."

"She's quite frail now," Kathleen said, "you should call on her."

He rubbed his arms. "These old bones . . ."

"That's what Mrs. Dooley said. About herself, I mean."

Father Michael nodded. "I'm sorry."

Why do priests always nod their heads? Clarice wondered.

"I didn't know Clarice and Clay existed until I found their names and birthdates recorded in Mother's cookbook. Like they were a big secret or something."

"Secrets?" His eyes shot up to the ceiling then back to Kathleen. "Yes, I'd say your family was loaded with them."

Clarice leaned across his desk. "Then help us, Father."

Father Michael made a steeple with his hands. "I cannot reveal what was told to me in the confessional." His hands collapsed. "But, some of my parishioners have said things through the years. And well, because of my interest in Laura, I've asked questions."

"I know my father sent her away," Clarice said. "I'm hoping you will tell us why."

Father Michael gave her a stern look. "That was between Laura, your father, and God, my child."

Clarice pressed her lips tightly together. *The damned confessional.* "Then tell us what you can, please."

He picked up a crystal pitcher, poured a glass of water, and took a slow sip. "Laura's father was James Slattery."

"Slattery?" Kathleen rolled the word on her tongue. "I never knew what Mother's middle initial, S, stood for."

Father Michael eyes brightened. "It was Slattery, for sure, and Laura's mother was Irene."

"Our middle names," Kathleen and Clarice both said.

He nodded again. "Good Irish names." He frowned and looked back and forth between them. "But you girls don't even know your grandparents' names?"

"Nor anything about them," Clarice said.

"Well, I can tell you that her father, James, labored on the killing floors at the stockyard amidst the stench and shrieks of animals being slaughtered."

Clarice's stomach churned. "It sounds awful."

"He never got the smell out. But James being a new immigrant, it was the only job he could get."

Clarice nodded. "Then he did what he had to do to survive. I respect that."

"And then Laura was born." His words sang like a melody. "If a father ever loved a daughter, well, James adored Laura from the moment he saw her. With her dark curly hair and blue eyes, she was the spittin' image of him." He looked at Clarice as if for the first time. "You look some like her."

Clarice twirled her finger around a loose curl. *People keep saying that.* "Go on, please, Father."

"But then James lost his job. He got another job at the lime plant, but he lost it too. Irene, poor woman, had to get help from St. Vincent de Paul Ministry to survive." He shifted in his chair. "She, well, she wasn't equipped to deal with things after James uh . . ." he twisted his hands.

"Uh, what?" Clarice said.

"James, well, he just left. Disappeared from their life. That's all I can tell you."

Heat flushed through Clarice's body. "The confessional again, Father?" She stood, then paced across the room and back. "James and Irene, and our mother, Laura, are all gone. So, you can tell us now."

He stiffened. "Anything told a priest in the confessional booth is secret forever, even if the person is long dead."

Clarice opened her palms in the air. "Well, that's convenient." She sat down. "All right then, you said you married my father to my mother, so you must have known something about them."

"Well, I didn't realize he was Red Roark's boy when I performed the ceremony."

"Red Roark?" Clarice said, puzzled.

"He's your father's father; your grandfather."

"I don't have a grandfather," Clarice's words were crisp, cold.

"You asked me to tell you, child."

Clarice's mouth quivered. "Then go on please, Father."

He took another sip of water, then pulled a white monogramed handkerchief out of his desk and dabbed his mouth. "Well, your grandfather, Red, got shot down on the street along with two of his men. Betrayed by one of his own everybody said." He frowned. "It seemed that Red got mixed up with the Irish Mob and the policy racket. I think that's what they call numbers now." He tapped his fingers on the desk. "It happened a lot back then. Still does with that sort of thing."

Clarice stiffened. *Can I believe anything this old priest says?* "My father is German," she said. "There is no Irish in him."

"Oh, there's Irish, all right. He grew up in Bridgeport as Patrick Roark, lived in the flats on . . ." he stopped. "You didn't know this, child?"

Kathleen touched Clarice's shoulder. "Pardon me, Father, but would she look like that if she knew?"

"Would you like a drink of water?" he said.

Clarice glared at him. "Just tell us what else you know."

He rubbed his forehead. "I only know some of it," he said. "The rest I have been told or surmised."

Kathleen leaned toward him. "Tell her the truth please, Father, if she's ever to have any peace about her parents."

He pinched his wobbling throat. "Well, young Patrick was just sixteen when his father was killed."

"Who's Patrick?" Clarice said.

Father Michael eyes were stern, chastising. "Your father's name was Patrick Roark, the son of Red Roark and Paulette. They called him 'Red' because of his carrot colored hair, I suppose. I will have to look up his given name. But young Patrick was black Irish like his mother."

A giant fist squeezed Clarice's throat. She could not believe she was sitting here listening to this old man with his preposterous tale and yet . . . she searched into his face, *priests don't lie.* The tight little office became a barred cage. Her heart pounded as she gripped the sides of her chair.

"I'm confused," Kathleen said. "First you told us James Slattery was our grandfather, and he just, well, disappeared. Now you're saying this man, Red Roark, was our grandfather."

"I'm talking about Clarice's family now. Red was her grandfather on her father's side."

"Tell me the rest," Clarice demanded. "All of it!"

Father Michael cleared his throat, took another sip of water. "Like I told you, Red got shot down on the street along with his two men. Some said it was the Irish Mob, others said it was robbery, no one knows for sure. But Patrick was only sixteen when his father died. And his mother, poor Paulette, was frail and sickly. Patrick was sickly too, as I recall."

"Let me get this straight," Clarice said. "Who exactly is Patrick Roark?"

"Why, Patrick is your father, child."

Clarice voice quavered. "You had better explain this to me, Father, because I don't understand it."

He dabbed his handkerchief in his water glass and patted his forehead. "Well, Patrick's mother died shortly after Red got killed.

I performed her last rites, and that made Patrick an orphan. He took off shortly after." He scratched his chin. "Most figured he went out west like so many others did back then. But someone told me he came home five, maybe six or so years later all filled out a nice-looking man. Yet I did not recognize him when I married him to your mother. One of my parishioners told me later who he was."

Clarice's eyes burned. "That can't be right!"

"I didn't believe it myself. I thought I had committed fraud by marrying them, but I checked court records, and your father had legally changed his name from Patrick Roark to Walter Pruitt."

Clarice's heart thumped. She crossed her hands over her chest as if to contain it. "Why would he do that?"

"Because of the Irish killing his father, I suppose. Perhaps he felt he might be in some danger."

"He used to belittle the Irish," Clarice said. "Yet, our servants, our cook, and my governess were Irish."

"And our mother," Kathleen said.

"We seek out the familiar," Father said. "It's basic human nature."

Clarice buried her face in her hands.

Father Michael pushed himself up, walked around his desk, and placed his hands on Clarice's shoulder. "You're upset, child. Let us seek solace in God's sanctuary."

Clarice brushed his hands away. "You just told me my father isn't really my father, that he is someone named, Patrick Roark, and you want me to seek solace in your sanctuary. I don't believe this!"

"Why would he lie to his own daughter?" Kathleen said. "Deny her of who she is?"

Silence fell over them like a tombstone. The outside church bell rang as if to announce their new-found ignorance.

"We came here to find out about our mother," Clarice said. "And other than some tripe about my father changing his name, and my grandfather in the Mob, you haven't helped us at all."

Father Michael looked at the ceiling. Hands trembling, he crossed himself. "Father in heaven . . . what have I done?"

Clarice shot up. "Don't 'Father in heaven' me, Father. I will take care of this matter myself!"

CHAPTER THIRTY-FOUR

"This place is a dump." Clarice said as she plopped in a corner booth across from Kathleen.

Muffled voices blended in Kathleen's head along with a Cab Calloway song from the jukebox.

"But then Manny's Diner has always been a dump," Clarice added. "And that's just how I feel. Dumped on."

"We learned more than we bargained for from Father Michael this morning."

"Yeah. Like my father is an imposter, and my grandfather was in the Mob, maybe even killed by the Mob. And our grandfather, James," Clarice snapped her fingers, "he just poof . . . disappeared. Hell, what else went wrong in this family?"

Kathleen rubbed her temples. "No wonder everything was so secret."

"You don't like this either, do you?"

"I used to get angry at my dad for not telling me about my mother, but at least I knew who *he* was."

"Don't count on it." Clarice's said. "Don't count on anything as far as our fathers are concerned." She ran her hands through her hair.

"Funny how we still don't know much about our mother, but we're sure learning about our fathers. Yours at least."

"And I wonder what Felicia knows?"

Kathleen bit her lower lip. "Would it make any difference to you?"

"I've always felt there was something between Felicia and my father. But if she knew about him being that, that Patrick Roark and kept it secret, well . . ." she banged her fist on the table. "I wish we had never gone to see that ridiculous priest!"

The waiter rushed to their booth. "What's wrong? Can I get you something?"

"No," Clarice snapped. "I mean, yes. Bring me a bowl of French onion soup." She nodded toward Kathleen. "Bring her one, too."

The clear soup soothed Kathleen's scratchy throat. Swirling the cheese with her spoon, her stomach tightened. *Secrets? Should I tell her that I found Clay?*

Ignoring her soup, Clarice's eyes darted to the jukebox, to a woman at the next table, to the scurrying waiter, to the ceiling, and then back to Kathleen.

With that restless look on her face, Kathleen flinched. *I won't tell her now.*

Clarice rubbed her neck. "I can't let Father get away with this."

Kathleen twisted her watch. *She's planning something; scheming to get her way.*

Clarice stared at her soup, picked up her spoon, waved it the air. "By damn, I've got it!"

"Got what?"

Beads of sweat popped on Clarice's forehead. "How to get what I want!" She fumbled through her purse, pulled out a twenty-dollar bill, and pressed it into Kathleen's palm. "This will take care of lunch and enough for a taxi back to Felicia's."

"But, but where are *you* going?"

"To see my lawyer," Clarice said, "and then to see Clay."

Kathleen blinked. "About Clay," she said, "there's something I need to tell you."

Clarice threw her open her palm in the air. "Not now." Eyes gleaming, she swiped her napkin over her face, dropped it on the table and picked up her purse. "I've got to go."

* * *

Two days later, Clarice sat across the warehouse desk from Walter with fire in her eyes. "You betrayed me, Father!"

Walter's matted hair lay in greasy strings, his chin a mass of stubbles, grease stains and ink splattered across his wrinkled white shirt.

Having rehearsed what she'd wanted to say, Clarice was taken aback by his ragged appearance. "What's happened to you, Father?"

Walter's face puffed. "You come in here accusing, and you ask *me* what's wrong!"

Clarice looked at the papers strewn over his battered desk, to the forms pinned haphazardly to a cork board, his Alaska picture, books scattered over a table and thought of his home office lined with bookshelves. She jerked. *But he never read them. They were only for show . . . why didn't I see that?*

Walter cleared his throat. "What do you want, Clarice?"

"The truth."

"Truth about what?"

"About why you turned my mother out, and . . ."

"You've been asking around town about me, so I figured you know by now."

"I want to hear it from you, Father."

"And if I won't tell you?"

"Then I will do everything in my power to ruin you."

"Your power? Hell, you're just a twenty-two-year-old spoiled brat."

Clarice rubbed her temples. *Why has it come to this?* Then suddenly, she knew. *Everything about him is false.* "I went to Albuquerque," she said. "I found the girl, the one who put the classified ad in the paper."

He banged his fist on his desk. "Damn that Felicia. She wouldn't leave it alone."

Boiling inside, "Why didn't you tell me my mother died?" she said.

Walter shrugged. "It seemed easier not to."

"You let us suffer to make it easier on you?"

"What would you know about suffering? I've given you everything money could buy."

"While you deprived us of our mother!"

Walter shrugged again. "I thought it best."

"Best for you, you mean." She gripped the arms of her chair and raised halfway out of her seat. "And why didn't you tell us we have a half sister and brother?"

"A brother?" Walter snickered. "Isn't one lunatic brother enough for you?"

Her face burned. "You know about Henry?"

Walter put his hand behind his neck. "I've followed that family. The lame father who works at the Santa Fe railyard and barely gets by, the pitiful girl, and that brother in the lunatic asylum." His mouth twisted. "Clayton will be in an asylum too, someday. Just you wait."

"You're the one who treated Clay like he didn't exist!"

Beads of sweat popped on his forehead. "It was your mother's fault. She brought tainted blood into this family!"

"Tainted blood?" Clarice's voice quavered.

"Laura told me that her father died when she was a young girl, and I believed her. But then someone tipped me off that she and her mother hid him away at Cook County Insane Asylum." His eyes looked like dark caves, "I saw the man myself. He was a raving maniac! Your mother denied it of course, but . . ."

Clarice's head exploded. "That's it?" She steadied her hands on the sides of her chair. "That's why you sent my mother away?"

Walter's face contorted like he'd swallowed a cockroach. "I couldn't let her be around you children after that."

"Was it catching, Father?"

Walter's voice shook. "She had already ruined Clayton. She would have ruined you, too, if I hadn't got rid of her. Someday you'll thank me."

"Mrs. Dooley told us what happened to Mother after you kicked her out. How she tried to see us. But you and your lawyers blocked her."

Walter smirked. "Mrs. Dooley, huh? A simpleton and a lousy piano teacher."

Clarice felt like she was falling into a swirling hole and might never come back. She gripped the sides of her chair again and realized she did not want to come back. Barely recognizing her own voice, she said, "If you hadn't sent my mother away, she might not have got the consumption. She might not have died."

Walter's face turned ashen. His lips trembled. "She never loved me. She, she never made me feel like a man."

Instantly, Clarice's head cleared. "You used her sick father as an excuse when it was just your manhood at stake?"

Walter slumped. "I had no choice."

"You had choices, Father. You chose to become German. You chose to change your name from Patrick Roark to Walter Pruitt, you chose—"

"What the hell!" Walter shot up.

Clarice stood and faced him. "Oh, I know who you are, Mr. Patrick Roark. I know you're Irish, not German. I know your red-headed father got gunned down by the Mob. I know you . . ."

Walter dropped back onto his chair. "So . . . that's out, too."

Clarice hovered over him. "My wonderful father. My prince. The man I modeled myself after. The man I adored." She sucked in a deep breath. "You're a liar and a fraud, Father. You put our business in jeopardy with your mob money." She took another quick breath and let it out slowly. Her face tingled. "I see . . . the Mob . . . your father in the Mob. It makes sense now. You must have *tainted* blood too!"

"Good Lord, Clarice. I've made mistakes, yes. But I saw no way to remedy them."

"Well, I have a remedy!" Clarice pulled legal papers out of her briefcase and shoved them across his desk.

Walter's eyes darted from Clarice to the papers then back to Clarice. "What is this?"

"You keep the house, this warehouse, what properties you have left, and your liquor dealings with the Mob." Her hands trembled. "I keep the State Street store."

Walter glanced at the papers and let out a soft laugh. "What makes you think you can do that?"

Clarice gave him a wicked smile. "I own two thirds of the company now. Clay signed his shares over to me."

Walter brushed the papers aside. "Like hell you do!"

Clarice retrieved the papers and thrust them back in front of him. "The one on top is your resignation letter as company president. The next one relinquishes your third of the store to me."

Walter looked at the papers as if they were poison. "What makes you think I would sign something like that!"

"Sign, Father. Or I'll see that the right people in this town know exactly who you are and all the things you are involved in."

Walter's face turned ashen. "It's Bradford, isn't it? That trip you made to Los Angeles."

Clarice cocked her head. "Do you think Robert is stupid enough to—"

"Everything was fine until you saw that damn classified ad in the *Tribune*. That was Felicia's doing."

"I'm glad she did, or I wouldn't know why you sent my mother away. Or that you, dear Father, are an impostor!"

Walter flexed his hands. "We had a good thing going, Clarice. And then you—you and your damned curiosity just couldn't leave it alone."

"And now I know why." Clarice picked up the fountain pen. "Sign, Father. Our partnership will be terminated, and your secrets will be safe."

Walter's face contorted like twisted steel. "Well, you won't want to see your precious Felicia again when I tell you *her secrets*. Just ask her about Annie Parsons . . ."

Clarice stared at the stranger across from her. *How could I have defined myself by him? How could I have worshiped him?* She dipped the pen into the inkwell and handed it to Walter.

He lamely scrawled his name as directed.

She waved the papers until the ink dried. "Thank you, Father. You finally made the right choice."

Walter's eyes shined like glass marbles. "And what are you going to do when your sons turn out to be lunatics like your two brothers?"

Clarice looked him in the eye. "I'll love them, Father." She shoved the papers into her briefcase and started toward the door.

"Clarice . . ." Walter's voice trembled.

She turned around. "Yes, Father?"

"I only wanted what was best for you."

She looked at him for a long moment. "Somehow, I believe you, Father. But I'll be deciding that from now on."

CHAPTER THIRTY-FIVE

Clarice gripped the steering wheel until her knuckles turned white. "I am so angry at Father, there's simply no way I'll go back to Felicia's right now." Her eyes locked straight ahead. "I can't believe he put our mother out because her father was in the insane asylum. As if it were her fault."

"Or her father's," Kathleen said.

Driving slowly past grand houses with porte-cocheres and limousines, Clarice shot her a knowing look. "He treated Clay as if he were a lunatic, too. Damn him!"

"When Henry went to the asylum, my dad blamed himself for not being a good enough father."

"It wasn't your dad's fault. And it wasn't Henry's or our grandfather, James's, fault either. I think it's a sickness just like any other sickness. Those mighty doctors will figure that out someday."

Kathleen's stomach tightened. "I think about Henry all the time. I guess I blamed myself some, too."

Clarice slowed down and pointed to a four-story sprawling mansion. "This is where my father really wanted to live. He used to put down Marshall Field, the Palmers, McCormick and the rest, but he longed to be right up here with them."

"I've never even seen houses like these."

"Our house is pretty big," Clarice said, "but nothing like this." She let out a soft laugh. "But Father was right about one thing. I did have everything money could buy."

"My dad didn't have much money, but he had a garden, and we never went hungry. My happiest times were working beside him picking peas and pulling weeds."

"And my happiest times were dressing manikins, going over sales reports, and walking the stores with my father late at night."

Kathleen smiled. "Funny, how different our lives have been."

"We don't have much control after all. If Father hadn't turned our mother out, then you and Henry wouldn't exist, and I wouldn't have known any of this. I wouldn't have known you."

Kathleen glanced at Clarice and caught her smile.

"Me and my what ifs. Father said it was my damned curiosity that stirred this up." She glanced at Kathleen. "But it was you who wouldn't let it go."

Warmth flowed through Kathleen's chest. "From the moment I saw your names in her cookbook, I knew I had to find you."

"And what if you hadn't?"

Kathleen smiled again. "I would have missed out on all this."

Clarice threw back her head. "You're pretty gutsy, you know. Moving out on your own; coming to Chicago to find me. And then I acted so wretched."

"That you did," Kathleen said. "But I could see you were hurting like me."

"You're pretty smart for a hick kid from Albuquerque." She drove a few more blocks then turned off the avenue onto the highway. A road sign pointed north to Niles Center, and she glanced at Kathleen. "Shall we?"

"Henry and I tromped all over that cemetery once, but we couldn't find Mother's grave."

Clarice kept her eyes on the road. "We'll find it this time. We must, or we'll never be free of our anger." She looked in the rearview mirror, steered to the right, and then turned north toward Niles Center.

* * *

The setting sun cast a soft glow as they stood over the mottled grave marker. "Poor Laura," Clarice said, "buried with all of her secrets and regrets." She fumbled through her purse, pulled out her handkerchief, and wiped the stone marker. "I can't stand all this dirt on her headstone. Let's clean it; make it right, so others will know our mother is here."

Kathleen pulled her nail file out of her purse, knelt beside her, and dug lichen out of the inscriptions.

Long minutes later, their hands smeared with dirt and moss, they stood, and Kathleen read the inscription. "Laura Slattery Pruitt Howe." She looked at Clarice. "Dad put all her names on her marker to include you and Clay."

Clarice gave her a sharp look. "You can't be sure of that."

"I'm sure," Kathleen said. "After Mother died, Dad went to your house to tell you and Clay, but your father wouldn't let him in, said he would tell you himself."

"He never did. But Clay sneaked downstairs the night your dad came and heard it all. He never told me until I got back from Albuquerque after seeing you."

"What if he had told you back then?"

Clarice heaved a sigh. "Maybe I wouldn't have been such a brat. Maybe I would have been kinder to you." She shrugged. "Who knows?"

Kathleen knelt again and traced her mother's date of birth with her fingers. "August 28, 1888. Funny, I never knew her birthday."

"Died January 10, 1915," Clarice read. "She was only twenty-seven."

Kathleen's chest tightened. Her eyes glued to her mother's inscription. Her hands trembled. All over, she trembled.

Clarice knelt and braced her arm. "What's wrong?"

"I found her."

Clarice steadied her onto the ground in front of the marker. "Found who?"

Kathleen pressed her hands to the sides of her face. Her voice quavered. "Every morning when I woke up, I ran to Mother's bed and said, 'wake up, Mama, wake up.'" Then, as if outside of herself, she heard her own panicked voice as a four-year-old. "That morning I ran to her bed, and her face looked like wet sand. I pressed my ear on her chest and I couldn't hear the gurgles. I screamed for Dad, and he came and put his hand over her cheeks, then put his fingers on her wrist." She looked at Clarice. "Dear God. I found her dead!"

"And you just now remembered it?" Clarice said.

She rubbed her fingers over the middle of her forehead. "Somehow, I knew, but I couldn't remember." She grasped Clarice's arm. "Now I want to remember it." She stared at the grave marker. Sweat spilled down her forehead as she wiped her brow with the back of her hand. "It's like that dirt was covering her memory, and then we cleared it. Perhaps us being together like this, seeing her grave for the first time, I don't know." She squeezed Clarice's hand. "I'm sorry."

"I'm the one who's sorry," Clarice said. "When I saw your names in the obituary. I thought Mother was living happily in Albuquerque with you." She stared at the grave. "I was bitter and angry. And wrong."

Kathleen blinked back tears. "And I made you and Clay into my fantasy family."

The setting sun cast its last glow as slivers of light danced on wind touched leaves. "This is too strange," Kathleen said. "Too weird."

Clarice breathed a long sigh. "How could you keep it buried for so long?"

"All these years, and I didn't know . . ." She crossed her arms over her chest. Her heart fluttered, trembled, and then resumed its imperceptible beat, beat, beat. "I think I needed to feel safe first."

CHAPTER THIRTY-SIX

Wisps of red hair hung gracefully from Felicia's puffed pompadour as she stood at her buffet and popped the cork on a champagne bottle. "It's been a long day, ladies." Her green eyes shined as she filled three long-stemmed glasses, placed them on a silver tray, and then carried it to Kathleen and Clarice.

Clarice reached for her glass. *She's my definition of beauty, inside and out, and my only friend in this world.* Her father's words still jarred her. *"You won't want to see your precious Felicia again when I tell you her secrets. Just ask her about Annie Parsons."* She took a quick sip of champagne. *Secrets? Annie Parsons? Who cares? Someday I might, but not tonight. I only care about holding my own life together.*

Felicia raised her glass. "To Kathleen, who had the courage to place that classified ad in the *Tribune.*"

Clarice raised hers. "To Kathleen, who came to Chicago and stuck with me, even when I didn't want her around."

Kathleen laughed and raised hers. "To Felicia, who put up with us both."

"And to Laura," Felicia said, "for having such intelligent daughters."

Kathleen looked at Clarice. "Maybe she can rest in peace now."

They sipped champagne, and the room took on a festive flair. Clarice looked excitedly at Kathleen. "If you decide to stay, we'll look for an apartment right away. There's one close to work. I've been eyeing a two-bedroom flat. One where we can share the kitchen and walk to the store together."

"I don't know yet," Kathleen said softly.

"You can work in jewelry. Maybe go back and forth to Albuquerque on buying trips and bring back some of those turquoise rings and necklaces. And you can model them at special showings."

"Maybe you'll come to Albuquerque and open another Pruitt's. Start over again."

Clarice laughed. "A Roark's is more likely."

Margaret came to the doorway. "Someone named Clay is on the telephone, Miss Clarice. He says he's your brother."

Clarice set her glass on the table. "Clay? Calling here?"

"He said to hurry, ma'am."

Clarice raced down the hall to the wall phone with Felicia and Kathleen close behind her.

". . . slow down, Clay, I can't understand you . . . yes . . ." Clarice glanced at the clock. "He's likely at the warehouse now. He sleeps there like he used to. I'll try to reach him." The earpiece fell from her shaking hands and dangled on its cord.

"What is it?" Felicia said.

"Clay's friend said the Mob ordered a hit on Father." Her lips trembled, "For tonight." She grabbed her stomach. "It's my fault; I shouldn't have taken . . . please, God, don't let them harm him."

Kathleen picked up the dangling earpiece. "This is Kathleen, Clay . . . I see . . . yes. Yes, we'll call him. And you be careful." She knelt next to Clarice. "Clay says they're headed to the warehouse now. And for you to warn your father. What's the number?"

Clarice's hands shook. "I can't remember. Oh, God, help me!"

Felicia gripped her shoulders. "The number, Clarice."

"I can't think, I—" Clarice jerked the earpiece from Kathleen's hand. "But I can dial it." Heart pounding, she tapped her foot, waited, tapped her foot again and waited. "Answer, the damn telephone, Father!" After several more rings, she slammed the earpiece on the hook.

"Clay's headed to the warehouse," Kathleen said. "Call the police."

Clarice dialed zero, and the operator put her through. "Police, yes, this is Clarice Pruitt. There's an emergency . . . Walter Pruitt . . . yes, he's my father. The Mob put out a contract on him, and they're on their way to his warehouse to kill him . . . yes, I said the Mob, at his warehouse, 1294 Randolph, on the corner." She screamed into the telephone. "You'd better show up, damn it!"

Clarice caught her breath. "That policeman said they already have an arrest warrant for Father; that they'll send somebody when they can." She looked helplessly from Kathleen to Felicia. "We've got to warn him!"

"I can't call Robert," Felicia said. "The switchboard operator goes home at nine." She grabbed her purse. "I'll get the car."

* * *

The warehouse loomed like a dark fortress flanked on both sides by dilapidated buildings. Felicia cut off her headlights and pulled onto a side street with a view of the front parking lot.

"There's a light on in his office," Clarice whispered, "but I don't see his car."

A siren wailed in the distance.

"Maybe the police changed their minds," Kathleen said.

Clarice grabbed the door handle. "I've got to warn him."

Felicia grabbed her wrist. "Wait for the police."

"To hell with the police!" Clarice tried to jerk free, but Felicia held her tight.

A tall slender man skirted the side of the warehouse and turned the front corner. The street light caught a glint of golden hair.

Clarice gasped. "Clay!" She cupped her hand over her mouth. Sweat popped on her forehead.

A black sedan roared around the corner and pulled up to the front loading dock. "Pruitt!" a gruff voice shouted from the car.

Clay sprinted toward the front door.

Car doors flew open. Two men jumped out, leveled their weapons, and bullets ricocheted off the brick wall.

Clay gripped his arms over his chest, spun like a tornado, and collapsed on the pavement.

Clarice screamed, and Felicia pushed her down.

Another blast of bullets shattered the night; then silence.

Kathleen groaned. "They killed Clay!"

Guns still raised, the men turned, and started toward Felicia's car.

"Get down!" Felicia cried. She punched the starter, the car jerked then died, and she threw herself on top of Clarice.

Siren blaring, a patrol car rounded the corner.

The men lowered their guns and dashed to their car. Tires squealed as it backed out of the loading dock and sped away.

Red lights flashed in a blinding swirl as a patrol car screeched into the parking lot.

Kathleen sprang from the backdoor and tore across the pavement toward Clay.

Clarice broke loose from Felicia with a fierce grunt and took off behind her. *I've got to save him; dear God don't take my Clay.*

An officer hopped out of his patrol car, drew his pistol and shouted, "Halt!"

Kathleen and Clarice charged past him.

"Halt or I'll shoot!" His voice boomed.

Still running, they each raised their hands in the air until they reached Clay and dropped to the pavement.

The officer whirled around and pointed his gun at Felicia. "Out of that car, lady. Now!"

"Don't shoot," Felicia said, then stepped out with her hands in the air.

The officer glanced toward Clarice and Kathleen, then motioned Felicia toward the patrol car. When she approached, he holstered his gun, pushed her face on the hood, patted her down and handcuffed her. He glanced toward Clarice and Kathleen again, and then shoved Felicia into the backseat and slammed the door. He drew his gun and walked carefully toward them.

Clay lay face up, covered with blood.

Clarice pressed a corner of her blouse over the gaping hole in his chest.

The officer holstered his pistol, pulled out a handkerchief, knelt, and wiped Clay's face. "Who the hell is he?"

"My brother." Clarice pleaded: "Get him an ambulance."

"And who the hell are you?"

"Clarice Pruitt. I called the precinct." Tears streamed down her face. *I can't lose Clay.* "Get help!" she cried.

"Ain't nobody comin', lady. I overheard yer call at the station and decided to warn Mr. Pruitt myself."

Clarice stared at the officer. "You're the same one who was behind my store last month. You arrested him."

He looked at her through narrowed eyes. "Uh, Yep." He nodded toward Clay. "A shame, huh. 'Cause it looks like yer brother took the bullet for his father."

Clarice let out a guttural roar. "Get him an ambulance!"

CHAPTER THIRTY-SEVEN

One month later, Kathleen stood in Walter's snow-covered driveway and looked at his mansion in awe. "It looks like a castle," she said.

Clarice let out a soft laugh. "Right out of Grimm's Fairy Tales, only with an armed guard."

"You said your house was big, but I never could have imagined something like this."

Inside the living room, Kathleen's mouth gaped open. "I see why you thought my dad's house was so small."

Felicia came down the stairway. "Clay's awake," she said. "The new nurse just got here and she's dressing his wounds."

Clarice frowned. "A new nurse?"

"The agency sent her."

"Thanks again for staying with him," Clarice said. "The guard's watching the outside, and I'm going to get one for inside in case it was really Clay the Mob was after, him having been a part owner of Pruitt's."

They walked silently through the somber rooms, and Kathleen touched her chest. "I feel sad here."

"Your mother was never happy in this house," Felicia said.

"None of us were happy here, except Father," Clarice said. "And I'm not sure he was." She tugged her sweater. "This house helped him feel important."

They walked into the kitchen, and Kathleen's eyes widened. "Wow. This is almost as big as my dad's whole house." She glanced at Clarice. "My stepmother, Bea, would love cooking here."

Clarice paced a few agitated steps, then stopped. "Right here is where Father told us he sent Mother away, and that he wished he'd sent Clay with her."

Kathleen pressed her knotted fist to her mouth. "That's how you found out?"

"Father just blurted it, and then Clay slugged him. Clay left after that." She wiped her forehead. "We all left."

As if to escape, they walked into the dining room. Clarice ran her finger across the oak table and nodded her approval. "This house has been vacant so long the cleaning service worked two full days before we could come home."

In Clay's room, the nurse stood swabbing his chest with iodine. She glanced at Clarice. "I'll be finished in a moment, ma'am."

"Who are you?" Clarice said, crisply.

"I'm Nurse O'Connell."

"What happened to Nurse Taylor?"

"She quit. Quite suddenly, I understand. The agency sent me to care for Mr. Pruitt now that he's home from the hospital."

Clarice walked up beside her. "And what are your credentials?"

Without looking up, "Twelve years of hospital nursing," Nurse O'Connell said, and then placed a fresh gauze over Clay's chest and secured it with white adhesive tape. She dipped a washcloth into a porcelain bowl, wiped his face, and patted it gently with a towel.

"I've hired a guard for inside," Clarice said. "I do not want him left alone."

Nurse O'Connell placed her hand over Clay's forehead. "That won't be necessary, ma'am. I'll take good care of him."

An obscure doubt settled in Clarice's chest. She pulled back slightly, then gave her a hesitant nod. "All right then. But I want to be informed of any further personnel changes. Do you understand?"

"Yes, ma'am. I understand."

"You may take your break now."

"Then I'll eat my lunch in the kitchen. Call me if he needs something." Nurse O'Connell pulled the white sheet over Clay's chest, dropped dirty bandages into the newspaper-lined trashcan, and closed the door behind her.

Clay smiled. "Don't fuss over me, Sis."

Her eyes bore into his. "You were gunned down, damn it. And we don't know what else might happen."

"Those bullets were meant for Father. Not me."

Clarice felt her face flush. "We can't be sure of that."

Clay looked at Kathleen. "I hear you're leaving us."

"Now that I know you're going to be okay," she said. "You gave me a scare."

"I wish you'd stay," Clay said, then glanced at Clarice. "We both do."

Kathleen took Clay's hand in hers. "I've got to go home and face my own demons."

"What kind of demons?"

Kathleen squeezed his hand. "I want to make peace with my dad." She hesitated. "And Henry." The corners of her mouth curved up. "Kind of like you, maybe."

"I understand," Clay said. "And I hope Henry gets better."

"The doctor at the asylum said there was nothing more they can do for him. But I want to talk to the doctor myself."

"They're doing research," Clay said. "They will find help for him someday."

"Henry being in the asylum has nearly destroyed my dad." Kathleen shook her head slowly. "Nearly destroyed all of us. But Dad blames himself."

Clay's mouth quivered. "In our own way, Clarice and I blamed ourselves, too. It seems we were sort of mixed up."

Kathleen sniffed, then laughed. "We were all mixed up. But not so much now, I hope."

Clay looked from Kathleen to Clarice to Felicia. "Thank you for staying with me in the hospital. I wouldn't have survived without you three."

Clarice's voice trembled. "I couldn't bear losing you, Clay."

"That's good, Sis. Because it looks like you're stuck with me again." He glanced around the room. "What irony that Father signed this over house to me."

"Father's assistant, Toby, said Father handed him the deed the afternoon before the shooting, and then took off with a redheaded man named, McKenzie. Toby didn't know where McKenzie took him, but it looked like he had a gun under his coat. So, we don't know if Father is alive or dead."

"He gave me the house because he didn't think I could survive on my own."

Kathleen looked at him slyly. "He didn't know you."

"And we didn't know him," Clay said. "I blamed Father for everything. I just wish . . ."

"If I hadn't taken his store away from him; if I hadn't threatened him . . ." Clarice's chest heaved. "I just wish we had been honest, instead of trying to protect each other."

"Let's start now," Clay said. "We don't really know what Father was like; we only know the results of what he did."

"And now we'll have to answer for ourselves," Clarice said. Tears welled behind her eyelids. "When you're better, we'll go visit that Jane Addams settlement house and see if we might turn this place into something good."

"And remember," Felicia said. "Robert offered you that job at his foundation to find ways to help the homeless."

Clay grinned. "Guess I'll have to come out of hiding."

Clarice waved her index finger. "Well, you didn't 'hide' when you thought our Father was in danger. You risked your life to save his."

Clay sighed. "I just wish we knew what happened to him."

"He cleaned the warehouse of cash," Clarice said. "But he left all the merchandise, uh, the liquor, I mean."

"Maybe he went west again, or down south this time."

Clarice felt a sudden tightness in her chest. "Or maybe the Mob got him, like they almost got you."

"I'm just grateful you're all safe," Felicia said. She glanced at her watch, pulled her car keys out of her pocketbook, and dangled them in the air. "Kathleen has a train to catch."

Tears wet Clarice's cheeks. "You'll come back to me. I can't lose you after all this."

"You and Clay can come to Albuquerque," Kathleen said. "You can open a dress shop or a jewelry store and start all over."

Clarice hugged Kathleen, and then held her at arm's length in front of her. "Well, we found out what happened to our mother."

"That's what I came for," Kathleen said. "And we're not the same, you and me."

"No! Oh, no," Clarice said. "And thank God."

Kathleen hugged Felicia. "You made it possible."

"You were the courageous one. You took the first step."

"Into the lion's den," Kathleen said, and then laughed. She looked at Clarice and ran her hands over her own red ruffled sleeves. "Thank you again for my new outfit. I love it." She touched Clarice's hair. "And I like your new finger waves; like Jean Harlow."

"Who is Jean Harlow?" Clarice asked.

"The new movie star. She's glamorous. And I like your outfit too. A little like a man's suit, but it fits nice and looks great on you."

"Perfect for my first day back to work," Clarice said. "I can hardly wait."

Kathleen walked to Clay and kissed him on the forehead. "So little time and yet, I feel like I've always known you."

Clay smiled. "Me too, little sister. And stay safe."

Kathleen took a long last look at Clarice, mouthed, "I love you," and then followed Felicia down the stairs toward her journey home.

* * *

Clarice's mind buzzed as she shifted into gear and started her drive to Pruitt's. *Funny how I fought so hard to keep Kathleen out of my life, and now she's part of it. And how I tried to keep Clay all to my-self, yet she found him anyway. Just the kind of thing I would have done.* She sighed. *They fit together perfectly like I knew they would, and it's all right; feels good in fact. There are three of us now . . . maybe four if Henry ever gets better.*

She turned into her parking space, walked through the main entrance, and felt the old excitement as pneumatic tubes swished up carrying tickets and cash, while others whirred down with receipts and change. Two smartly dressed women sat in front of a mirror trying on hats. Soft music hummed in the background. A shoe clerk knelt by a little girl's foot measuring for high top shoes while her mother looked on. A silver-haired saleslady dusted a glass case filled with dazzling jewelry. She savored a whiff of Evening in Paris as she passed the perfume counter.

She walked through Women's Wear and smiled at Molly the manikin standing proud in her black sheer, long-sleeved, Madame Cutie top with a ruffled collar and crocheted-lace cinched at her waist and a matching skirt and nylon stockings. *Madam Cutie is hot right now.*

She stood in the center aisle and her eyes swept the store. *All this, these people, are mine now. And I can run it the way I want to! Maybe I'll change the name from Pruitt's to Roark's. Maybe I'll get a loan and add on. Maybe . . .* her heart raced.

She entered her office and was startled to find Walter's bookkeeper, Beale, sitting behind her mahogany desk with a cigarette dangling between his lips. Two men in dark, double-breasted suits sat in chairs across from him.

Her face grew hot. "What are you doing at my desk?"

Beale hooked his cigarette between his fingers and looked up casually. "I'm going over the books."

Clarice's eyes bore into him. "You have no right to go over my books!"

Beale leaned back. "Prohibition is almost over ma'am, and we need to branch out. This store is a respectable front for our operations."

"Not this store!"

Beale smiled politely.

Clarice's hands flew to her hips. "I'm the sole owner now. So, stub out that cigarette and get out, or I'll have you arrested for trespassing."

He sat up straight and nodded toward a man across from him. "This is Mr. Ferris McKenzie; your new boss. He's an old friend of your father."

McKenzie? An icy hand squeezed Clarice's throat. She clenched her fists. "Where is my father?" she demanded. "I know he left the warehouse with you. So, what did you do to him?"

McKenzie raised his eyebrows. "Your father, *Mr. Patrick Roark*, stole money from his own father, and it got his old man killed. He sweet talked a lady banker in Fairbanks, Alaska, and then slipped out of town with an *undetermined* amount of funds. He came back to Chicago and changed his name to Pruitt, then opened this fine department store." He shifted to the side of the chair and crossed one leg over the other. "Oh, and he married a beautiful Irish girl, your mother, I believe, and then he kicked her out on the street." He fingered his chin. "It seems there's some insanity in the family."

Clarice's head roared. "How can you know that?"

McKenzie smiled, coolly. "And when this depression caused Pruitt to lose his other stores, we set him up nice. He would have lost this store, too, if we hadn't bailed him out." He pulled a silver cigarette lighter out of his pocket, tapped a pack of Lucky's, and lit another cigarette. "But it seems that Pruitt got greedy; went behind our backs and found his own sources for liquor. But not before he filtered money into a special account for you."

"I never touched that damn money!"

"Yeah, well, that's too bad. This store might be in better shape if you had."

She shook her fist at him. "You corrupted my father. But you can't touch me."

McKenzie motioned her to a chair. "Sit down, please, Miss Pruitt."

"I don't want to sit down!" She waved her hands through cigarette smoke. "You men may look respectable in your three-piece

277

suits and slick hair, but you're just the 'Chicago Outfit' of thugs." She pointed to the door. "Get out of my office now, or I'll call the police!"

McKenzie's eyes narrowed. "I wouldn't do that if I were you."

Clarice jerked the telephone toward her and picked up the receiver. "You can't tell me what to do!"

McKenzie blew smoke in her face. "Your beautiful new half sister just boarded a train to Albuquerque, car number thirteen, seat twelve, third aisle window seat on the left. She's wearing a red, ruffled blouse with a tan bolero jacket and skirt. I believe you bought it for her last week from our Women's Wear." He looked Clarice up and down. "And you bought this fine-looking suit for yourself, too. You have good taste, Miss Pruitt." He tapped his cigarette in the ashtray. "It would be a shame if something should happen to your newly found sister."

Clarice dropped the receiver. "My sister has nothing to do with this!"

"And your brother, Clayton, well—"

"Your thugs nearly killed him!"

"That was a shame by the way. Perhaps your brother got caught in a round of bullets meant for, well, for somebody else. But he'll be all right, now that he's under the care of a capable nurse, a Mrs. O'Connell, I believe."

Clarice's stomach jerked as if he had hit her.

"After surviving all that, well, it'd be a shame if Clayton disappeared like his father."

Clarice gasped for breath. "They're innocents! Leave them out of this.

McKenzie's steel blue eyes bore into hers. "That, Miss Pruitt, will be up to you. All you have to do is cooperate, and they'll both stay safe."

Clarice turned away from his icy stare and walked to the window. Black clouds drooped over the lake like limp arms. A faint outline of a steamship faded into the distance. She squeezed her eyes shut and pictured Nurse O'Connell's hand on Clay's forehead.

Kathleen's bright face, "Maybe you'll come to Albuquerque, open a dress shop or a jewelry store and start all over." Her eyes stung.

Feeling the silent menace of the men behind her, her heart raced. *I can't . . . won't. Won't cooperate with them.*

A bolt of lightning shot across the sky and illuminated the clouds. Thunder cracked. *I've got to protect them. And I will. All I need is time.*

"Miss Pruitt?"

A sticky lump clumped in the back of Clarice's throat. She swallowed. Rocking slightly, she fingered her waves, then turned around and faced Ferris McKenzie with a blank stare.

"All right. What do you want me to do?"

THE END

AFTERWORD

To my readers who may have cringed at the words "lunatic asylum, insane, maniac, shame," among others: I cringed too. I sought to portray how mentally ill persons were perceived in the 1920's and 30's, and the lack of information, treatment and concern they were shown. We now know it is caused by biological factors such as brain chemistry, genes, and family history.

One in five Americans have experienced a mental health issue, and one in twenty-five live with a serious mental illness such as schizophrenia, bipolar disorder, or major depression. Statistics show that people with mental health problems are no more likely to be violent than anyone else. We now have medications to help reduce symptoms, and more are being developed which have enabled mentally ill persons to be productive members of our community.

CPSIA information can be obtained
at www.ICGtesting.com
Printed in the USA
FSHW011250101219
64938FS